About the Author

Steve France was born in Birmingham. After school, he left England, took casual jobs and travelled. He spent a year hitchhiking across America and Canada, before returning to Europe and finding adventure travelling through Iran and Afghanistan to India, China and beyond.

After years of travelling and realising that the world was both bleaker and more beautiful than he ever imagined, he returned to England, met Amanda, and married.

They now spend most of their time travelling and when not travelling, live in Cheshire.

Hiding with The Sugar Stealers

Steve France

Hiding with The Sugar Stealers

Olympia Publishers
London

www.olympiapublishers.com
OLYMPIA PAPERBACK EDITION

A CIP catalogue record for this title is
available from the British Library.

ISBN: 978-1-78830-980-6

This is a work of fiction.
Names, characters, places and incidents originate from the writer's
imagination. Any resemblance to actual persons, living or dead, is
purely coincidental.

First Published in 2021

Olympia Publishers
Tallis House
2 Tallis Street
London
EC4Y 0AB

Printed in Great Britain

Dedication

To Mandy

Chapter One

I suppose it all really started when I walked out through the doors. I mean, stuff had happened before that, lots of stuff. For a start, I had this stupid immigration guy asking me a million stupid questions and before that I had been cooped up like a battery hen on a plane for what seemed like a week. And before I'd left, I'd been telling anyone who would listen, 'Yeah, I'm going to America.' I'd say it as cool as anything, as if it was just like having breakfast or something. I was 17; it was the 70s. I lived in a crappy part of Birmingham. In the 70s no one from that part of Birmingham went to America. I didn't know anyone anyway. As far as I knew, not even rich people went to America, not that I knew any rich people.

People used to ask me, 'What you gonna do?'

'Just travel around,' I'd say. 'I'm just gonna Greyhound around for a while.'

'Just Greyhound around.' It was a crappy thing to say. As soon as I'd said it that first time, I wished I hadn't; it sounded so stupid. But people seemed to like it, they drooled, so I just kept saying it over and over. Whenever anyone asked me, I'd just say, 'I'm gonna Greyhound around' and then watch them drool. When you're 17 you get a kick out of seeing people drool. Really, I was scared big style, but I didn't want to admit it. You don't like to admit stuff like that when you're 17, so I just said stuff to make them drool.

Anyway, when I got off the plane, I was dying for a leak. Once I'd held off going for over 24 hours. That was my record.

But today, I was dying. I don't know why; maybe it was being in the air so long. I just knew I was dying. I could have gone on the plane, if I could have been bothered to walk the mile to the crappy little toilet and then wait in a queue for hours, but I don't like going to the toilets on planes. Tell you the truth, I don't like planes. I don't mind taking off and landing and stuff, but I'm scared big style in between. I just sit there thinking of the million miles of wires and billions of parts that can go wrong. When I'm on a plane, I just sit there counting the seconds, waiting for some wire to break or some crappy part to overheat or seize up or something. I usually start to sweat and just want to get off, but it's hard to get off at 35,000 feet. They say that flying is the safest form of transport, but what good is that gonna be to me when I'm falling out the sky because some crappy wires have gone wrong?

I guess working in a car factory for a while hadn't helped. I needed money for this trip, so I did a few crumby jobs for a while before I left. One of them was in a car factory. I couldn't believe it when I saw how badly they built cars. The cars we built had loads of wires missing, I'm telling you, there was loads of everything missing. In that factory, nothing much got done all week, but towards the weekend it got even worse. Everyone used to joke, 'Make sure you never buy a car built on a Friday.' Trouble is, it wasn't a joke. When I'm in a plane now, I always worry in case it was built on a Friday.

Anyway, I wasn't going to go for a leak on that plane, so as soon as it landed, I was ready to go big style. But then I got held up by this stupid immigration guard I told you about. He really did my head in. I thought I was going to have to break my 24-hour record because he asked me so many questions, so when I got through, I just had to go. I ran across the hallway and into the first restrooms I saw. I didn't see any urinals, but I was dying, so

I just ran into a toilet. It was kind of odd that there were no urinals, but I wasn't thinking straight. When I'm dying to go to the toilet, I never can think straight. Now there is probably some crazy Gestalt psychologist or someone who can tell you all about figure and ground and stuff and they'd be able to tell you why I can't think straight. I don't know anything about that stuff, though, I just knew I wasn't thinking straight.

Anyway, as I was going, I started to feel better, but then I heard voices.

'What you gonna do tonight?' one asked. It was a high-pitched whiney voice, with a southern drawl. Apart from the immigration guy, it was the first American accent I had heard since I had landed, and it was all whiney. I hate whiney voices.

'Going down the Stork Club,' came a reply in the same southern drawl. They giggled. It sounded southern.

'Shit,' I thought, 'I'm in the ladies.'

Now I don't know why they do this, but often toilet doors have a little gap at the bottom between the floor and the bottom of the door. It's kind of like they are saloon doors. You know, like those saloon doors in crappy cowboy westerns. I don't know who thought it was a good idea to have saloon doors in a toilet, but it was a good thing for me that today they did. As quiet as I could, I got down on my hands and knees and peeked out. Shit, there are girls in here.

Now, given the southern drawl, I was half expecting to see Scarlett O'Hara in her best plantation crinoline, but it was just a couple of teenage girls. Teenage girls dressed in bellbottoms and tank tops. It was the 70s; people wore crap like that. I just stared out and watched. They were putting on some lipstick in front of the mirror and tidying up their hair and stuff. You know, doing what girls are conditioned to do. They were giggling and messing about, but most of the time they just kept puckering up their lips and putting on lipstick. I noticed how close their faces were to the glass, and how it looked as if they wanted to kiss themselves. They were so close to the mirror, their warm breath condensed on the cool glass, and for seconds, bits of their face disappeared behind the mist. I couldn't see much, just their backs, and sometimes their half-hidden faces behind the mist on the mirror. But they were girls, I was 17, it was better than working.

I don't know why, but I started thinking about accents and how I could never date a girl with a southern drawl. I kept thinking that every time she spoke, I would end up imagining I was Clark Gable or someone. I'd have to wear that indignant, cocky, I'm a 'smart-arse' look all the time and bang on about not giving a damn. It sounds crazy, I know, but here I was, crouched down on the floor in a New York toilet thinking about Clark Gable with his stupid, pencil-thin moustache and all. It cracked me up. Maybe dating them would be funny for a day or two, I thought. She would ask me what I wanted to do at the weekend and I could pretend I was in the movies and say I didn't give a damn. But I'd get bored. I could never date a girl with a southern accent. Just thinking about it cracked me up, though.

When you think about it, it's weird how accents can affect people. See, I don't like Welsh accents either. Like if someone from south Wales says 'huge', they say, 'uoogh'. I'm telling you, when I hear someone say 'uoogh', it always does my head in.

It's not just Welsh accents either. There are loads of accents I don't like. If I listed them all, though, you'd stab yourself in the eyes. I'm telling you you'd die of boredom before I could list them all. Mind you, if you heard me, you wouldn't like my accent. People think that the Birmingham accent makes people sound stupid. It does too. See, I've noticed when I'm watching the telly, like a play or an advert or something, and if they want to make someone sound stupid, they give them a Brummie accent. Then, when they need a lowlife crook or someone, they make them sound Scouse. They do it all the time. Sometimes I wonder who made up all this crap and why we all judge each other, but most people do. Most people I've met are always judging people. I know I am.

Anyway, I had stopped crouching down and was sitting on the toilet waiting for things to settle. My legs were starting to hurt from being all crunched up and I had got a bit freaked in case they saw me peeking out from under the door, so I tucked my feet in so that no one could see them under the gap at the bottom of the door and waited. I waited for ages, you know, while I was thinking about Clark Gable and Welsh accents and stuff, but then I noticed it had gone quiet. Relieved, relieved, I decided to have another quick peek out from under the door. They'd gone.

'Thank God,' I thought and decided to get out quick whilst it was quiet. I hadn't realised how much I had started to sweat, but as I dashed out, I noticed it was pouring off me. I think it was because I'd already had a grilling from that immigration guy and then I started to think what might happen if someone saw me coming out of the ladies. Maybe I could just tell them I was dying for a leak and couldn't think straight, maybe I could confuse them with some Gestalt stuff. I wasn't sure; nothing sounded convincing, I started to sweat even more. Fortunately, there was no one outside, but the whole thing had freaked me out, so I dashed straight into the men's room. I saw the urinals. I had got it right this time. There was no one about, so I walked over to the sinks to run some water on my face. Normally, I don't like too much water on my face, but I was sweating big style and my eyes were burning hot, so I let the water run for ages and just kept splashing it on my face. That's when I got angry. I was pissed off that I was so hot. Pissed off that that immigration guy had held me up so long. Pissed off that Welsh people say 'uoogh'. Pissed off that they call them 'restrooms'. I started to think that maybe if the toilets were marked more clearly and not called stupid 'restrooms', then maybe I wouldn't have got into this mess. When I get myself into a mess, I always find myself looking for someone or something to blame. I've noticed a lot of people do that. I know I do it. I reckon if they gave out medals for blaming people when stuff goes wrong, I'd win gold. No problem, I'd get gold every time.

But anyway, right there, right then I was real pissed off that stupid Americans call them stupid restrooms. Maybe the Americans think toilets sounds vulgar, I thought. Maybe that's why they have come up with this restrooms crap. I hate bullshit like that, but the world is full of that kind of bullshit. Like when the army shoot one of their own soldiers and they say it was 'friendly-fire'. 'Friendly-fire'. I bet Mrs Cooper is really chuffed when some crappy four-star general knocks on her door to tell her that her son was killed by 'friendly-fire'. Who comes up with this bullshit? It does my head in.

Now I don't make a habit of going into ladies' toilets, but as I was splashing that water over my face and looking around the men's room, I started to think about how small the ladies was seeing as though they don't have urinals and all. I guess if women designed them, they would probably make them bigger. Maybe these had been designed by men. I guess almost everything is designed by men. Maybe the bloke who designed this airport didn't think about it much. Maybe. Or maybe he just didn't give a damn.

'Shit,' I thought, I've got to get Clark Gable out my head. I cooled myself down and went back out into the long corridor marked 'exit'. It had felt as if I'd been stuck in here forever, but I could see the doors. I guess that's when it all really started.

Chapter Two

Airports are airports. Lounges, long corridors, luggage, people rushing around. I could have been anywhere. To be honest, I was shit scared to leave the airport, but there were so many people rushing about I just wanted to get out through those doors. I walked out and took a breath of hot New York air. There were people everywhere. More people rushing around. It was noisy too. Horns, the screech of wheels, yelling. I thought about going back in and back to the toilets. Maybe that's why they are called restrooms. It started to make sense.

'Yo, where you going to, bro'?' This small guy appeared from nowhere and tugged at my arm. 'Where you headed?'

I was travelling light, but he lunged towards me and grabbed my bag. I had a yellow rucksack with me. It contained everything I owned. My life was in that bag. I grabbed it back. 'Downtown, Manhattan,' I said, as if I came to New York all the time.

'Here bro', here. I'll get you a taxi.' He moved quickly. 'Quick,' he said, 'Quick.' I was getting the feeling everything in New York moved quickly. 'Quick,' he said, 'Quick.'

'No, you're okay,' I said. 'I want to take a bus.'

Astonished and disappointed in equal measure, he looked at me to say, 'No one takes the bus.' He dropped my bag and brushed me aside.

'Where's the bus sto…?' He was gone. I was learning you need to be quick in New York.

I thought about chasing after him, but there was an old guy sitting on his battered old suitcase who looked up. He was rolling a cigarette, but he looked up.

'Over there.' He tilted his head a little and nodded as if he was indicating it was across the street. He did it as if he didn't want to use up much effort telling me. As if rolling that cigarette was the only thing he cared about right now. That, and maybe saving energy. He looked back down at the half-rolled cigarette in his fingers and carried on.

'Thanks,' I said. 'Thanks,' and watched him smoke as I waited in line. The tip of his cigarette pulsed furnace red when he sucked, then calmed to dark, dusty, dead, black ash. With each draw, the cigarette pulsed, and the ash lengthened, and the line lengthened, and smoke came and went.

I waited about half a cigarette and then the bus pulled in. Now I don't know why, but I don't remember much about that bus ride. I think it took about an hour, but I couldn't really say. Even if you paid me, I don't reckon I could tell you. That's the funny thing about time. Sometimes it just goes.

I guess I saw lots of stuff from that bus, but the big thing I remember is the sound of the engine. It really whistled. Every time the driver changed gear, I remember the high-pitched tone and the whistle. Sometimes it sounded like a jet engine. It's funny, because I can't get on a bus anymore without listening to the engine. Then, I remember driving past this great big, massive cemetery. It went on forever. I'm telling you it just went on and on. There were thousands of tombstones everywhere you looked; they were right there, right in front of your eyes. That was the first time I realised how many dead people there are. Right there in front of everybody. Right by the highway. And I noticed the smoke rising from the crematorium. Dark, dusty, dead, black ash. And the smoke came and went.

I honestly can't remember much else until we got nearer to

the city and it got more built up. There was lots of traffic, overhanging traffic lights and 'Don't Walk' signs, where some people walked, and some people didn't. There were hot dog stands selling franks the size of my arm and flies circling spilled fried slices of onion. And jets of steam. Steam pumping out of vents from the pavement and subway below. It looked hot and messy. The bus started to crawl.

Now I don't much like cities. I don't like the way everything is all crammed in on top of everything and I don't like crowds. I like space. I started to think New York may not be a good idea. You would think that coming from a big city like Birmingham would mean I would be okay with cities, but I'm not. I reckon if you had been brought up in Birmingham, you wouldn't like them either. I know a lot of people from Birmingham that don't like cities. Some of them don't like much at all.

As the bus ground closer to downtown, it suddenly dawned on me I didn't know what I was doing. I'd bought a plane ticket, landed, and now I was on this bus. Back home I had made out I was the big 'I am', I told everyone I was going to 'Greyhound around'. It made people drool, but really, I hadn't worked out any stuff at all. No plan, nothing. I had some vague idea about going out west to see some stuff before I headed to Texas, but I'd never really mentioned it to anyone and didn't have anything sorted. It was just kind of an idea, a crazy idea and so here I was, on a bus heading for the East Side bus terminal, downtown Manhattan, clueless. Back home, I kept making out I was this big 'I am' and telling everyone what I was going to do, as if I was a politician or something. But I didn't have a plan, not a clue, like a politician or something.

I was going to need somewhere to stay, though, so I started looking out of the window for places. You know, cheap hotels and stuff. Even from a bus window it's easy to work out New York. The avenues run north-south, and the streets cross, east-west. It's a grid. The lower street numbers start at the southern tip of Manhattan and the numbers increase block by block going north. The north is rougher. I was more north than you want to be. It was rough, rougher than I wanted it to be.

Making crappy cars without most of their parts, back in Birmingham, hadn't paid too well, so I hadn't saved much. I needed cheap. I kept looking out the window and saw a few shitty places that looked as if they wouldn't cost too much. Trouble was, they looked like the sort of places where you'd get shot up or end up with a knife in your belly. I stayed on the bus and counted down each block. I figured I couldn't stay on too long but getting off too soon would mean I wouldn't see tomorrow. It was stressful, real stressful.

I'm not sure why, but suddenly I signalled I wanted to get off. I think I probably panicked; it looked as if things were starting to get expensive. I grabbed my rucksack and listened to the engine wheeze as the driver slowed down through the gears. I got off. I swallowed. I started walking.

Wandering around the streets of Manhattan, lugging a bright yellow rucksack in the heat isn't something you wanna try, but I needed a place to stay, so I just kept walking. I kept looking up and thinking, here I am, it's New York. I was still shit scared, but part of me kept saying to myself, 'I bet they're drooling now.' I thought about Baz with his clumsy legs and Gateley who was great at drawing cartoons and Skinner who told me I'd never make it this far and all the others too and thought about them drooling.

As I walked, I kept looking up. I looked up a lot. Maybe it was because you hear about the skyscrapers and things in New

York and that's why I just kept looking. To tell the truth, though, I wasn't much impressed. See, none of the buildings were as tall as I had imagined. I mean, they were tall, but not the 'Jack and the beanstalk' tall of my imagination. I thought they would be bigger, much bigger. It got me down.

Now, I reckon happiness depends more on what you expect than what you get, so it was a let- down. One big let-down. I think the Germans have a word for when you feel like that. You know that feeling, when what you get doesn't live up to what you expect. I know it's a long word, you know with about a hundred letters or something, but I just can't remember what the German word is.

Anyway, not remembering that stupid German word made me think every language should have a word for it. I don't think there is a word in English. There should be. If there was, I reckon 'shittungap' would work fine. You'd have to pronounce it as if it was German, though. Yeah, I said to myself, these buildings are 'shittungap'. When you think about it, life is full of 'shittungap'.

I was in New York. I should have been on top of the world, but those lousy buildings had started to make me feel down, and I was having to make up words to keep my spirits up. I stopped looking up and started looking for hotels and that's when I saw The Majestic. It sounded okay. It looked shittungap. I was even more depressed. I needed somewhere to stay, though, and the shabby Majestic looked as if it might be cheap. I went in.

It was airless and bleak inside. Airless, bleak and brown. I looked around and noticed everything was brown. The worn-out carpets, the paint-peeling walls, the lampshades, even the dirt on the carpets and walls. Everything was brown. If you can avoid it, never stay at The Majestic, not even if you like brown. I ain't at all fond of brown, but I was tired, so I checked in. I thought it would be cheap, but it wasn't. It seems brown in New York costs you. It was a crumby, lousy place, but it wasn't cheap, just brown.

I waited for the lift, but it was out of order. Then, though it didn't look like the sort of place that deserved one, a porter came over and took me up a few flights of stairs to my room. He was a tall, awkward-looking guy who made the stairwell seem oppressively small. We climbed them in silence. It felt as awkward as he looked. I followed him along a dreary corridor, and he fumbled for the keys as we arrived at my room. He opened the door. The good news first, it was brown. Shittungap. It was small too, and the awkward-looking fellow looked even larger.

There was a single bed, covered in wrinkled sheets that looked as if they hadn't been changed. The room was dusty. There was no bathroom or anything, just a crappy-looking sink leaning against the wall next to the bed. I hate sinks in rooms. It's sleazy. When I see sinks in rooms, I always think about the million people who couldn't be arsed to get up in the middle of the night to walk miles to the toilet and so pissed in sinks instead. I mean, I can hold off for 24 hours, so if only young guys like me used it, it would be fine. But it looked as if loads of creepy old guys had stayed here. Old guys who pissed in the sink. Thinking about it made me want to throw up, but the porter was hanging about, so I had to hold everything back. I hate that feeling, you know, when you have got to do something, but you can't, and you hold it back.

I needed to get rid of him quick, but I read the signals — he wanted a tip. I'm not accustomed to tipping and I wasn't exactly flush with cash, so I fumbled around for some change. I found a quarter. I dropped it in his outstretched palm. It fell on to his hand like one lousy drop of rain on a barren desert thirsty for more. No chance, I thought. He hesitated. I hesitated. I hesitated longer. He left.

'Thanks,' I said. 'Thanks for nothing,' I thought, but I didn't say it. I just said, 'Thanks.'

The room seemed bigger without him, brighter too. I dropped my yellow rucksack by the bed. It stood out like one of Wordsworth's golden daffodils against the desert of dirty brown. It looked like if I squeezed it, my hands would smell of lemon. I was reluctant to lie on the bed, but I was tired. Tired won. I tried to think about daffodils and lemons, but I couldn't; my head was full of brown.

They say you sleep better in warm, quiet, dark places, but this place was hot. Much too hot. Noisy and light too. Noise gushed in from the traffic rushing by in the street below. The crumby drapes didn't cover the window, so car lights and siren lights lit up the room like a firework display. I tried to close the drapes, but I couldn't; they were too small. I noticed some bubble gum stuck dry on the window. It was all gnarled and bleached and it was stuck solid to the frame. I imagined how, when someone took it out the wrapper, you know, just after they bought it, it was bright pink and smooth and fresh, and how it came to be just this dried-up bit of spit. I thought about the person who might have chewed it, and how long ago it might have been. I wondered if it was a young kid, like me, full of expectation or just some old guy who was too lazy to hit the bin and who pissed in the sink. By rights I shouldn't have slept, but I did. I slept right through.

I had a fuzzy head when I woke the next morning and looked out the window. In New York you need to be high up in the building to see sunlight. The buildings submerge the streets in shade so that even on bright days, the lower floors and sidewalks are left in a half-light. Looking up you can see a narrow strip of blue, like a river between the building tops, but the light can't seem to pierce its way to street level. I was on the third floor; outside looked grey. Inside I was turning brown. Grey looked a lousy option, but I checked out.

Outside, I looked back at the crumbling building. The Majestic. I imagined that crappy four-star general knocking on Mrs Cooper's door again. 'Mrs Cooper, your son has been killed by friendly-fire, but you may take some comfort from knowing he spent his last night at The Majestic.' The Majestic, who comes up with this bullshit?

It was early, but I hadn't drunk a thing since I was on that plane and then I was so stressed out I hardly had a thing. Food on planes is crappy anyway, so I hardly ate a thing. Opposite The Majestic was a diner. It looked a bit creaky, but I could see people drinking, so I went in.

Compared to The Majestic, it looked bright. You know, it was light brown, less dust. Steam belched out from a couple of coffee machines that gurgled away behind the counter and a few people were smoking. The smoke just clung to the damp, hot steam and hung in the air like a smog. It looked a bit like a November night in Birmingham.

There were a few people sitting on swivel, high stools by the counter. Without thinking about it, they unconsciously rotated their chairs. You know, as people who perch on swivel chairs seem to do. I bet they didn't know they were doing it, and never even thought about how stupid it looked. I thought about all the stupid stuff we do. Trouble is, most of the time we just don't notice what we are doing. I reckon if some Martians landed or something, they'd crack themselves up looking at all the crazy stuff that people do. I reckon there's a lot of stuff we do that we all think is normal and we never stop to think about. You know, no one questions anymore. If we did, I reckon we would go nuts. That's why no one wants to stop and think about it. That's another reason why I don't like cities; it's worse in cities. In cities everyone just keeps rushing around and swiveling their chairs and stuff, just so there's no time to think. In cities, no one stops. No one thinks.

There were some high stools by the window too, so I bought a coffee and a couple of donuts and went and sat there. I could see The Majestic across the street as I gazed out of the window. I sipped on my coffee and swivelled on my chair. I don't think anyone noticed, but I thought about how stupid it would have looked. I imagined someone looking in from the street and seeing all of us swivelling on our chairs as if we were three-year-olds in some mad house. I wished I was outside, just so I could have seen it; it would have cracked me up. I wished some Martians had landed and asked us why we were doing it and we could all say we didn't know why.

The streets outside were starting to fill with people and cars and buses and yellow taxis. It felt as if I was in a scene from *Kojak*. I just kept gazing out the window thinking about some Martians landing and asking Kojak about his lollypop, but then this old guy came and sat down next to me. There were plenty of free seats, so I don't know why he sat down by me, but he did. I hate it when people sit by me when there are plenty of free seats; it does my head in. I didn't want him to sit by me, so I kind of ignored him, but he glanced across at me. He nodded and mumbled, 'What's up?'

That's another thing I hate. You know, when people say things like 'what's up?' I never know what it means. In England, I know loads of people who say, 'What's new?' I don't know what's new. 'What's new' depends on loads of things, like what you already know or what somebody else has told you. How on earth should I know 'what's new'? 'What's up' is just as bad. It does my head in when people say stuff like that when they meet me.

I thought I'd better answer, though, so I said, 'Hi.' That seemed more than adequate and anyway, I guessed he didn't really care too much what was up or not.

He was an old guy. He looked as if he had more enthusiasm for his bagels than for life. He looked tired, all creased up and worn. His face was all crunched up like a boxing glove that had been stuffed in a cupboard that was too small for it. His eyes were sunk deep too. It looked as if someone had pulled out his eyeballs, gouged out most of the flesh above his eyelids and stained them with ink, before shoving them back. You know, a bit like what they do in those crazy *Monty Python* sketches. I reckon if I was sitting there with his mum, and I told her he was ugly, she wouldn't even argue. Now if your mum wouldn't argue, then you know you are an ugly bastard. I reckon everyone he'd ever met had probably thought he was ugly, but I bet no one had told him, though. To tell you the truth, he looked scary and I really wished he hadn't sat by me, but he did, so I was stuck with it.

When I'm in spots like this I always just keep my head down. Just chew on your donut and stare out the window, I thought to myself. I thought it was working too, but then he started speaking.

'Where you from?' he asked

'England. Birmingham, England,' I replied. Shit, I thought, let's hope he keeps this short.

It went quiet for a while, so I thought it had worked too, but then he said, 'Do you know the Beatles then?'

I smiled. It seemed the right thing to do. He's joking, I thought, he must be. But he stared at me with his inky eyes and didn't blink. He looked serious. He didn't look like the sort of guy who joked. I bought myself a few seconds by chewing slowly on my donut.

I started to think about saying 'yeah, I know them real well'. You know, like I was best buddies with John Lennon, I just wanted to see him drool, but I didn't. He didn't look like the sort of guy that drooled either.

'No,' I said, 'England's a big place.'

He paused again, then said, 'I've seen a map.'

That caught me off guard. I wasn't sure what to say, so I just said, 'Huh.'

'Huh' is my favourite word; it can mean anything. If you say 'huh' with a smile on your lips and the faint echo of a laugh in your tone, it sort of means, 'ah, that's cute or amusing' or something. But if you want, you can spit it out and lower your tone while you're exhaling and all. If you do that, it can sound like you're real pissed about something. You can say 'huh' any way you want to, and it can mean anything. That's the good thing about words; they can mean anything.

'It might seem big if you live there,' he said, 'but it ain't that big. I've seen a map. England wouldn't even fill Texas.'

I felt obliged to say something. 'I thought I might go to Texas sometime, but I guess it is quite big.' I was hoping I wouldn't offend him. He looked like the sort of guy you didn't want to offend. I started drinking my coffee fast.

'Texas ain't that big,' he said, 'I went on a road trip there once. Crossed Texas on my Harley in a day. Texas ain't that big. Mind you, you could drive fast back then, no black and whites hiding on every bend.'

I started to imagine him when he was younger before his face got all crunched up and all. I smiled.

'If you want big,' he said, 'Yeah, if you want big, try Canada.'

'Huh,' I said. It seemed the safest thing to say.

It went quiet, but it looked as if he was getting ready to spar some more. He was. 'My map said England is in Great Britain. Are you from Great Britain, then?'

'Yeah,' I said. I hadn't thought about it much, but I said, 'Yeah, England is part of Great Britain.'

He came straight back. 'Well, who decided it was great?'

He looked at me in an accusing manner as if it might have been me. But he looked as if he really wanted to know. You know, as if he'd been mulling it over for some time and had to find out. I really wasn't sure what to say. I had grown up there and, to be honest, I never thought it was that great myself, but I wasn't sure that was the answer he wanted. Trouble was, I really had no idea who had decided it was great, or why, for that matter. Everyone just said it, 'Great Britain,' as if it must be true or something. I guess the person who decided it was just thought words can mean anything.

'Dunno,' I said as I swigged down my coffee fast.

'Hey,' I said, 'talking of maps, do you know where I can get one of New York?' I thought the change of subject might help me out a bit, so I repeated myself. 'Any idea where I can get one?'

'Why do you want a map?'

It kind of seemed obvious, but I went along. 'I just flew in yesterday. I wanna look around, find a cheap hotel and stuff. Do you know any cheap hotels?'

'Nothing's cheap in New York,' he said, but then he went on, 'You could try that one.' He glanced out of the window and nodded at The Majestic.

'I stayed there last night,' I said, 'but it was a bit brown for my liking.' I smiled but soon realised the irony was lost on him. 'I need something cheap.'

'If you want cheap, go upstate, maybe even Canada. You ain't gonna find anything cheap in New York.'

He said it as if he had fallen out of love with the place. I knew how he felt.

Well, I'd finished my coffee and I thought this might be a good time to get up and leave before he came back to all that Great Britain stuff, so I stood up and said, 'Well, thanks, it was nice to have met you.'

I really didn't know why I said that cos he hadn't been any help and it wasn't nice to meet him. Trouble is you just kind of slip in to saying all this sort of crap. Sometimes it just seems the safest thing to do. We were taught to play it safe at school. Maybe that's why I play it safe so much. I remember we had this English teacher, Mr Brooks. Brooksey, we used to call him. Hey, it's English today with Brooksey, we'd say. Now it's funny how when you're a kid you feel the need to add a 'y' to one-syllable names. Like Jones became Jonesy and Spinks became Spinksey. Now for some reason you never did it with two-syllable names. We never shouted Tomkinsey when we wanted Tomkins or Ashtoney when we wanted Ashton. It wouldn't sound right, so we never did it. I don't think anyone would do it, not that I've ever checked or anything. I don't know who makes up these rules and stuff, but I'm telling you if you had a one-syllable name, you were gonna have a 'y' added whether you wanted it or not. But anyway, it was Brooksey that came up with that advice to play it safe. See, I used to like writing poetry. I was good at it too. Brooksey even told me I was, and always gave me good marks.

But when it came to exam time, he always used to tell me to write an essay instead. 'Writing poetry in exams is too risky,' he used to say. 'Poetry is subjective. You might get someone who marks your paper who doesn't like your style of poetry. Better to play it safe and write an essay.' I remember him telling me that as if it was yesterday. 'It's not safe,' he said, 'better to play safe if you want to pass your exams.'

I stopped writing poetry after that. I was crap at essays, but that's what I wrote, even though I was crap at them. You can't blame Brooksey, though; he was just telling me how it is. And that's how it is. Play it safe.

I probably would have got in a big strop if it had been another teacher saying that to me, but I kind of had a soft spot for Brooksey. We all did. I think it's cos he used to read to us during English lessons and so we didn't have to do much. The best was when he read Chaucer to us. That always cracked us up big style.

See, we were studying Chaucer and had to read all that Canterbury Tales crap. Brooksey would read one of the tales to us, but he wouldn't read it all normal like, not in everyday language. He used to read it as if he lived in Chaucer's time and so he pronounced everything all weird and stuff. When he came to a word like 'knight', he wouldn't pronounce it as we do now, he'd say 'ker- nik- tah'. He used to read the whole tale in this crazy, authentic language used in Chaucer's day, as if we were actually on this stupid pilgrimage. Now none of us had a clue what he was on about, and anyway, how were we supposed to know if that's how they pronounced things then? He could have told us any bullshit. But we liked Brooksey and it cracked us up. It sounded good too, a bit like when you listen to hip hop.

Sometimes he would stop to analyse a passage. As if we cared. But that's what he did. I remember one time he went banging on for ages about these couple of lines in some tale or play or something about the dangers of making a slip between cup and lip. He kept telling us that the pilgrims used to pass a bowl around and drink from it whilst walking on this stupid pilgrimage they were on. Anyway, this one loner wouldn't take a drink cos he realised everyone was dripping saliva and all into the bowl when they drank. You know, all that back wash and splother. After that, I never ever drank out of the same bottle as someone else again. I still don't, I just imagine all that saliva and stuff at the bottom of the bottle. And that was Brooksey all over. He helped us work out how to play everything safe.

Anyway, that's why I reckon I said 'nice to meet you'. It's hard to break habits sometimes, so I just said it, as if I was on autopilot. I didn't even think about it until after I said it.

After that, I got up to go, but as I did, he grabbed my arm. It wasn't aggressive, though, you know, it was like when you are best buddies or something.

'YMCH', he said. '9th and 34th, it's as cheap as you'll find.'
'You mean, the Youth Members Christian Hostel?' I asked.
'Yeah,' he said.

'Thanks again,' I said, but this time I meant it. I never went into that diner again, but I found plenty of places that were about as smoky and steamy. I met plenty of guys like him too. America is full of them.

Chapter Three

Might as well try the Y, I thought, so I headed south. It didn't take long to walk a dozen blocks, but I started thinking about the place. I knew the Y had something to do with Christians, but apart from that, didn't know much at all. I wondered if maybe you had to be a member? Or maybe a Christian? I even started wondering if I was a Christian. Who knows? As a kid, if I was with someone who was asked about their religion, you know, when they had to fill in a form or something, they always said C. of E. I started saying it too. I didn't really have a clue what it meant, I just used to say it. I started thinking that if it hadn't been for some king or other wanting to get divorced, then I would probably have to tell everyone I was Catholic. But since old Henry kicked up a bit of a fuss so he could change all the rules, we all have to say we're C. of E. I'm not sure if many people give a monkey's what they are, to be honest.

But someone is always making up crappy rules. Manipulators making up rules. Look at all the statues, well-dressed white men. Trouble is, nobody questions it. I mean, who said females couldn't be heirs or couldn't vote? Who puts in all the blocks to stop them getting to be CEO or President? Probably the same nut-jobs who don't let them design toilets.

And anyway, most of the rules just depend on where you're born. You get loads of different rules then. Like you could be born in ten different places and just because you're born there, you'll be fed with all this different bullshit. Accident of birth. They make out that it's the only thing you should believe and get you waving flags and stuff, but down the road someone is telling someone else a load of different shit. And you start to believe all your shit and they start to believe all their shit. And then everyone starts killing each other to try and prove their shit's right. Crazy thing is all the crap that everyone is being told was all written down in some crazy forgotten language on scraps of papyrus about a million years ago. I'm telling you, where I went to school most people couldn't even remember what someone told them ten minutes ago, so how are you supposed to trust what someone said a million years ago? But the trouble is, the people who spout out all this crap, they tell it as if they were there, and your life depends on it. Henry used to do that until he wanted to get divorced and needed to change the rules. People fall for it. Anne Boleyn did, and look what happened to her.

Anyway, I started wondering whether maybe the people at the Y might have a load of rules and ask me about my beliefs, and if I go to church and stuff. I wasn't really sure what I would say. I mean, I hadn't worked out what stuff to believe. I knew what I'd been told to believe, but that's different. At 17, I still hadn't worked it all out.

I had been to church, though, at least I could tell them that. I never went frequently like, but I went a couple of times after I joined the Life Boys when I was a little kid. Now, if you wanted to stay in the Life Boys, you had to go to church every Sunday. You had to wear your uniform too. It was a bit scary, when I first went to that church. It was massive and cold. Even though it was full of people it felt cold. I was proper nervous, but I walked in all proud, cos I was in my uniform. I thought it was all going to be fine, but then some spindly old hag started yelling at me.

'Take off your hat,' she yelled. 'Take it off.' She did it right there in the church, in front of a load of people. She made a big song and dance of it too, as if someone had made her hat queen for the day. I hated her for that, the way she yelled at me in front of everyone, so I just ran out the church. I never felt like going to church again after that. I left the Life Boys too, cos no one could tell me why God didn't like me wearing my hat in church.

It didn't stop me praying, though. Even though I didn't go to church, I kept praying. See, that was because I bought this book that was full of Bible stories and pictures of Jesus. I bought it in this crappy department store in Birmingham called Henrys.

Well, I was walking around Henrys as bored as hell, past all the kettles and vacuum cleaners and bedsheets, but then I came across this bookstand. I didn't read much as a kid and I only stopped by these books because they were stacked on one of those rotating stands. I tried to spin it just for something to do. You know, the same way as people feel clothes on racks, when they're shopping even though they ain't planning on buying anything. It was easy to spin, so I just kept spinning it around. Around and around until it was dizzy. Henrys didn't seem so bad when it was dizzy. I caught my mum looking at me, and for a second, I thought she was going to yell at me for messing about. But she didn't. My mum didn't yell much. She just asked whether I wanted to buy a book. Now I know my mum didn't have much money, but this book had a picture of Jesus on the cover and he looked nice. He was wearing these cool robes and had nice long wavy hair and stuff. He looked like the sort of person that would have been okay with me wearing my hat in church. I thought maybe he was looking out for me, and maybe that was why no one yelled at me, so, even though we didn't have much money, I said yes.

I looked at my mum. She was smiling, she looked happy. The sales assistant was smiling and looked happy, Jesus was smiling and looked happy. I tried to picture myself smiling. I wondered if smiling made you feel happy. Anyway, that's how I came by this book. The sales assistant placed it in a small brown paper bag and crouched down to pass it to me. She bent down and made herself look small in the way adults do when they want to reduce their height to that of children to make them feel safe.

After that, I started praying a lot. I read that book almost every day. Then I stopped. When I got older, I could never figure out why all the pictures of Jesus looked the same, though, you know, why he always had really pale skin and soft hands and stuff. Some of the stories said he was a carpenter that worked outside in the heat of the sun, but he always had such pale skin and soft hands.

Well, I was thinking about all this stuff and wondering whether they would let me in, when I saw the sign. It hung above a door about a block away. It was a vertical sign with large individual letters, one below the other. At first, I thought it said the YWCH, but as I got closer, I realised that the M had fallen from the bracket holding it to the wall. It had slipped upside down and was hanging by one bolt. It looked as if it didn't want to be there. From a distance it looked more like a W half obscuring the C. As I got closer, though, I realised it was the YMCH. It was one of those crappy neon signs which they have everywhere in New York. Trouble is, neon is fine when it hums in the dark and all the fancy colours are flashing and reflecting off windows and painting passing cars and stuff, but during the day it looks real crappy. You can see all the dirty pathetic tubes of glass, wound on to bits of wire that are going rusty. It made the place look tacky. Tacky like The Majestic.

There were a crowd of guys hanging around outside. Most of them were smoking; some were chewing gum. They tipped their heads back and blew the smoke into the air. Most of them chewed gum with their mouths open, and I could see the pink splodge of bubble gum swilling around in their mouths like some old pink shirt scrunched in a wash tub. They smoked and chewed as if there was no tomorrow, and a few started brawling. It looked a bit like a scene from *West Side Story* or something, but without the stage lights to make them all look wholesome.

I brushed past them and said 'hi', but I don't think anyone even noticed; nobody said anything anyway. I went in. It was as creaky as anything. I wished I hadn't worried about what they might ask me, though, cos checking in was a piece of cake. No one asked me any questions at all. Not one. I reckon Charles Manson could have walked into that place, and nobody would have given a shit.

I walked past a few more guys on the way to my room. A few more guys, smoking and chewing and drinking and brawling. I'm not sure if any of them were Christians, but they looked the sort of guys who would have worn their hats to church. I bet if anyone had told them they couldn't, they would have just carried on wearing them anyway. Wearing their hats and chewing.

I took the lift to the millionth floor and walked down a couple of long corridors towards my room. It was depressing. Long dark corridors, rows of doors, graffiti and floors covered in spit and gum and God knows what. It was noisy too, lots of uncomfortable noises. Noises like people chewing with their mouths open, but louder. Much louder.

My room was small. It had a bed and a sink. Another room with a sink. It was full of young guys, though, so maybe they don't piss in sinks. It didn't help. It did have a window, though. Thank God. I pulled back the blinds and looked out.

The building was built around a quadrangle, so the inside

rooms looked across at each other. About a thousand years ago, there was probably a courtyard at ground level, but now it was just a rubbish tip. I watched as people tossed crap out of the windows. Bottles, cans, remains of takeaways. It clanked and smashed on the layer that had built up at ground level. It looked deep. I reckon if someone jumped from one of the windows, they'd probably bounce off the rubbish below, as if it was a trampoline. A trashy trampoline made of glass and cans and crap. I wondered if anyone had jumped; it looked like the sort of place where people had. If I had to stay for more than a week, I reckon I would jump.

I hid my rucksack under the bed and went out. The bed was too low, so a bit of my rucksack poked out. Poked out as if it needed to get away. I needed some air and anyway, I wanted to get out and see New York. I knew I couldn't stay here for long. Everything was expensive and scary. I thought maybe I could put up with it for a couple of days, tops. I needed to get out and see. Maybe after that, I would head north, just as the old guy in the diner had told me.

I kept thinking about different places I had heard about in films and songs and stuff, and so I went out and walked. A startled fish, I darted about that city with my heart pounding. In no pattern either, just zig zagging from place to place as fancy took me. Way down to Battery Park and the Statue of Liberty. The Twin Towers, Chinatown, Broadway, Greenwich Village, Central Park. I even went to Bryant Park looking for a statue of Tesla. I couldn't see one. That pissed me off. Like Tesla was trying to make sure everyone in the world would get free electricity, but I couldn't even see a statue. Just GE ads.

When I was near Bryant Park, I went to the New York Public Library building. I like libraries sometimes. You know, when you are in a city and it gets all crazy, you can go into a library and find some space. It's quiet and people stop rushing around. It's as if some of the stuff in all the books has somehow worked its way into people's heads and they start to think. I thought about how many words there were in all the books in that library, you know, like when you think about how many stars there are in the sky even though you can't see them all. I thought about how the words stay the same, the same words as yesterday and the day before. And how the words were the same the year before and the year before that. I looked at some of the people strolling around and fingering through books. I thought about how the people would change and how they might look next year, even though the words in the books would still be the same. I thought about the people who'd been into that library years ago and how some of them had grown old and how some of them might even be in that cemetery I passed on that bus.

For the next two days the sun shone. I felt good, just as I had in Henrys. It looked as if everyone was on their way to somewhere and I felt as if I was too. Except at night. The nights were gloomy. It was so noisy in the Y. Fights, yells, screams, bottles smashing in the quad below. My heart pumped, and I heard the blood rushing through my ears. I don't remember hearing anyone laugh in there, though. I don't think anyone ever laughed in that Y. I'm not even sure people smiled.

I had got through a lot of money fast, so I decided I needed to get out. New York felt like a fast city in a bad mood, and I'd had enough. I needed space. I thought about what the old guy in the coffee shop had said about heading north. I thought about how his face had got all creased up living here. I decided to head north, Niagara Falls. Just because.

I checked out and headed for the bus station. It was still early, but I thought I'd hang around for a night bus. That way, I could sleep on the bus and save myself some money. To get to Niagara, I had to take the bus to Buffalo and it wasn't leaving until 9.45. It was noon. I had a long wait. I crushed my bag into a locker and walked.

I must have walked for hours, nosing in ten-cent shops and dreary dive-bars, past poolhalls and past cardboard-couched bums in doorways. And on and on past cafés and diners and a thousand sad, faded red-brick alleys leading to nowhere. Walking and walking into the electric fried smell of the city. The sweet, salty, sickly smell of street vendor carts bloated with bagels and hot dogs and mustard and ketchup mixing with petrol and the sweat of a hoard and sometimes, just sometimes, the oh so sweet, scent of a Fifth Avenue perfumed princess. And drowning in sound. The roaring, soaring mad, crash, smash and bash, bedlam racket that is New York.

I was lost but ended up near Times Square. I hadn't seen it, so I went to kill time. I'd seen it on TV, when they show everyone bringing in the new year and stuff. They always have the seconds counting down on the clock until midnight strikes and the crystal ball falls. Then they show pictures of everyone cheering and hugging and kissing each other and everything.

They always make it out to be this really big deal, as if the only place in the world to be at midnight on New Year's Eve is Times Square. The Americans are great at making out they're genius; it makes me puke.

Well, I'm telling you Times Square is all bullshit. The way they've built it up makes you feel as if you're really going to knock your socks off, but when you get there, you're not even sure you're there. I'm telling you, when you're not sure you've got to a place and you are there, it must be crap. It is.

37

For a start, it's not even a square. Most of New York is based on grids, so you would have thought building some great massive square would have been a piece of cake. But Broadway slices through it at an angle, so Times Square ain't even a square. I reckon if you looked hard enough at a Picasso painting like *Guernica* for long enough, you might find a shape like it, but I'm telling you it ain't a square. Now Plaza Mayor in Madrid is a square. So is St Marks in Venice and Red Square in Moscow, but Times Square isn't. It's just more American bullshit. I bet if some American hero like Hemingway or someone had ever been to Times Square, they would have died of embarrassment. I'm guessing Hemingway would have gone back to his place in Madrid and stumbled across Plaza Mayor, all pissed up, shouting, 'Now this is a square!' I bet you if you search carefully around some of the small little alleys near Plaza Mayor, you'll find some of his graffiti where he scribbled, 'All squares are not equal.' Just look closely, you'll see. I'm telling you, you'll find it.

I didn't hang around for long. Just long enough to see the bums, begging outside the crappy shop fronts and all the crumby advertisements flashing on the hoardings. I was hoping I'd see Jane hopped up on Bennies, cuddling her baby. If I had, I'd have gone right up to her and goo-gooed her kid and bent over and tweaked its cheeks and said stuff like 'boy, ain't you a cutie', even though I wouldn't have meant it and don't even like babies. But I didn't see her. I just saw the roadworks, digging up the place like a graveyard, tarmac on black tarmac, lies on lies. And the bums and lots of trash cans overflowing with empty plastic pop bottles and God knows what. It did my head in. Next time I see Times Square on the TV on New Year's Eve I'm just going to think about all the poor sods crowded into this crappy little part of New York waiting for a clock to count down to midnight and a lousy crystal ball to drop. I bet most of them will be freezing their socks off and dying for a piss. There ain't nowhere to go for a piss in Times Square, not even a crumby sink. I guess that they'll have to ask the bums what they do. That's if the arseholes who celebrate New Year there can bring themselves to speak to bums.

I wished I had never gone to Times Square. After going there, I felt 'shittungap'. So, even though it was early, I headed back to the bus station. When I got there, I kind of wished I had just gone and spent some time in Central Park and looked at the trees or something, cos the bus station was a full-on dump. At least it was empty. I was bored and wanted to kill some time, so I did that thing where you walk around and try not to tread on the cracks between the tiles. It was a cinch and I was glad too, cos the grouting was old and dirty, and I didn't fancy treading on it, even in my trainers which had thick soles, as thick as a mattress. But it was too easy, and I got bored and so found myself a bench and sat down. The bench was hard as concrete, but I managed to stretch out and used my rucksack as a pillow. There was still no one about, so I just lounged around and tried to sleep. But it was uncomfortable, and I couldn't sleep.

I tried to sit up straight like when I was a kid. See, I had this teacher at junior school that used to make everyone sit up straight. He used to make us sit up straight all day. Clasp our hands behind the back of the chairs, so our backs were straight, and our shoulders were all square and stuff. All day we had to do it. It would help our posture, he said. It did too, but mostly I forget and now just lounge about instead.

I liked Mr Bagshot, though. You wouldn't have thought he was the kind of teacher I would like. None of the other kids did, but I quite liked him. He was strict and everything, but I liked him.

He was ancient, about sixty I reckon, and he had grey hair greased back with hair gel or something, but he always stood up real straight. He was tall as an oak tree, and when he got excited about things, would wave his arms about. When he did that, he looked like a great massive oak tree bending in the wind.

He had some funny ways too. He gave us spelling tests where we had to spell words in front of the class. He'd shout out a word and then if he called your name, you had to spell it out loud. When you got it wrong, he would make you stand on the desk. You even had to say when it was a capital letter. If you just said 'e' when you were spelling something like England and not capital 'E', he would tell you that you were wrong. Even if you spelt it all correctly, if you didn't say the capital, he made you stand on the desk. I tell you, by the end of some tests, almost everyone was standing on the desks. Trouble was, most of the class were crap at spelling, or forgot about the capital thing. Most of the kids hated him for doing that, but I could spell okay and always remembered the capital thing, so I didn't mind.

It was a good job I did sit up, though, cos the place started to fill with people. They all rushed to grab the seats, but it got so full people had to sit on the floor. Some of them sat down slap bang in the centre of those square tiles, but some of them didn't seem to care and they sat on the grouting between the tiles. Even though that grouting was filthy, some of them sat right on it anyway.

My bench got crowded and I was squashed between some fat geezer and the wall. That got me mad. I hate sitting next to people I don't know, especially if I'm squashed, so I went and sat on the floor by a water fountain. The floor seemed cleaner there, from all the water that spilled over onto the tiles, so that's where

I sat.

I sat there and when I felt like it, gulped water from the fountain. Sometimes, when I didn't have much money for food, I would just drink water instead of eating. I reckon those water fountains probably saved my life while I was in New York. Free, cold water that dripped through streams in the Adirondacks and gurgled and roared its way through the mountains and the pipes of the city. All that way, just to reach my dry cardboard throat and save my life. I was bored as hell, just waiting for that lousy bus. You know, just leaning against that water fountain, waiting. I still had hours to kill, so I started drawing on my rucksack. Mainly, just for something to do, but to be honest, it still looked too new and I wanted to scruff it up. It had a few marks because I'd been squashing it under beds on dirty floors in the hotels and all, but it still looked too new. New, like a shiny lemon you'd buy on pancake day.

I scrawled 'New York' on to my pack. I took ages drawing those letters, as if I was some specialist tattoo artist or something. Really, I just wanted to kill time, so I drew real slow. The black, black ink stood out against the bright yellow fabric. I looked at it and thought I'd do it every place I went. Just write the initials of different places on my pack. I stared. 'N.Y.' I wondered about tomorrow and the day after that. I wondered about all the places I'd seen on a map and of the west that lay out before me like some exotic, embroidered carpet. I thought about the colours I might find and the places I might stay and the people I'd see. The never-ending highways and dusty roads, and the cities full of hustlers and the ordinary folk doing ordinary things. And the pretty waitresses serving me breakfast on my way through the wilderness and to an ocean on the other side. I wondered what I might find there.

Whilst I was scrawling on my pack, a few bums came up to me and asked for handouts. I reckon I didn't have much more money than them, but I was taking a bus across a carpet and they were stuck here. Poor bastards. I found a few dimes and gave them what I had. Most people just ignored them or told them to get lost. Maybe that's what you do if you get hassled by bums all the time, who knows, but that's what most people did, just said 'get lost'. One couple told everyone to get lost. They were well dressed and kind of looked out of place.

Most people looked as messed up as me, you know, wearing jeans, trainers and crappy T-shirts and stuff, but this old couple were dressed up as if they were going to a ball. The old man was wearing a suit and the old lady was wearing some fancy dress. She even had beads round her neck. They looked fake and all, but she was still wearing them. They didn't seem the type of people who would have much time for the poor bastards stuck in this dump. The old man looked down his nose at people, as if he thought everyone should stand in the gutter and the woman looked as if she wore gloves to blow her nose. They were in the crappy bus station, though, so I reckon it was all just show. A lot of America is all show. If you had money, you'd never come to this crappy bus station.

Anyway, after they told this bum to get lost, I heard them cussing him. They were saying how he should go and get a job and all and how he would only waste money on alcohol and drugs and stuff. People who say that sort of crap do my head in. Like I'm guessing that if this bum went for a job, him not having an address and having ripped trousers tied up with string might go against him. I'm guessing a lot of companies have some dress codes and all which don't allow string round your dirty ripped pants.

Looking at all the cigarette butts on the streets and the liquor stores and bars, I reckoned just about everyone here looked as if they spent most of their money on alcohol and drugs anyway. It's better than going mad. Trouble is people get all crochety when bums spend their money the same way.

Anyway, the fancy, over-dressed couple got on a bus going south and I was heading north. It looked as if I was with the other poor bastards. Time dragged in that bus station; I tell you, it dragged. This wasn't how I imagined it would be back in England, but that's how I spent my last night in New York. Talking to bums, who made a crust by selling their blood and me leaning against a water fountain cos it had the cleanest tiles, and scribbling on my rucksack, thinking about what might be.

I was glad to get on the bus.

Chapter Four

If you ever leave New York, leave it in the dark. It's lit up like a Christmas tree and things always look prettier in the dark. I started to like it. I shouldn't have really. I started to think of all the cities across the world that, just like here, were lit up like Christmas trees for no reason at all, other than that was the way it is. All those lights on for no reason.

On the way out, we passed a Greyhound bus, driving down 51st street and I thought about England. About how I drove in a daze down the Bristol Road in its haze with sleepy eyes on my way to work. Where I worked or pretended to. Shuffling papers or fixing bits to cars until my brain was numb. Then, come half past five, drove back in a bleaker daze, gazing into the evening, where I'd meet up with Cookie and Ali, not cos I liked them much, but because I was in need of some human warmth. And we'd drink snakebites and pints of mild, because they looked like Guinness, and because they were the cheapest froth you could get. Then I'd go home drunk, and fall into an uneasy sleep, but never find dreams, cos the factory stole them, and put them in some shredder.

I took a last look at New York. After leaving the city, there wasn't much to see or do, so I just listened to the sound of the engine for a while and then tried to grab some sleep. I grabbed myself an aisle seat and dumped my bag by the window to claim both seats. You know, as if I was out west, looking for gold and staking a claim. If the bus had been full, I probably would have had to sit next to some fat bastard who snored all the way, but the bus was empty, so most people were sprawled out across a couple of seats. So that's what I did, just sprawled out across a couple of seats as if I owned the bus company.

Trouble is, during the night the bus stops for passengers. The new passengers boarded and looked for seats. Some wrestled their way to the head of the queue so they could get first pick of the seats. Everyone was trying to grab a double seat so they could sprawl out and get some kip. I watched the scrum form by the bus door, the pushing and shoving, just so they could get on first. I started to wonder what it might be like in some crazy emergency on a plane or a ship or something. You know, if people are going to beat each other up for a bus seat.

The people already on the bus didn't want anybody to sit down next to them either. They tried to put the new passengers off, anyhow they could. The regulars sprawled out across both seats and pretended to sleep. Some even snored. I knew they weren't asleep really, cos they'd been sitting up and stuff before the bus pulled into the station, but they pretended to snore. Lots of people hiding in the dark on a bus. Strangers hiding.

I got lucky; no one sat next to me. But I caught on quick; by the second stop I pretended to snore too. It all worked out okay. I'm telling you compared to the Y and The Majestic, the night bus was bliss; I slept like a baby.

It was getting light when I came around. The Indian ink of the night dissolved into a watery haze. Things brightened. A shaft of sunlight streaked through the window and blazed on my yellow rucksack. It was as bright as a spotlight magnified on glass. I looked out of the window at the fields and the trees flying by. And the space, the expanding galaxy of space. Joy at last. No dim, red-bricked alleys or grey, shabby, suffocating tenement tombs. I felt like sunshine.

The bus pulled into Buffalo at around six. The station was a lot smaller than New York, but just as dreary. Water fountains, hard benches, bums and crowds of people. It looked messy. Outside, there were some Moonies and they crowded around me and smiled and danced and chanted. They smelt like joss sticks. I didn't hang about and got the local bus to head out to the Falls. I'd had enough of buildings and people, I wanted space.

Americans love the outdoors. Natural spaces and forests and mountains celebrate with campgrounds everywhere. I'd heard there was one near the Falls, so that's where I headed. It was empty. That suited me fine.

I didn't expect it to be so empty, but it was early summer and so I guess that helped. The good thing about travelling in the 70s, though, was that you could rock up just about anywhere and check in. No queues, no reservations, nothing.

See, half of the people on the planet couldn't travel during the 70s. Chairman Mao had a Little Red Book and that meant about a billion people were stuck just south of the Gobi Desert. And not long before that, Churchill, Roosevelt and Stalin had stuck their pins in a map over a couple of gin and tonics and their 'iron curtain' went up. Then, chuck in a whole load of Africans who are busy trekking miles just to get some drinking water and you aren't left with many poor bastards going on holiday. Couldn't move an inch. Poor bastards. Maybe in the future, there will be freedom of movement to cross borders. Maybe. I reckon it won't last long, though. Before long, a load of bigshots will whip up some nationalistic crap and start building walls and stuff. It'll work too; people don't even wanna sit next to someone on a bus.

Not being able to move an inch would kill me. It did my head in when I had to apply for this stupid visa just to come to the

States. It wound me up big style to think that some loser in an embassy somewhere could look at my picture and decide I wasn't getting one. Some arsehole who wouldn't even have to give me a reason. Trouble is, there are always some big 'I ams' calling the shots. Just ask the people of the Chagos Islands. Just ask them why they were kicked out of their homes by Britain. I bet the bigshots who came up with that are the same losers who decided Britain was Great. Great at keeping it quiet. That's what I should have told that old guy in the diner in New York when he asked me about it. 'We're great at keeping stuff quiet,' I should have said.

Thinking about all that stuff started to wind me up, but I calmed down a bit, cos American campgrounds are genius. A young kid with a bony face and gleaming eyes checked me in. He was sitting in a small wooden gatehouse the size of a chicken shack listening to a radio blasting out the blues. He rocked to and fro in a rocker, as if he was sitting on a porch on a hot, sweaty Alabama evening, dreaming of being older and darker. Nodding in time, imagining he had a soul.

'Where can I camp?' I asked, taking note of the tempo and squeezing it in at the end of a bar. We listened to the piercing scream of a blues guitar solo and imagined the gracious, delicious, effortless, black fingers dance across the frets. Only black fingers can play the blues that way.

'There's plenty of space. Take your pick.'

So, with the effortless, black-hand blues in my ears, I did. Took a pitch the size of a football field with a tree or two for shade, and a table and barbeque where I knew I could feast. I pulled the small tent I had with me from my rucksack and imagined I was with a chain gang. Hitting the pegs into the hard, hard ground and hurrying. Hurrying and keeping time along with the distant, haunting, blurred buzz of the sax. I could have pitched about twenty of my tents on the space I had, but I like space. Space and the slow beat, desperate, sad-eyed blues. It suited me fine. To sleep without being surrounded by the jerks who stayed in those crappy hotels. No stinking sinks. And the blues. Just fine.

I put that tent up in five minutes flat. Pitched it under a tree and then just lay inside for a while. The ground was hard. Hard as if it hadn't seen rain for a month. But after New York and those crappy hotels it felt marshmallow soft. Soft like floating in a warm ocean. Under the shade of the tree, I could hear the birds rustling in the trees. I listened to them singing whilst I looked up at the small patch of beige canvas. The sun was shining, and the dappled light cast shadows. The leaves and branches fluttered in the breeze and fragments of shade danced. I lay there, listening to the birds and watching the patterns appear and disappear. I reckon I could have stayed there forever, as if I was words in a book in a library. See, I used to go camping when I was a kid and it reminded me of that. You know, when I was a little kid, camping with my mum and dad when everything was safe. Now, there ain't much to do in a tent after dark, so my dad used to make shadow animals on the side of the canvas. My mum would hold a torch and shine the light, and my dad would make shapes with his hands. He'd put his hands between the light and the canvas and make shapes. Loads of shapes, casting shadows on the wall of the tent. He'd twist and contort his hands and fingers into all sorts of crazy forms. I don't know how he did it, but he did. That's when all these creatures would appear out of nowhere and dance. Birds swooping down, then rabbits, horses and butterflies. A tent the size of a garden shed, but at four, filled with all those shadow puppets, it became jungle, forest, fantasy. Sometimes it seemed as if it was the whole world. These days I keep stuff in, but then, I jumped around like crazy. I yelled and screamed at those shadows. You know, like when you are bursting and you need to shake the joy, before it blows your head off. I jumped about and tried to grab the shadows. Hands clasping at shadows. A bursting heart, grabbing. I couldn't keep still. My mum said I had St Vitus's dance. I never knew who St Vitus was, I still don't, but my mum said I danced just like St Vitus.

Now, lying on my own, lonely atoms in a small space, I looked up at the canvas, and watched the breeze forge shape and pattern on my world. I hoped for swooping birds and rabbits or horses. I hoped for the magical. I knew if my mum and dad were here, I'd see them, I knew I would. But they weren't here, and so I only saw shade. Twisted shade and formless shape. Trouble is, they wouldn't ever be here either. They wouldn't ever be anywhere. See, I don't like talking about it, but fact is, my mum and dad were killed just before I left. That's the reason I came to the States really, cos they were killed. See, they were just driving along, minding their own business, when this crazy madman came around the corner on the wrong side of the road and smashed right into them. Bang, straight into them, head on and all; they didn't stand a chance. Crazy bastard Todd J. Rumplan, driving like a madman on the wrong side of the road.

See, my mum and dad never had much money, but they had a car. It was only a small, cheap little car, but they used to drive about in it all the time. Nowhere in particular sometimes, just out of the city and into the countryside. Just to get some peace and fresh air and stuff. I used to go with them too, when I was small. My dad even bought me this make-pretend driving wheel which he stuck to the back of his seat. I'd sit in the back and would steer like mad making out I was driving. I'd drive all over Birmingham like that. I thought I was Stirling Moss or someone cos I had driven all around Birmingham and I was only four or something.

Anyway, on the day my mum and dad were killed, they were just driving around on their own in the countryside, minding their own business. That didn't make any difference to that crazy madman, though. Todd bastard J. Rumplan. Todd bastard J. Escapeplan more like. Afterwards, there was talk that he was drunk and stuff, but they never got the chance to prove it. My mum and dad hardly drank at all, so everyone knew they weren't drunk for sure. My dad would have half a shandy at Christmas sometimes. Half a shandy, that was mostly lemonade. My mum drank even less. Sometimes she'd go crazy and have a snowball. A crappy shandy and snowball at Christmas, that's all they ever drank, but some crazy maniac got drunk and killed them.

Trouble was the police didn't even give him a breathalyser and he never went to court. Talk about a stitch-up. See, he was this big American hotshot, some diplomat or politician or something, and so he just got on a plane and went back to the States. Diplomatic Immunity, they called it. He has Diplomatic Immunity.

'So, he can get pissed up, kill someone and just fly home?' I asked. 'No investigation, no prosecution, no extradition.' That pretty well sums it up. I tell you, who are the shitheads who make up these crappy rules and why do we fall for it? That's another reason why I got so pissed off with that scumbag immigration guy asking me all those stupid questions just to get into his stupid country. I felt like saying, I've got diplomatic immunity, but I didn't. It wouldn't have made any difference cos I'm not a bigshot or anything. I'm nobody, so it wouldn't have made any difference. I bet when that crazy madman with his diplomatic immunity got back, he didn't have to answer any questions, not one. Not yet anyway. Glazed, I gazed at the roof of my tent looking at formless shadows pinned onto canvas and thought about my mum and dad. To tell you the truth, it started to get me down. See, before I'd left England, I'd tried to get some justice. I'd spoken to MPs and the press and stuff, but I was just a seventeen-year-old kid, and he was a big hotshot. I was wasting my time. They gave me all that 'we're on your side' and 'we're going to help you' crap, but nothing happened. Diddly-squat. That's why I needed to do something myself. That's why I needed to get away.

Thinking about it started to do my head in, so I decided I had to get out. I was hungry but thinking about that car crash and stuff made me feel sick, so I just headed out to the falls to try and take my mind off stuff.

I liked the falls. Before you see the falls, you hear them. But before you hear them, you feel them. Senses imagining and building anticipation. The forceful flow of falling water forms a fine spray that dances in the air and when the wind whispers, gently showers your skin. A fragile, pale veil of mist, transparent space emerging. You know, cos you can feel it on your skin. But then, as you get nearer, you hear. The rumble of distant thunder. A thousand dancers trampling on stage. Then you see them. The enormous presence of frantic gravity ripping apart hydrogen and oxygen and bursting tremendously.

I really wasn't sure what to expect. I'd heard about Niagara and all. The American marketing machine makes sure everyone hears about everything in America, well, everything they want you to hear about, but I didn't really know what to expect. If I'd created this big picture in my head and everything, I bet this would have been more 'shittungap', but I hadn't pictured anything, so I wasn't disappointed. Sometimes it's better when you expect nothing; that way you're never disappointed.

Looking at the water thundering over the edge was great and all, especially at night when it was all lit up in fancy colours, but what I liked best was just dangling my feet in the river. I reckon most people just look at the falls and forget about the river. Everyone remembers the money shot. But I liked the river. I wandered along that riverbank for miles. It gets wide and wild in places, but I went right up to the edge and dangled my feet. And that's what I did most of the time, just sat by the river and dangled my feet. I bet in the future, some crazy Health and Safety guy will build a great big fence about a million miles from the river, and some lousy marketing guy will charge everyone about a million bucks to get past the fence. I'm telling you, that's what they'll do, but this was the 70s, you could just rock up at places and do anything you wanted to.

After days by the river, I felt better, but I was hungry. New York was so expensive. I'd spent too much money on hotels and that bus and stuff, and I couldn't really afford to eat. I was hungry.

I found a store and bought salad and bread and made up about a thousand sandwiches. Like this massive buffet for an army or something. God, I was a greedy bastard. I tell you I'd been dreaming of food. Nothing fancy like, just fried eggs and simple stuff. A week without it and I was already dreaming of food. I started wondering if all those poor sods starving in parts of Africa dream about food all the time. It made me feel guilty.

That pissed me off, because then I went off the idea of eating. I was gunning for a feast, but then I couldn't bring myself to eat it. Guilt. I mean, I hadn't done anything to those poor sods in Africa, but I felt guilty anyway. So, I had all this stuff lying over the picnic bench and couldn't eat. Couldn't eat a thing.

I stared at my lousy million sandwiches. Just stared curiously. Dump it? Leave it? Take a photo? Who takes pictures of food? I'd never taken a photo of food, who does? But I was still feeling guilty, I don't know why, but I thought maybe taking a photo would help. Maybe taking a photo made it feel worthwhile or something. I don't know, I just remember taking this stupid photo. A photo of a million sandwiches stacked up like the leaning tower of Pisa. I almost didn't bring a camera with me, cos I ain't big into photography or anything, but I got one in England just before I left. I happened to be in town one day, and it started to rain as I walked past this second-hand camera shop. That's the only reason I bought it. To be honest, I didn't really want a camera, but I went in anyway. It was raining heavy and I thought I could kill some time just looking at the cameras and stuff and make out I was David Bailey. I thought I might get some assistant to tell me all about the different cameras until it stopped raining, and then just tell him I'd have to think about it. I bet assistants get really wound up when people ask them a million questions about the crappy stuff they sell and then just say 'I'll think about it'. I bet under their breath they're cursing like crazy and then go home and stick needles into dolls they've made of customers and stuff. Well, some of them anyway.

The rest just roll their eyes. That seems to be what most people do. I reckon that's what I'd do if I was an assistant, I'd roll my eyes. Maybe I'd say 'huh', too.

Anyway, that's what I was going to do when I went into the shop, but this assistant was proper helpful, and so I started feeling a bit guilty about wasting his time. He showed me loads of different cameras and explained how they all worked and stuff. After about half an hour I knew a hell of a lot about cameras, I tell you. A hell of a lot. He showed me loads of stuff, but for some reason, I took a shine to this old Russian camera. It just took my fancy. It was a Fed. It was scratched all over and looked like something Yuri Gagarin might have used on his early space flights, but it looked sturdy, you know, as if it would last forever. The assistant banged on about how great it was, and I don't know why, but I kind of liked it. I ended up liking the assistant too, so I bought it. It even came with a brown leather case. The case was a bit scratched but was real sturdy too.

So, that's why I had this camera with me, and how come I took a crumby picture of my sandwiches.

I had to load a reel of film and I remember thinking how I should invent some fancy camera that will take thousands of pictures, without worrying about loading film, or processing. It wouldn't help Kodak any, and it would probably mean that everyone would spend all day taking stupid pictures. People always waste time doing stuff if it don't cost nothing. I reckon they'd take pictures of everything. They'll probably have a million pictures of themselves.

What they look like with their hair back, hair up, hair down. Pictures of what they had for dinner and what they look like eating their dinner and what they look like on the toilet afterwards. I don't know why anyone would want to do that, but I bet if I invented a fancy camera which don't need film, that's exactly what people will do. I bet you there will be a million jerks with a million pictures that they never look at. I thought about all these poor sods starving in Africa, and all these people with a million pictures of hamburgers and ice creams with chocolate sauce and hundreds and thousands sprinkled, just because. I started to wish I hadn't taken that picture. I hoped no one invented that camera too.

Anyway, in the end I got hungry, so I ate those sandwiches for days whilst I dangled my feet. Three days at the Falls. I even took some of those lousy sandwiches with me and gave them to bums I met in the park. Some of them said thanks and some didn't. Some grunted, and some of them threw them back at me and asked me for beer instead. I would have given them a beer if I had one, but I didn't, just sandwiches, wrapped in napkins, getting a bit dried out.

I had felt down in New York, but I started to feel better. Better enough to think about where I wanted to head next, you know, things I wanted to see. I kept thinking about Texas and why I was here, but I wondered if I should slow things down. Slow down and build anticipation. Take some time to work it all out, you know, who I was, what was the answer. I dangled my feet.

For some reason, most of the world's great waterfalls are at borders. Victoria Falls, Iguazu Falls, Niagara Falls. I guess it's just that rivers and waterfalls create natural boundaries and so when some big shots are carving up countries after wars and stuff, rivers and waterfalls are neat and convenient boundaries. I'm guessing that when some fat-arsed general is given the job of carving up some land, to save breaking a sweat, he just says, 'That river will do.' That's providing that there's not some oil or gold or something just the other side. I don't know, but I know that a lot of falls are at borders. Niagara is too. Bang between the States and Canada. When I'd been at the falls, I looked across the river at Canada and wondered what it was like. A lot of the people I'd met told me the view of the falls was much better from the Canadian side. Maybe that was all bull, but what the heck, I thought, I'll go to Canada.

Chapter Five

Getting into Canada is easy. There is a bridge across the river. I just walked across. There is a checkpoint about half-way across and that's where you get asked loads of stupid questions. He was a fat guy, just like the fat guy in New York, and he asked the same stupid questions. I reckon they must all go to the same training centre to learn how to eat so much and how to ask the same stupid questions. He did my head in.

'Are you carrying any drugs? Are you carrying any firearms? Any explosives? blah, blah, blah.' I started to think about winding him up and telling him my rucksack was full of cocaine, but he didn't have to worry because I had diplomatic immunity. He didn't look as if he would get it, though, so I didn't.

People who ask stupid questions wind me up big style. One day, I'm going to say something crazy right back just to see what they say. I really will too, something real stupid just to wind them up, but I didn't really feel in the mood today. I just wanted to get across the bridge.

So, I just said, 'No, just my clothes and tent and stuff.'

Now immigration guys don't smile much, they just stare at you as if you've killed someone. That's how he looked at me anyway.

'Why you coming to Canada?' He carried on staring.

He was pissing me off big style, but I just thought I'd give him a bit of flannel. You know, butter him up a bit just to see if he might relax.

'I've been told the view of the falls is better from Canada,' I said. I didn't get much of a reaction, so I thought I'd pile on a bit more flannel. 'I've heard Canada is beautiful, I'd love to get chance to see some of it.' I said it all gushing, and to be honest, it made me feel a bit sick, but I said it anyway. He just stared.

To be honest, I didn't know why I was coming to Canada and I didn't really care whether he let me into his stupid country or not. I almost told him that there and then, while he was staring at me, but I didn't. I just gave him more flannel.

'It's a beautiful country, I've heard.' Your move, I thought.

Now, I really didn't know why I was coming to Canada. I had heard the view of the falls was better, but that was no big deal. I think the main reason was because when I was at school, I knew this kid who was brought up in Canada. He lived in Toronto or somewhere until he was about eleven and then he came to the UK with his parents. He was in my class at school and we sometimes talked about Canada. At eleven it sounded exotic and all and maybe that's why I thought about coming to Canada. I wasn't sure. Really, I'm not sure why I do anything.

The kid's name was Neil, but we called him Jim. Jim wasn't his real name but that's what everyone called him. We all did. He looked as if he should be called Jim. I bet even his mum called him Jim. He was real bright, though, much brighter than anyone in our school. I remembered wondering whether the Canadian schooling system was much better than ours and wondered whether that's why he was so bright. Maybe it was or maybe it wasn't. Who knows? I bet the Canadians say it is and the Brits say it isn't. Then everyone waves flags. Maybe it was just that he was a real smart kid. I never really found out, I guess I never cared that much; all I knew was, he was real smart.

I was pretty quick at school myself when I was that age, but I was never as smart as Jim. I was just good at remembering stuff.

I found it real easy to remember stuff; it just came natural and I soon worked out you could breeze through school if you remembered stuff. I've got a good memory and if someone tells me stuff, if I can be bothered, I can remember it dead easy.

Sometimes it's as if someone has just told me something like two minutes ago. I remember stuff that easy. Sometimes, I wish I could forget stuff, some stuff you want to be able to forget, but I can't. I remember almost everything.

Sometimes, I try to forget stuff by imagining I'm carrying this big eraser with me. I picture myself rubbing out all the memories and stuff, but it doesn't work. I don't know why I do it really cos it doesn't work and now I have all these other crappy memories of trying to rub stuff out with an eraser.

School was a cinch, though, when you can remember stuff. Like we had to take all these tests and exams and things, but really it was just seeing what you could remember. So long as you remembered what they told you it was fine. It could have been a big load of bullshit, but if you remembered it, you were fine.

Teachers were always asking us stupid questions just to see what we remembered. I remember in this English class once the teacher asked us what assonance meant. We were reading Caesar and Cleopatra or something by Shaw and after a certain passage, the teacher just asked us what assonance meant. I just yelled out what he'd told us a couple of weeks before. I was going to say it's when the writer can't be arsed to find a proper rhyme, but I knew he wouldn't like that, so I just told him the crap he had told us a couple of weeks ago. 'It's when there's a resemblance of sound between syllables, when a word sounds very similar to another word, so it makes it feel like a rhyme, but it isn't an exact rhyme.' I was gonna add how it can create the sound of despair, but some of the other kids looked fidgety, so I kept it brief.

'Right,' he said. 'Well done.'

All I'd done was remembered something and I got a 'well done'. I tell you, you could breeze through school as long as you remembered stuff. I lounged back in my chair like some big 'I am', with a stupid grin on my face. I remember some of the other thickos in the class looking at me as if I was some kind of genius or something, just cos I remembered something.

After that class, one of the thickos came up to me. Alan Walthams it was. He was this great big guy, twice as big as me, maybe three times, he was big anyway. He was into sport and everything and was good at rugby. I hated rugby, and I was crap at it, but they made me play it anyway. I reckon they made all the little scrawny prats like me play it just to see us get half killed. But Al was great at it, even played for the county or some hotshot team like that. Anyway, when he came up to me, I was half expecting him to punch my lights out or something for answering that question. Some of the kids couldn't answer any questions and so they got pissed big style when somebody did. Well, I was expecting to get a good battering, but he didn't even touch me. Instead, he just asked me how come I was so smart.

At first, I thought he was taking the piss, but I think he genuinely wanted to know. He wasn't that smart, and I think he genuinely wanted to know. I don't know, but I think he'd worked out that if he didn't make it in rugby, he needed something else to back him up. See, he was in this 'in-crowd' that thought they ran the school, so normally, I would have said something just to get him off my back, but I didn't. I just levelled with him.

'I'm not that smart,' I said, 'I just remember stuff. Maybe I find it easier to remember stuff than you, just like how you find it easier to play rugby than me.'

'You'll be okay,' I said, 'when we leave this crumby school, no one's going to give a shit if we remember this stuff or not.'

He looked at me as if he didn't buy a word of it, but he smiled and put his hand on my shoulder as if we were best buddies. We weren't, but just for that second it was as if we were. It was as if I'd suddenly joined the 'in-crowd' and he was smart.

Now if Jim had been there, he would have come up with a load of witty comments. He always had something witty to say. One time, we were being hassled by this other guy from the thicko club and he kept calling Jim 'son'. He was poking away at him saying stuff like 'watch your back, son', 'I'm gonna get you, son'. Now, he was the same age as Jim, but he kept saying 'son', as if he was a big 'I am'.

Jim just kept listening for a while and then just said, 'You know, my mum calls me son. She says I'm so bright, she just has to call me sun.' Jim used to come out with stuff like that all the time. He cracked me up. As I told you, he was much smarter than me. Anyway, I think maybe the reason I was coming to Canada was because I had met Jim at school, no other reason than that. I wasn't going to say that to the immigration guy, though.

'What's in your bag? Open it up.' He hadn't melted.

I fumbled with the straps of my rucksack. I was nervous as hell. I hadn't done a single thing wrong, but immigration guys talk to you as if you've murdered someone, so I just fumbled around with the straps.

He took a look inside. I think he was about to poke around a bit, but he saw all my grubby underpants and he pulled his hands away as if he was putting them into a nest of rats. I reckon you could smuggle anything you want in your bag so long as you shove a load of grubby underpants in your bag.

'Okay, shut it up,' he shuddered. 'How long you planning on

staying?'

Long enough to come and blow your house up, I thought, but I just piled on more flannel. 'I'd love to get up to Toronto and Ottawa and places like that, they sound great, but I've got things to do in the States, so maybe two or three weeks, tops.'

He said nothing, but he stamped my passport. 'Next.'

I was in Canada.

I spent another couple of days by the falls on the Canadian side. They were right, the view was better from this side, but the place was full of resort hotels and you couldn't get down to the river, so I decided to move on. I inked Niagara U.S. and Niagara Canada on my pack and moved on.

'I wouldn't bother taking a bus,' she said, 'you should just hitch a ride. I do all the time; it's easy.'

I wasn't expecting the girl in the Niagara Tourist Office to say that to me, but she did. I was thinking of going to Toronto and went in to ask her where I could buy tickets for a bus, but she said, 'Don't bother.' I couldn't imagine anyone in a tourist office in the UK telling me that. I bet they would warn me off hitchhiking and tell me of all the dangers, you know, just like Brooksey telling us how to play it safe. But the girl in Niagara Tourist Office suggested I hitch a ride, so that's what I did.

I had all my stuff with me and the main route to Toronto was just by the tourist office, so I headed out to the road to give thumbing a go.

Now it's funny how when you try something for the first time, it always seems awkward. After you have done it a few times, it all just goes on autopilot, but the first time it's all awkward and uncomfortable. You know, like your first day at school or when you first kissed someone. I remember my first kiss. I wish I didn't, but I do. Her name was Jeanette, and we

61

were both about 13. We met at this stupid kids' disco and used to see each other there every Friday. I went to an all-boys school, so didn't see a girl all week, but we used to meet up on Fridays, and started hanging out. We seemed to get along, so I guess she kind of became my first girlfriend, not that I really planned it. But we just used to hang out together and it just kind of happened.

Anyway, after that I started to get real worried about having to kiss her. I remember worrying all the time about all sorts of crap. I used to think about which way I should tilt my head for that first kiss. Which way should I tilt my head, for crying out loud, but I did, I used to worry about all sorts of crap. See, I used to worry in case she tilted her head the same way and instead of kissing we just banged noses, you know, a bit like what Eskimos do. I mean, I didn't know which way she was going to tilt her head, how could I, I'd never kissed her. I'd never kissed anyone. I thought about asking her, 'Which way you gonna tilt your head?' Honestly, I thought about asking her, I was such a prat. I didn't, but then I just kept stressing about it. I was a real prat.

Then, I started thinking, maybe we'll get lucky and both tilt our heads the right way, just by pure chance and all, but then I wasn't sure whether I should close my eyes or not. I imagined that maybe I might take a peek mid-way through the kiss and stuff, but then I thought, what if she's peeking too? Jesus, I thought, that's going to really freak us out. Imagine your eyeball about half an inch from someone else's eyeball. This girlfriend thing seemed like hard work. I used to worry about everything and so we didn't kiss for ages. When we did, I then started worrying about how long the kiss should last. I had no idea, so in the end I figured I'd kiss her when they played a record at this crumby disco and stop when the music stopped. Now pop records usually last about three minutes. I'm not sure why, but I reckon it's because that's about as long as you want to kiss someone for, before you pass out. I remember kissing her all the way through Paranoid by Black Sabbath once. Jesus, that was crappy. Ozzy Osbourne kept banging on about finishing with his woman cos she couldn't help him with his mind. I reckon he wrote that cos he was stressed out about all this girlfriend crap too. I tell you, it was real hard work, I worried about everything. It's funny, though, cos after a while I stopped worrying about all that crap and then I didn't even think about it when I was kissing. I could even think about other stuff while I was kissing her. I used to think about all kinds of stuff. I reckon she did too. She never said she did, but I reckon she did.

For a while, I thought Jeanette was the best name in the world. But that wasn't for long. See, one Friday, I saw her knocking around with a smart-arse named Pete James. He was about a year older than me and was real cool. His hair was longer than mine, and he was a real good dancer too. Trouble was, he was real good, I mean real good, moved like treacle. Everyone knew it, but what was worse was he knew it too. He had all the moves and went on the dance floor strutting around as if he was Mick Jagger and all. All the girls used to dance around him as if they thought they were Pan's People or something. It did my head in. Anyway, I saw her knocking around with him one Friday and we never kissed again after that. We never spoke much either.

It's funny, cos after that I went right off the name Jeanette. It sounded as if she should be some crumby hairdresser from south Wales or something. Jesus, that freaked me out big style, having to kiss someone named Jeanette from south Wales. I reckon that would kill me. Well, I know it sounds crazy, but because I hadn't hitchhiked before, I was stressing out about that too. I started worrying about where I should stand. In the road by the kerb, back on the pavement? Should I stand up straight with my arm out all purposeful or look a bit more casual as if I hitchhiked all the time? I always over-analyse stuff, so as I stood there, I started looking at my outstretched arm. It was real pale and skinny, and I could see the tendons on the underside of my wrist sticking up through the surface of my skin, like a rail track. My hand was in a bit of a fist shape with my thumb sticking up. Maybe Darwin or Wallace would have written papers about opposable thumbs and hitchhiking if cars had been around on the Galapagos. If they had, I bet Wallace would have written it first, but then everyone would say it was Darwin.

Christ, I hope I'm doing this right, I thought, but it didn't matter, cos I didn't even wait a minute, and someone stopped.

He lowered the window, leant out and asked, 'Where you headed?'

'Toronto,' I said.

'Jump in.'

It was a Ford van. A black van, big enough for ten people, but there was only me. I climbed in, and so there was just me and this guy on our way to Toronto. And I don't even remember his name. But I wish I did, because it was my first ride and he deserved that. But I don't. But I remember the road and how straight it was. Straight as an arrow, well, most of the time. Straight and flat, so we got there in no time at all. Just me and this guy whose name I can't remember. So, it was as easy as that; I always thought it would be.

Now it's a good job someone stopped so quickly. You see, I don't have much stickability. I guess there is a proper name for it, but I don't know what it is, so I just tell people I don't have much stickability. If things don't work out real quick, I give up. When I stood by that road, I was thinking if I didn't get a lift in ten minutes, tops, I would take the bus. If that guy hadn't picked me up, I would have never hitched again. He did, though, and now I hitch all the time. Now, I don't even think about it.

Toronto was fine, but it was another city with too many people, so I didn't stay long. Just long enough to write Toronto on my rucksack and think about where Jim had grown up and how it didn't seem so exotic anymore. My bag was starting to look as distressed as a Leonard Cohen love song. I scribbled a few of the places I'd been to, on the side. Parts of the canvas had started to scuff, and the bright yellow had faded a bit. It started to look like a bag that was owned by someone. I wasn't sure who, but you know, someone.

I decided I'd spend a bit longer in Canada. I'm glad I did too. Getting rides was easy. Rides came quick. Ed and Candy in their beat-up Buick, The French-Canadian guy that couldn't speak much English. Dee in her big flash company car and business suit driving at 90, saying she had places to be. Telling me it was a man's world and how she had to move fast just to keep up. Until she got pulled by the cops. He sauntered over and peered in the window and Dee went all girlie and fluttered her eyelids, and the cop went all gooey, and said, 'Just be careful.' And she drove off and told me she could wrap men around her finger, and I said, 'Sure, he deserved it for being so stupid.' And she stopped at a diner and bought us both lunch on her business card and we drank too much beer and went away happy.

And the parks that I slept in and the bins that I scavenged for food when I saw nice families throw their half-eaten picnics away. And the fresh, fresh air that is Canada.

A lot of the time, I just travelled around to see where I got. Usually, just for the hell of it, hoping Jane would turn up with a lock of your hair. I thought about all that flannel I'd given the immigration guy at the border about wanting to see Canada, and it kind of made me want to go up to Ottawa just as I told him. So, I did. I went to a few other places too. Along the banks of the St Lawrence Seaway up to Montreal. Beyond Quintes Isle and on to Quebec where I drank coffee at cafés as if I was sitting in France. Then on to Halifax and New Brunswick, and to where the space opens up, and the cold wind rips skin off your fingers.

I scribbled names on to my rucksack after each place I got to. It was so scuffed up, it looked like a pineapple by the time I got back to the States.

Chapter Six

Thumbing through borders is as tough as sawing through concrete. No one wants to pick you up in case your bag is full of goo goo beads. And even if you're clean, they probably worry they'll get held up for hours, while Captain America grills you on a fryer. I tried to get a lift but gave up after an hour and decided to walk. I walked miles from Maple Grove to the border. I've got skinny legs that ain't fond of walking and they ached terrible by the time I got there.

The Canadian guy waved me through as if he was glad to see the back of me. He didn't even know me, but that's how he looked at me. As if he never wanted to see me again. But then I had to go through all the usual crap to get back into the States. The American guard was the usual, three parts hate and seven parts misery. Fat too. You know, as if he'd been to training school to learn how to fill his face full of donuts and crap out accusations. As if he had tattoos of Sidney Gottlieb. I didn't like him and pictured him at home with his fat wife and fat kids guzzling beer and yelling at the New York Yankees.

I knew the score by now, though, so I had all my answers ready and just kept smiling as if I enjoyed being beat up. I knew he'd poke around in my bag too, so I stuck all my dirty underpants right at the top. Even smeared a couple with sauce, just for good measure. God, I was waiting for him to get sticky hands. Stick his hands right on to that brown sauce. To tell the truth, I could have put up with his stupid questions all day, just so long as he poked around in my bag and got a load of sauce all over his stinking, prying mits.

He did too. Then he shuddered. I tell you he shuddered. Shuddered as if he was best mates with Eddy II and knew he was next. That cracked me up. It was all I could do to not wet myself.

I don't know why these immigration guys make such a fuss anyway. I'm a scrawny little kid who ain't made of much, so what do they think I'm gonna do? Maybe they think I'll get a gun and turn up as a shooter in some school or college or something. As if no one who lives here does stuff like that. Thinking of him with a poker up his arse cracked me up, though, so even though he burnt me for hours with all his 'judgy' looks, and all his 'judgy' insinuations, I just took it. Didn't even mind.

Anyway, as I told you before, I got used to all this 'judgy' stuff. Everyone's always judging.

I'm terrible, I judge people all the time, usually in two seconds flat. I'll look at them and think I don't like their eyebrows or the way they hold a pen or something. It can be anything, but it's in two seconds flat. I tell you someone could give me a million quid and if I didn't like them, it wouldn't make no difference. I'd just take the million quid and say, 'That's very nice of you,' but as I walked away, I'd still be thinking I don't like the way you handed it to me and I don't like your eyebrows much either.

I'd take that million quid straight to a bank, though. I'd stuff it all in a plastic bag and slap it down on the counter right in front of a bank teller. I'd probably pick the weedy, scrawny one, but sometimes you ain't no choice cos they're all like that. Then I'd say something like:

'I'd like to open an account, my good man.'

I would definitely say 'good man', even though I wouldn't like him, but I'd still say it, because it was a million quid and that's what people with that sort of money say.

While he stared at all the notes just flopped inside, all loose, like a load of old lettuce leaves, I'd eye him all over. I'd look at his shirt and notice all the wrinkles cos I'm betting it wouldn't have been ironed properly and I'd look at his tie and think he should have gone with a Windsor knot, rather than one of them other crappy knots that never do up right. And this teller would be looking in the bag, while he was giving me the once over. He'd get all suspicious and start thinking, what's this kid doing with a million quid and why's it in a plastic bag and ask a load of stupid questions. He'd look at me as if his shirt was whiter than mine even though I bet you it wouldn't be, but he'd just look at me as if it was and he ran the bank or something. Then he'd tell me to wait and call the manager, and we'd both just stand there in this awkward silence, waiting and judging each other.

Then the manager would stroll over holding his pot belly and rubbing his eyes, as if he was getting forty winks, and someone had just disturbed him. Disturbed him right in the middle of a dream where he'd run off with Suzie who was the only decent girl in the bank. The one who greeted you at the door when you came in and had nice ankles. And so, he'd be all grumpy and start to ask me all the same stupid questions. But then he'd suss I was all legit and so he'd change his tune and the teller would change his tune, and they'd start polishing my shoes and licking my arse and bringing me cocktails while I waited.

Then, I'd watch as they counted all that money and when they got to the end, I'd say, 'Excuse me, my good man, would you mind passing me a fifty-pound note?'

I'd watch his eyes light up, cos he'd be thinking maybe I was gonna give him a juicy tip cos I'd come into all this money. But I wouldn't. I'd just take that note and, instead of using a match,

I'd use it to light a cigar. I'd do that, right there in the bank in front of the pot-bellied manager and the teller and anyone else who'd be watching. I swear I would. I'd just sit there and take my time sipping on that cocktail and puffing away on that cigar. Even though I don't like cigars, that's what I'd do.

So, I took all his judging and answered his stupid questions and about two cigars later found myself back in America. America, the home of the brave.

Chapter Seven

Bradley was from Duluth, Minnesota, but I met him when he picked me up just outside Bar Harbor. I'd been travelling around Canada for a couple of weeks, but I wanted to get back to the States, I had things to do. I crossed the border and found myself in Maine. I knew I wanted to head out west and then back, but I had plenty of time and I didn't really care which route I took to get there, so I thought I would take a look at Maine. Back in England, I'd poured over this big map of the States, and used to think about all the places I'd heard of and might go. Sometimes, I'd draw lines with the quickest routes out to San Fran. I'd ink in a route, then think about a way back east. Next day, I'd change my mind and try different roads. Maine hadn't even crossed my mind, but I was here now, and it looked as if it had a neat coastline. I noticed a place called Bar Harbor. I didn't know anything about it, but it sounded neat, so I tried to get a ride.

There's really only one main road into Bar Harbor after you leave the interstate highway after Bangor, so that's where I stood. I only had to wait a few minutes when a mustard-coloured Toyota Corolla pulled up. Bradley was driving.

'You're heading to Bar Harbor, I guess,' he said.

'Yeah.'

'I live there, jump in.'

Bradley looked older than me, redder too. He had a mop of red hair. Not long, but thick as a scourer. Heavy, thick, red hair. If I had just seen him walking down the street or something, I would have thought he was Scottish. Some mad Scots guy who hated the English. I like Scots, especially ones who don't like the English, so I liked Bradley. I liked him straight off, just cos he looked as he did, even though he wasn't Scottish at all.

'I almost didn't pick you up.' he said. 'Then I saw your Union Jack on your rucksack.' Before I'd left England, a load of people had told me that Americans love the Brits. They love our accents, they love the 'old country', they're into nostalgia and all that stuff. Make sure you put a big Union Jack on your rucksack, so they know you are a Brit. I never took any notice. That's one of my problems, see, I never take any notice of people. Trouble is the last thing I wanted was some crappy flag on my pack. I don't like flags. I mean, I do like flags and all if you mean the patterns and the colours, but I don't like what they stand for and how they are used. So, I never did put a Union Jack on my pack.

As it happened, though, there was a small Union Jack flag already on it. It was part of the logo or some 'Made in Britain' crap. I was going to rip it off and I would have too, because I needed more space to scribble all the place names I visited onto my pack, but I hadn't got around to it.

'You want to get a great big Union Jack and stick it right on the top of your pack so everyone can see it. Americans love Brits, you'll get rides all the time, really easy if you do that,' he said. 'If I hadn't seen your flag, I wouldn't have picked you up.' He was jamming home the point. The advice seemed to be overwhelming and I started to think I had been a bit stubborn about all that flag advice. But I never did put a flag on my pack. I'm stubborn like that, so I never did. I hate the way people use flags.

It was only a short ride to Bar Harbor, but the countryside looked raw and meaningful and Brad was easy to talk to. We talked a lot and he told me about Bar Harbor. When we got close to the town, I asked him about places to stay.

'I'm thinking of staying a couple of nights. Do you know if there is anywhere to camp near here?' I asked.

'Yeah, plenty of places,' he said, 'but you can stay at my place, if you want. It's small, rented for the summer and I'm at work in the day, but you can crash if you want.'

'That would be great,' I said. I felt I ought to say more, something more substantial, but I couldn't think of anything better to say. If something is crappy, a million words come to mind, but when something is good, I get stuck. So, I just said 'great'. Another word wouldn't come.

Anyway, that's what happened, and that's where I stayed in Bar Harbor. In my sleeping bag on the floor in Brad's apartment. It was right in the centre of town amongst all the other painted weatherboard buildings and just a short walk from the sea. I liked Brad's apartment and Brad. I liked Bar Harbor.

Later, I got to know more about Brad. He had a degree in Politics from Washington DC. But he had just drifted since. Casual job to casual job. He seemed restless. He was smart and could have done anything if he had wanted, but he didn't want to do anything. Not right then anyway. The world didn't offer enough, or only offered deceit, so he drifted drearily. Disillusioned, he had the intellect, but not the desire to pursue much that was American. I found out later that he was a big fan of J F Kennedy. I reckon he felt that's when America died. America became Vietnam and Nixon. Napalm and tricky Dickie.

'It's going from bad to worse,' he used to say. 'God knows who'll be in charge in 50 years?' At 23, he was marooned in some half-lit limbo, deciding whether he should sell out or drop out. Drop out and look for something out west like Sal Paradise in Kerouac's *On the Road*. As I got to know him, I put money on

Sal.

Anyway, for the time being, to pay the rent, he wore his grown-up, sober face that he kept in the drawer by the door. He wore it to work, in a hardware store in Bar Harbor. A two-faced Bar Harbor summer. He worked most of the day but gave me a key, so I could come and go as I pleased. I wandered around the gentle fishing village and along the roaring, ragged, rugged seashore. I went out to Arcadia National Park and Cadillac Mountain and felt the first rays of dawn. Soaked in America's first sunlight, I walked glorious trails and met curious people who were passing through like me and glorious people who were born there and would never leave. Old men, glorious men who had the ocean and the wind written into the deep lines of their faces and who smoked pipes and sang shanty songs when they weren't too drunk to remember the words.

I could see why Brad had chosen to spend a summer here. The polite streets full of ice cream parlours and boisterous pubs full of singing. And the lobster pots bubbling and bobbing on the ocean, as if nothing mattered much.

During the evenings, after work, Brad would take me to meet some of his friends and we'd go for shoreline walks and then, to bars. We drank a lot and ate a lot. A lot of everything, but mostly lobster. Maine smells of lobster.

'Ever had lobster?' he asked, one night.

I reckon the closest I'd come was greasy cod and chips wrapped in the *Birmingham Evening Mail*, so I thought it best to be straight. 'I don't think so.'

We headed off to a lobster pound. A pale blue beach shack full of driftwood, and lobsters in gurgling glass tanks. We sauntered around and ogled. Ogled the tanks and the lobsters and the smiling girls wearing skinny tops and daisy dukes and showing off their suntans.

'Which one do you want?' Brad asked. 'Have a look around and pick the one you want.'

We went back to the tanks. Five tanks with too many lobsters to count. To be honest, I had no idea how you can tell a good lobster from a bad one. At least humans have job titles, like politician and estate agent.

I just closed my eyes and pointed. Maybe that's what everyone does, but I didn't feel so good.

The lobster was crawling about, minding its own business; then I pointed. I got someone to do my dirty work and throw it into boiling water. When I thought about it, I didn't feel too good at all. Trouble is, I'm a big stinking hypocrite really, cos if someone had slit a chicken's throat and cooked it, and I hadn't seen them do it, I'd go ahead and eat it. I just didn't like being the bastard executioner. I tell you, I'm just a great big bastard hypocrite really. Maybe one day, everyone will go vegan or something, but I bet right now, the world is full of bastard hypocrites like me.

I felt queasy. I felt hungry. I was curious. I smiled at the sun-tanned girl, dripping rivers of soft, golden butter down her white cotton blouse. Shit, I'm a hypocrite. The lobster tasted nice.

We sat in that lobster pound for hours, eating, talking, and that's how I found out a lot about Brad. He asked me lots of questions about England and about where I grew up and stuff, but I never really said too much. I prefer to ask questions rather than answer them, so I usually just told him bits, then changed the subject or got him talking about himself and America and politics. I didn't tell him about what happened to my parents or anything. If we ever got close to talking about it, I just changed the subject and banged on about some place in England that I reckon he would like to visit.

Brad loved politics, though, so it was easy to get him to talk about that. He told me loads of stuff about how the system works and what he thought of American politics. Nixon was news. Nixon and Watergate. I kept asking him stuff about how their system worked. I asked him loads of stuff about senators and diplomats and governors and where they were based and how they went about their daily routines and stuff. Sometimes he looked at me as if I was asking him a load of crazy questions. I was, but he loved politics, so he just kept talking. Brad told me a lot.

'You seem pretty interested in politics,' he said to me. 'Ever wanted to go to DC?'

'Hadn't really thought about it,' I said. 'I'm planning on heading out west. I want to see California and stuff, but then I'll probably head back to Texas.'

'God, why do you want to go to Texas? It's full of oil wells, ranches and crazy people who want to execute everyone.'

'Yeah, I've heard,' I said.

'You'd like DC. It has a lot of interesting stuff. The Capitol Building, the White House, JFK is buried in Arlington, you know.' He seemed enthusiastic about DC. It's where he had lived when he was taking his degree and he loved talking about Kennedy who was buried there. 'You should go,' he said.

'Sounds like I'd like it, maybe I should try and get there before I head west.'

'I might go back to DC myself,' he said. 'I'm thinking of quitting my job, I'll keep the apartment, but might go back to DC, I haven't been for a while.'

I was a bit surprised. I knew he wasn't going to work in the hardware store forever, but he seemed to like Bar Harbor. I thought he would stay for a while.

'Yeah, I'll keep the apartment, but I think I'll quit my job and head down to DC. Maybe head across to see my best friend in Penn before I head back. You could come with me if you want.'

I was even more surprised.

'Sounds neat,' I said. It sounded lame, so I thought I'd better say more, 'When you thinking of going?'

'Tomorrow, day after tomorrow, who knows? Soon. Yeah, soon. I'll quit my job tomorrow.' He said it as if he was working it all out as he spoke. As if he worked it all out in two seconds flat. That's one of the good things about being young — sometimes you can work everything out in two seconds flat. Everything's black and white; it is, or it isn't. No grey.

And that's what he did. The next day he went to work and quit. He told me as soon as he walked in the house after work.

'I've quit, we can go tomorrow.' He was beaming. His friend Mary was with him.

'Do you remember Mary?' he asked, 'She's coming with us.'

The first night I arrived in Bar Harbor, we had gone out to a bar called Giddy's; Brad had introduced me to a few of his friends. It was June 30th, and the bar had a 'Half New Year's Eve' party. America does stuff like that. You know, create stuff that don't really exist just to sell stuff. But Mary had been there, at Giddy's, on the day that was called something, but wasn't really anything. Lots of people had been there, it was packed, so we hadn't really been introduced or talked much, but I remembered seeing her.

'Hi Mary,' I said, 'I think we met the other night?'

'Yeah,' she said, 'you're the English guy, I love your accent.'

I always felt I should say something polite back, like I love your accent too, but I didn't. I don't like American accents and I don't like Americans who talk more loudly than is natural. Trouble is, most Americans do. It's like when they are at school, they are all taught to build up their self-esteem and to speak out and stuff. But it just means they all shout everything at you, even when you're only an inch away. Mary talked like that. Unnaturally loud in an American accent. I should have told her really, but I just said 'huh'. I smiled, and I just said 'huh'.

The next morning, we were gone. I was sorry to leave Bar Harbor. I nodded at the lobster pots; they bobbed back. I felt sad, but happy too; it was good to be moving. It felt good not to need to worry about getting rides for a while and I knew Brad would tell me lots of stuff about places we'd visit. It gave me more time to ask him stuff about politics too.

We travelled south, passing cranberry fields and stopping in little towns. We browsed in bookshops that looked as if they would have first editions of *Uncle Tom's Cabin* and we were sad that nothing had changed. And we drank coffee, not cos we were thirsty, but because we wanted to and because the place looked neat and the owner smelt like cinnamon and ginger beer. Then we crossed the stateline into New Hampshire and we did the same stuff there too, even though the bookshop owner didn't smell of ginger beer, even though he didn't smell of anything.

We were heading to Mary's parents who lived near the White Mountains. On the way, we left the car and hiked a trail up to a waterfall. It was dark and we scratched and cut our legs against the branches of trees and bushes that hid in the black. Then we washed them in the icy water under the waterfall and it stung like hell. But then, because it was so cold, I couldn't feel a thing and my legs went numb, but it didn't matter cos my head was alive and the stars peeping through the canopy of treetops made me tingle.

I think Mary tingled too. See, she had a bit of a thing for Brad and hoped he might fall for her, especially on that walk up to the waterfall. But Mary was too American for Brad. The more time they spent together the more Mary seemed to like Brad, but the less Brad seemed to like her. I started to feel sorry for her, but I don't think Brad did. I don't think Brad liked Americans that act like Americans much. He didn't like Mary much anyway.

When things went wrong, Mary always got the blame. It might have been a problem with the car, or something I had done, or even Brad, but if it went wrong, Mary got it in the neck. Trouble is, sometimes that's just how stuff goes. It's as if people kind of have this halo or they don't. If someone thinks you've got a halo, you're fine. But when you don't, you're screwed. It don't matter what you do then, if you ain't got a halo, you're roasted. That was Mary's problem with Brad, see, she never had a halo.

I don't worry about that sort of crap now, though. It happened to me all the time at school. If a teacher liked you, even if you messed up, you'd be okay, but if they didn't like you, then you were dead meat.

I had all this halo crap in my German class at school. I didn't really want to learn German, but Mr Jackman told me I should. 'We're joining the European Community,' he said, 'German will be useful. All languages will be useful.'

I didn't really take much notice. I didn't like him much. I never liked the tweed jackets he wore, and his skin was a bit too red for my liking. The skin on his face was always a bit red and looked rough, as though if you touched it, it would feel rougher than his tweed jacket. I never touched his face, but I did touch his jacket once and it felt rough.

I never answered him when he told me all that stuff about the European Community and all. See, it seemed to me that most of Britain was still banging on too much about how it had won the war and stuff to want to join any community. But if I didn't take German, I had to do Technical Drawing. I didn't have a clue what Technical Drawing was, so I took German. Jackman probably thought he'd persuaded me to take it and probably smoked a cigar when he got home, but really it was just because I didn't have a clue about TD. I was pissed off big style, though, cos after I said I'd do that stupid German class, I found out he didn't even teach it. He was leaving that to Miss Rupin. German with Miss Rupin, you've got to be kidding.

Now, Miss Rupin was only about twenty-three or something and everyone knew she hadn't been teaching for long. She was nice enough, pretty too, with long black hair and a bit foreign looking. If she'd have kept her gob shut, people would have thought she was from Italy or something, but she couldn't teach German with her gob shut, so we knew she was from Stockport. Somewhere grim up north anyway. Wherever she was from, she couldn't teach for toffee. Like I'm sure she knew German and stuff, but she didn't have a clue how to control crazy kids. A mob of bust-up boys who only took German to get out of Technical Drawing. It wasn't too bad in some ways, cos she was pretty and all and she had nice soft skin, not like that Jackman geezer, but we knew we weren't gonna learn any German. Everyone used to mess about all the time. I did too. You know, not doing my homework, turning up late, skipping class and everything. You can't really expect a halo when you do all that.

Anyway, one day, the whole class decided to mess with her head big style. Just not turn up and leave her waiting in her room on the second floor where she used to try to teach German. Almost everyone it was, you know, all the class thickos and the bunch in the 'in-crowd'. They all went into the school yard instead and stared up at her as she looked out the window at them. They all started yelling abuse and started frog-marching like Nazi soldiers around the yard.

'Vee don't vont to do Deutsche today,' they were yelling. I think Deutsche was the only German word anyone knew, that and how to pronounce everything as if it starts with a 'V'. She looked terrified and kept yelling for everyone to come back. She'd lost control, though. She'd lost control from her first day. She was pretty and all for a teacher, but nice skin ain't gonna get you through. Not with a mob of bust-up boys.

Now that day, I didn't join in. I don't know why. I just didn't feel like it. I didn't feel like it, so I just went to her class instead. So, me and a couple of do-goodies just sat there quietly watching all this as she yelled out the window at the mad crazy mob frog-marching around the school yard.

After about ten minutes, everyone got bored, though, and came in. That's the trouble with pranks like that; after ten minutes you get bored and can't even remember why you did them, so everyone came in.

Now, Miss Rupin was crazy mad. She had put up with lots of crap before, but this really tipped her over the edge; she went crazy. She was yelling and shouting and looked as if she might have a fit or something, and her skin even turned red, a bit like Jackman's.

That's when she turned on me. Now I don't know why she turned on me, cos I'd just been sitting there quiet as if I was asleep or something. But she did. I didn't have a halo, see, so she turned on me.

'Bardell,' she shouted. 'Dylan Bardell, you're for it. You've gone too far, you're for it now.' Her head looked as if it might explode and that made me laugh, which I don't think helped. All the other kids started laughing too and then, yelling. They started chanting, 'Herr Vardell, you're vor it now.' They just kept yelling it over and over in their stupid German accents, saying everything with a 'V'.

To be honest, I couldn't even be bothered to tell her I was just sitting there all the time and that I hadn't been outside doing all that stupid frog-marching and stuff. See, I knew she didn't see a halo, so I would have been wasting my time. I guess I could have asked the do-goodies who had been sitting next to me to tell her, but I knew they would be shit scared to say anything. I'm telling you they were frightened of their own shadow and they wouldn't have said a thing. So, I just switched off for a bit while she hurled all this shit my way.

After it all died down, she sent me to see the Headmaster. He went banging on for a bit and even said something about the war and not disrespecting 'our boys'. Our boys who had made all these sacrifices. To be honest, I think he was more worried about some dead spitfire pilots than he was about poor old Miss Rupin. See, I think he'd been in the Air Force or something about a million years ago and so liked to bang on about it. I reckon he must have been in the Air Force, cos he had a handlebar moustache just like all those old pilots in war films. Anyway, I told him I was sorry even though I hadn't even done anything. But I told him I was sorry anyway. And he told me he was sorry too, but he had no choice but to give me the cane. See, they used to think it was a good idea to hit you with a stick in the 70s, so that's what he did, whacked me with this stupid stick he used to keep in the corner of his room.

Anyway, I was kind of glad he had this stupid handlebar moustache, though, cos it looked pretty funny, and it took my mind off stuff when he hit me. When he whacked me, his moustache even twitched a bit. I reckon it twitched more than my hand, cos I tried real hard to keep it still. It hurt like hell, but I tried to keep it still just to make out I didn't think it was a big deal.

I could have told him that I was in the class the whole time, but to tell you the truth, I couldn't be bothered. I knew he didn't think I wore a halo either, so he wouldn't even believe me. Anyway, I just took it. In a way I was glad I did, cos I wouldn't have heard all his stories about the war pilots if I hadn't, and I tell you that was a lot better than learning German. When I left his office, I thought my hand would be smarting really bad. You know, as if my hand was falling off sore. It had these bright red streaks right across the palm and looked sore, but to be honest, I couldn't feel a thing. That was what school did to you; it made you so you couldn't feel a thing. When I had been sitting in that class watching Miss Rupin trying to get control of that crazy mob, at first, I started to feel sorry for her, but after that caning, I didn't feel a thing.

I didn't bother going back to her class that day and just skipped school. I walked across some of the fields nearby instead. It was summer and the sun was shining. I reckon it must have been warm and the breeze might have felt nice against my face. But I couldn't tell, I couldn't feel a thing.

So, cos I was used to all that sort of 'you ain't got a halo' crap, I guess I should have felt sorry for Mary. I didn't, though. I didn't like her loud American voice and her whiney accent and her stupid centre of attention American ways. I should have felt sorry for her really, but I didn't, I didn't feel a thing.

The White Mountains were glorious, though, and Mary's parents had this real swanky looking place with a swimming pool and everything. They seemed real friendly too, but we didn't hang about. Brad seemed to want to get on, so we dropped Mary off. I think she was glad to get out. I think she'd lost interest in Brad. I don't think Brad noticed. I don't even think he noticed she'd got out as we drove on towards Boston.

We drove pretty fast on the way down to Boston, just stopping for fuel and leaks and trail mix. We bought so much trail mix, we put it in a bucket and must have dipped our fingers in more times than those pistons pumped. Faster too, even though he was driving at 80. The salty taste of the peanuts and the sweetness of the raisins, and the oats and the sunflower seeds got me dreaming of California. We must have eaten all the trail mix in Massachusetts by the time we got to Boston and when I licked my fingers they still tasted of salt.

Most of the sites in Boston relate somehow or other back to the American Revolution. This is where the colonials took on the British. I was Paul Revere on horseback, smoking tea, not tipping it. JFK was born here; Brad loved it. Brad loved lobster too, so we ended up at the Big Oyster House. JFK was supposed to have eaten there all the time, you know, all that favourite seat stuff. Restaurants in America are always doing that. You know, claiming so and so ate here or such and such happened here. I reckon most of it is bullshit, but the Big Oyster House bangs on about JFK, as if he was having breakfast there every day or something. Maybe he was, how would I know? There was a plaque and everything in this booth, saying this is where JFK sat when he ate at the oyster bar. Brad gave me a load of bull, but he loved it and loved showing it to me even more. So, we had more lobster, right there, in the seat where JFK ate his. Yeah. Smoking Boston tea, eating lobster. We talked more politics, I found out more stuff; the oyster house made more money.

I could never really tell if Brad loved DC or Boston more,

but after we left, he was dying to show me around DC. We headed south.

Out of the car into the oven-hot heat of DC. The air was as sticky as maple syrup and wet clothes glued as we wandered under a sky the colour of bone. The dry, magnificent bones of some ancient animal lay before us, vastly spread across the still, flat land. A skull balanced oddly on the only pillow in the dead, flat land. Ghosts circled. Grand and splendid, like a new Rome, but diminished by smaller minds to become no more than the too tidy desk of a too tidy man. Awaiting Caligula. We walked through the mummified white, dripping.

The Capitol, the White House. We wandered. The Smithsonian, the Kennedy Art Centre, the Watergate buildings. Brad talked breathless about Nixon and the reporters who helped unravel him. We looked for wanted posters. Manipulators wriggled.

On the last day in DC, he took me to Arlington Cemetery to JFK's grave. I didn't really want to go to a cemetery after what had happened to my mum and dad and all, I didn't want all the bad memories. But I still hadn't said anything to him about what had happened to them, so he didn't have a clue. Anyway, I knew how much it meant to him to go, so that's where we went on our last morning in DC. We didn't speak much. He was quiet and preoccupied. I reckon he was thinking about what America would have been like if JFK hadn't been killed. I was thinking about my mum and dad. Quiet and preoccupied.

Chapter Eight

We left DC and headed for Pennsylvania. Brad's best friend, Dan, was living near Harrisburg with his wife Marty. Brad was planning to stay there for a couple of days and then head back to Bar Harbor. He said Dan and Marty would be happy to meet me, so I could go with him and crash there for a night or two.

On the way we talked about JFK and Nixon and how the wrong guy had been assassinated. He told me a lot about the tensions in the States in the 60s. I was a few years younger than Brad, so I didn't know that much about it. I had been too young to ever get much more than headlines. But Brad had been a teenager in the 60s and had been old enough to get angry. He'd grown up watching Daisy Bates risk her life so that black kids could go to the same school as white kids in Arkansas. Nine black kids wanting education. He'd watched the clueless, cutthroat clan of white mothers and fathers spitting hate as the kids were escorted through the gates. He talked about the turbulence of those times. Segregation, the civil rights protests and Tommie Smith at the Olympics in Mexico, the assassinations of Kennedy and of Martin Luther King and Malcolm X. We talked about why it's always the good guys that get murdered.

I asked him whether he thought it was ever okay for someone to kill someone. You know, if someone was real evil and had done something real shitty. He was shocked. I don't think Brad would kill anything, except maybe lobsters. I asked him if some bastard had killed someone, should they ever be able to get away with it, like if they claimed diplomatic immunity or something.

'You talk about some crazy stuff,' he said. 'You're crazy.'

'Yeah, I know,' I said, 'but what do you think?'

'Well, no, no one should kill anyone. But no, I don't think people should be able to use privilege to get away with anything.' He paused. 'I'm not sure revenge is the answer.'

'I guess I agree,' I said. I just left it vague.

We arrived late at Dan and Marty's apartment. It was above a row of shops in a busy street, opposite a donut place. The neon lights flashed and lit up their room. They lit it up too. They were nice, just like Brad. I could see why Dan was his best friend.

Dan had been at Duke University in Durham, North Carolina, and that's where he had met Marty. He was tall. I reckon he must have been about seven foot or something. He had dark hair, almost black. It was thick, swept back off his forehead and hung over his collar. It looked a bit like Roy Orbison when he was singing Pretty Woman for the first time. Next to Dan, Marty looked small. I guess she wasn't really that small, but next to Dan she looked small. I guess next to Dan, everyone looked small.

I liked Marty, though, she was sweet. She had dark hair too, but it was short. When she wore a shirt or a dress or something it didn't even reach her collar, so I could see her neck. She had a nice neck. Long and graceful, longer than most necks I'd seen anyway. I don't know why, but apart from her neck, she always reminded me of a mouse. You know, a cute mouse, the sort of mouse you'd get in *The Wind in the Willows* or a Disney animation or something.

She didn't look anything like a mouse, but that's what I think of. A tiny Disney mouse next to big, desperate Dan with his black, Roy Orbison hair.

I spent a couple of days at their house and met a few of their friends, not that I remember much. I don't remember seeing anything of Harrisburg either. I don't even remember going out much. Trouble was, we smoked a lot of grass and ate a lot of donuts. I could see why they had rented a place across the road from a donut store.

Their house was always full of people too. People they knew who just used to come and go. Some of them stayed all night and some of them didn't stay any time at all, but there were always people coming and going. I don't remember them all, but I remember Cathy and Sue. They knew Marty from Duke and had moved up north just because. And then there was Wes. He was a black guy who played in a jazz band in New Orleans. He'd met Dan on a spring break once and had called in to see Dan and Marty on his way up to New York, where he was gonna play jazz in a piano bar in Tribeca. And there was Willy Kinchin and I don't even remember what he looked like or where he was from, but I remember him, cos I liked his name and wished I'd been called Willy Kinchin. I tell you, if I'd sent postcards that week, I would have signed them Willy Kinchin, but I didn't send any, so I just thought about it in my head.

At night, when a crowd had gathered, we'd sit in a circle, cross-legged on the floor as if we were Apache Indians. Not cos we wanted to be, but mostly cos there weren't enough seats and it was easier to chew the fat that way. We'd pass joints and tell stories and laugh and drink too much beer. I remember smoking this bong. A beer bottle turned pipe that filled up with so much smoke it blew your head off. I can still feel the rasp against the back of my throat and the hot smoke burning my lungs. At that moment, you could never figure why you did it, but then after a minute, you figured it all out. And then you couldn't remember much at all except that everything seemed lighter and the taste of those donuts. One time, when we'd all smoked too much and drunk too much too, I looked across at Sue. She had the sweetest smile and just for that moment, I reckon she loved me. And Joni Mitchell was playing and singing about frying pans being too big. And on paper, when you see it written down it don't seem to mean much, but the way that she sang it, it sounded as if she knew how we felt. You know, how it feels to be lonely and missing someone so bad that everything seems too big. But then I felt hungry, and cos I reckon Sue had fallen for me, I asked if she wanted to go across and buy some more donuts and she nodded and said yes. And so, we dashed out into the cold night air and didn't really care that it was hammering down with rain and about how wet we'd got. So, we ran across the road and flashed in the neon and the rain made our T-shirts stick so close to our skins that you could see our heart beating.

We waited for a long time to get them donuts. We didn't care much though cos we were messing and fooling as if we were lovers even though we weren't. When we got to the counter, we made out we were headed to Vegas and planning to get married and the server was cheerful and said she hoped we'd be happy. She even threw in an extra donut for free. Just as a present like. She crammed it in the 12-donut box and there wasn't really room, so it was all squashed and mangled. But that didn't matter cos we were all squashed and mangled. It seemed as if we'd been gone a lifetime by the time we'd got back. Wes had left to go and meet a friend and Willy Kinchin was playing guitar in the corner. Dan and Marty had gone to bed and Brad and Cathy were curled up fast asleep on the carpet amongst all the joint butts and the beer bottles and half-eaten donuts.

Me and Sue curled up too, as if we were really gonna go to Vegas, knowing in the morning, we wouldn't even remember.

Knowing by next week we probably wouldn't even remember what we looked like, or care either.

I liked Dan and Marty. I liked Brad too. I liked them all a lot. But it was time to move on. Brad was heading back to Bar Harbor. Dan and Marty were living. And Sue and Cathy and Wes and Willy and all the others, all had plans too. I would be heading out west. To the magnificent sunset west. It was time to move on.

Chapter Nine

So, after all that, I found myself in the back of a Ute heading for Columbus, Ohio. A '64 Falcon Ranchero. It felt cruel. For the last couple of weeks, I'd been travelling around with someone who had become a friend. We were strangers but had become friends. But that was gone. Life had been pretty good, I'd seen a lot and found out a lot, but it was gone. Over. Everything is temporary.

That's the thing about travelling. Two weeks before, I hadn't even met Brad, Dan or Marty, and chances are, I wouldn't see any of them again. Maybe I would, but chances are I wouldn't. When you travel, there isn't much space for the past. It melts like ice cream and there is only now. Every day, new. Now is new. People you knew shrink to dots on a page, and there is a story ahead. A story to be written in any colour you choose. Full of human joy or heart-wrenching solitude. Eager, ecstatic, fearful, alone. That's how it felt in the back of this pick-up truck heading for Ohio.

The guy who picked me up couldn't have been more different to Brad or Dan. They were both well-educated and seemed a bit lost. Lost, disillusioned, searching. I know that's how I feel most of the time. But the guy driving this pick-up truck was different. He was a farmer boy. He looked a bit like Howdy Doody with his cheery manner and checked shirt I looked at his hands. I could see he worked with his hands. He didn't seem like the sort of guy who spent a lot of his time thinking. You know, worrying about working it out. He seemed happy, though, happier than Brad and Dan. Happier than most. I reckon he'd never been lost in his whole life.

For the first twenty miles or so, I sat upfront in the cab with him. He didn't say much, just smiled. So, I smiled back, and in between smiles just looked out the window. He was cheerful, but just didn't say much. Anyway, not long in, he chuckled and told me he had to pick someone up and there wasn't enough room for us all in the cab. At first, I thought he was gonna throw me out, but he chuckled, and said I could ride in the back of the truck. 'It's great in the back of the truck,' he said. 'You gonna love it. I'd climb in there with ya, but I can't see, cos I'm driving.' He chuckled again and I chuckled back, as if it was the funniest thing I'd ever heard.

So that's what happened. He stopped and picked up his friend and after that, I sat in the open air in the back of his pick-up truck. His friend was another farmer boy, but he didn't have a Howdy Doody smile. He looked me up and down with a suspicious look, so I just nodded and climbed on the flat bed in the back of the truck.

It is genius in the back of a pick-up truck. I'd had a few rides in trucks in Canada and I loved them. The wind rushes past you and you can hear the whooshing of the air as you speed across the country. You see stuff. Fields, farms, flowers, birds. For ever. You see for ever. If I had a choice, I'd always travel in the back of a pick-up truck, but hitchhiking is like a box of donuts; you never know what you are gonna get.

That farmer boy drove that truck so fast I thought I would shoot right off the back, so I held on tight as we raced towards Columbus. Then suddenly, he pulled off the highway and drove down some dusty country roads. He was up front with his pal, so I didn't know where we were headed, but I was glad to slow down and just looked at the farm boys working the fields. I thought about stopping and looking for work, you know, waiting for harvest time. But I looked at my hands and thought about his and then thought about sunflowers and the sun of California.

We got to a farm, some run-down, rickety, single-storey, falling-down place, and his friend climbed out. He still looked suspicious, so we just exchanged nods, and as he walked off, I climbed back into the cab. To tell the truth, I was happy in the back of his pick-up truck, but cheery boy said 'hop back in the cab' with a chuckle, and so I did, with a chuckle, and hoped he might tell me about life in Ohio.

I asked him about Columbus. He didn't say much. I tried politics; he looked at me blankly. I asked him whether he'd travelled across the States; he told me he'd never left Ohio. I rambled on about England; he glazed over. I guessed he didn't have much to say.

Now when I was riding in the back of his truck, I had been leaning against these farm tools and crazy bit of machinery. It looked as if there were bits of a harvester or something in that truck, but all I knew was they had sharp bits that looked as if they'd cut your leg off. Bits that had dug deep in my back real bad when we hit bumps in the road. I thought maybe he might want to tell me about that. To be honest, I really didn't give a shit what it all was, but I couldn't take any more chuckling and I didn't know what else to say, so I asked him about it. Jesus, he never stopped. He must have talked about that stupid thing for the next hundred miles. He hadn't said a thing, but he couldn't stop talking about these stupid tools and bits of crappy farm machinery. I think he loved that bit of crap just as much as Brad loved JFK. That's the thing about hitchhiking; you never know what you are gonna get. I reckon he'd still be talking about it now if he had his way, but when we got near to Columbus, I changed the subject. He seemed disappointed. I started to ask him if he knew anywhere that I might stay. When I'd hitched in Canada, I sussed that this was a smart thing to do when you were getting near to the end of the ride. Sometimes, people knew of a place and then would go out of their way to take you there. Right up to the front door of the place, as if you'd booked a taxi or something. That was always neat when that happened.

But sometimes, they wouldn't know of a place and that's when I would start telling them how I didn't have much money and how some people had been real kind and let me camp in their garden or on their land and stuff. You know, I'd lay it on with a trowel, real thick, and tell them about how kind and helpful some people were, and how great people were to help out a young Brit trying to make his way across the country. I reckon sometimes, when I was really laying it on thick, if I could have heard myself, I would have thrown up. But usually, I just went onto autopilot and spouted out all this Charles Dickens, Bob Cratchit, 'help me if you can, mister' crap. Sometimes it worked and sometimes it didn't, but mostly, it did. Mostly people helped me out. They'd say stuff like, 'Oh, ok. Maybe you could pitch your tent in the yard.'

'That would be real kind of you if you don't mind, I really appreciate it.' I'd say it as if they'd just saved my life or something, I'd say it all gushing and dewy-eyed. I'm telling you sometimes I almost puked when I did that, but I did it anyway. Who knows, maybe sometimes it did save my life.

Well, I think if I had tried this with this guy about a hundred miles ago, he wouldn't have said a thing, but he'd got so excited telling me about this crappy farm machinery, that he seemed to have taken to me. Union Jack, I thought. This guy wouldn't even know what it was. But he knew about farm stuff. I reckon that bit of farm machinery saved my life in Columbus, Ohio. 'I don't have a yard, but you could sleep on the floor in the house maybe. I'll have to check with Ma, but if she's okay about it, you can sleep on the floor.'

The 'maybe' worried me. The guy was about 40 and looked as if he could wrestle a cow to the floor with his bare hands, but it seemed he lived with his ma.

'Wow,' I said, 'wow.' I'm not really a 'wow' kind of person, and almost said 'huh', but 'wow' came out.

And that's how I ended up seeing his ma sitting on the toilet at about two in the morning in this shack just outside Columbus, Ohio.

I reckon it almost killed her, as if she almost had a heart attack or something. See, I don't think she was keen on me staying at her place at all. When we got to their house, he took me to meet his ma. I stood around in the hallway and I could see them whispering to each other. I couldn't hear them, but you could tell she was looking at me all suspicious like. Same way his pal had done earlier. I reckon she was cursing him and asking him why he had brought a stranger to the house. I don't think my English accent and Union Jack were going to cut much ice. He was shifting about, looking proper nervous, you know, how people do when they shift their weight from foot to foot. You know how little kids do when they are dying for a leak or something. He looked at his mum and looked as if he was shit scared of her, but he glanced across at me and looked as if he didn't want to go back on his word to me. He'd lost his cheery look, though, you know, more like Howdy Doody when he's off-stage and shoved in a box. He shuffled even more and looked even more nervous. I got the feeling that he had never stood up to his mum in his life, so I watched as they whispered. I started to think I wasn't going to have a place to stay for the night. To be honest, I wasn't that keen on staying here anyway, but it was getting late and I didn't have many options. I played my ace.

'Just let me know when you need a hand moving that farm machinery out of the truck,' I yelled to him.

He looked back at me and then at her. And then at me and at her. He pulled himself upright, so he was about two inches taller and raised his voice too.

'He's staying,' he said. He stared right at her. 'He's staying.'

She stepped back as if she had been shot in the chest and muttered something under her breath. It sounded blasphemous. I don't reckon he had ever stood up to her before and it looked as if he had felt a new emotion sweep through him. He looked at me with a triumphant sneer on his face, knowing he was two inches taller. But it only lasted a few seconds. His expression changed. He stared into the middle distance for a moment and muttered to himself. I couldn't hear what he said, but it may have been, 'Oh God, what have I done?'

'Let me know when you need a hand,' I said. I thought it might break the ice.

The house was a crappy little shack in the middle of some run-down part of town on the outskirts of Columbus. Now I'm not saying that because I'm some bigshot or something. I come from a crumby part of Birmingham, and Birmingham is the pits. But just because I knew shit, didn't make theirs any better. I'm telling you the place was a dump. An 18-carat dump.

I reckon they didn't have much money. I mean, he looked as if he worked real hard and all. His hands were all rough and chewed up and stuff as if he'd worked real hard all his life. It just didn't look as if he'd made much money. That's the trouble;

working hard doesn't seem to make anyone much money. Finding some scam will make you money, but not working hard. I reckon this guy didn't know any scams.

I imagined that some future creepy President would suck up to gullible guys like this. You know, hard-working folk who live in dumps around Columbus, Ohio. He'd probably tell them a load of bullshit just to get their votes, because he'd be full of scams. I bet they'd give it too. I reckon folks like this would probably fall for crappy scams like that and they'd give their vote to anyone who promised them bullshit. I mean, look how he helped me out and I only talked to him about his crappy farm machinery.

Anyway, after all that crap, that's where I crashed for the night. In my sleeping bag on his living room floor. The house was small. There wasn't much space and every room joined the living room. The kitchen, the bedrooms, even the toilet. It was messy with lots of stuff lying around. There were even bits of farm machinery leaning against the walls. I'm telling you it was an 18-carat dump. They had this crazy dog too. It just kept charging about the room, sniffing around and sticking its nose into everything. I hate dogs, so I kept out of its way as best I could, but it just kept sniffing around.

The evening dragged and the place creeped the Jesus out of me, but I helped get that crappy farm machinery out of the truck and that seemed to take about twenty hours, so by the time we got back in, the old lady had gone to bed. Howdy went to bed too, and I unrolled my sleeping bag and tried to get some sleep.

Now during the night, that stupid dog just kept sniffing around. I hated it, but I reckon by morning, Ma ended up hating that dog more than me. I bet if she had a gun, she would have shot it right between its eyes. Right there in her living room.

See, what happened was during the night she kept having to

get up for a leak and stuff. You know, getting up a million times in the night to go for a leak just as old people do. The crappy toilet was just off the living room, so she had to creep past me to have her stupid leak. I reckon I must have slept through sometimes, but she kept getting up to go and it kept waking me up.

Now, I tell you, I wished I hadn't been awake the last time she went, but that stinking dog had been sniffing around me and so I was wide awake. I watched as she crept across the living room in her old creepy nightie and went into the toilet and closed the door. It was just a few feet away from where I was lying, so I heard everything. She had so much wind, I reckon she'd been chewing gum in a gas cooler. It was gross, I tell you. Gross. I felt as if I was going to puke. But then it got worse cos this crazy, mangey dog started sniffing around the door and poking its nose in as it had been doing all night. The door swung wide open while she was still sitting on the toilet. Right there in front of where I was sleeping, right there in front of my eyes. I'm telling you I almost puked.

The dog was sniffing around her legs and poking its nose into her knickers dangling down by her ankles. She pushed it away and cursed and swore and the dog was yelping and barking. She grabbed a toilet brush that was by the side of her and tried to whack the dog. The dirty, stinking head of the toilet brush bust off and flew across the living room like a hand grenade. It missed my face by a couple of inches and wedged itself under the cooker. But she hung on to the handle of the brush, and still in her hand, it came down hard on the dog's nose. It yelped and scurried off across the living room to the kitchen. I put my head inside my sleeping bag and thought of Brad and Dan and Marty and donuts and how I could have married Sue in Vegas. I tell you, when you hitchhike you never know what you're gonna get.

I didn't sleep much the rest of that night. I didn't go to the toilet either. Ma didn't either. The dog did, though, right in the kitchen next to the head of that toilet brush wedged under the cooker.

Next morning it was quiet. No one said much. The guy took me out to the interstate early. I don't think he fancied facing his ma. I didn't see her before I left either. Any of her. I'm not sure what she was going to do to him when he got back, for bringing a stranger to her house. I'm not sure what she was going to do to the dog either, but I reckon I would have sooner been the dog.

Chapter Ten

I reckon most stuff is just made up. Especially history and reputations and that sort of stuff. They tell you the story they want you to believe. Usually, they don't care much if it's made up and it's all bull, they just care about how many people they can get to believe it. Politicians do it all the time, countries do it too. Anyone who has power does it. That's the trouble — most stuff is just made-up bullshit.

It's like that with America. They want you to believe it's the best place on the planet and all, as if it's this great wonder country running the world and doing everyone a big favour. Everywhere you go in America, someone gives you a load of bull and tells you how great they are. You turn up at some crumby restaurant and they say, 'we've got the world's best pancakes', or you go to a baseball match and they call it the 'world series'. It's all made up. No one else plays stupid baseball and those crappy pancakes probably aren't even the best in the state, never mind the world. It's all bull, but it's what America believes. They've told themselves all this crap for so long they've started to believe it. That's what they want everyone else to believe too.

Really most of America is a dump. Soon as you leave some of the big cities in the east behind, and get into the mid-west, you realise it's a dump. I'm telling you, it's full of crappy little towns and cornhusker shacks and trailer parks flying the stupid Stars and Stripes. That's one reason why I hate flags. Some jerk living in a house on wheels, in the middle of Nebraska with next-to-nothing, has been fed all this bullshit about how great America is, and so they stick up a flag. Now, I reckon if you spoke to Harriet Tubman or Red Horse or some of the poor bastards who lived in Nagasaki, they wouldn't say it was so great. But they didn't write the story. They didn't even get a pen.

It's not just America either; everyone does it. Britain. Everyone. Everyone makes up a load of bullshit and does their best to sell it. It's just that America does it better than the others. I reckon if America is world class at anything, it's selling bullshit.

It don't matter where you look in America, you can tell they think they're the best thing since sliced bread, but I'm telling you, really, a lot of America is a dump. I bet there will be some fat-assed President talking a load of shit someday about how great America is and how he'll make sure it'll stay great and all that crap. I reckon there will be a load of nobodies in the mid-west lapping it up big style. They'll start waving their flags and sing 'God save America', as if their life depends on it, but I'm telling you, it really ain't that great. It never was. It never will be. It's a dump. Well, most of it anyway. See the National Parks and stuff are genius. It's just that Americans live there.

Trouble is, it don't matter whether something is true or not, it just matters whether the creeps making it up can get enough people to buy the crap they're spreading. Half plus one. Just get half the people and one more person to buy the bullshit and you can do what you want. Sometimes, you don't even need that many, but half plus one is a banker. Then you're left with this winner takes all shit, and people forget that they're sharing the same space. That's the trouble with democracy. Half plus one calls the shots, while half minus one waits in the shadows. It might be the biggest cock-up ever, but it don't matter if it's called democracy. People stop asking questions. They stop thinking about what's happened and whether it's a good thing or not.

That's why they don't like you asking questions at school. They just wanted us to remember stuff and not ask questions. I reckon if people started asking questions, it would all fall apart real quick, and they don't want that. It's better if no one asks any questions and everyone says 'it's okay cos it's democracy'. Then, nothing matters anymore, cos people just say it's democracy, as if it's magic or something.

And that's the big problem with America. The problem with all empires. All empires. The Greeks, the Romans, the British, everyone, they all just made-up crap. And that's what a lot do, just talk crap. Ask the soda companies how many plastic bottles they produce every minute and how that helps the planet. Silence. Open a bottle of pop and even the top goes sshhhh.

The British tried all this crap until the Americans learnt how to do it better. Like when I was at school, we were always told about how great Drake was. He was even knighted. Sir Francis Drake. You ask the poor sods in the Caribbean what they think of Drake and they'll tell you he was a marauding bastard of a pirate. Just a stinking pirate, robbing on behalf of Her Royal Highness. Her Royal Arsehole more like. Drake. Biggsy with a boat and some hoity-toity connections. See, trouble is, if you lived in the Caribbean, you didn't write the story. You didn't even have a pen. But some lackeys did. Lackeys with connections in high places. It didn't matter that it was bullshit, what mattered was how many people fell for it. And, how many people still do. See, Drake would have had diplomatic immunity. He could do whatever he wanted to, and it was okay, cos he would have had diplomatic immunity. Sir Dipstick Immunity.

I always thought that Drake crap was bullshit. One day, during a history class at school, when we were studying Drake and stuff, I just yelled out, 'Tell us about the Morant Bay rebellion and why they massacred 1,500 blacks after the Jamaica courthouse burning. Why are we always taking about Drake? It sounds to me like he was just a pirate.' Most of the other kids laughed. I don't know why they laughed, cos I was serious. The teacher clipped me round the ear for that one and told me I was wrong. He wasn't a pirate, but a great man and that's why he was knighted. A great brave adventurer, he told us. I don't know if he really bought that bullshit or if he'd just said it to so many kids that he'd started to believe it. And I'm pretty sure he'd never even heard of the Jamaica courthouse burning, cos they didn't want to talk about stuff like that. That was the trouble with school; they didn't want you to think about things and question stuff, just lap it up. Then, if you could remember stuff, remember all the crap you were fed, you could write it down in a paper. That's how you passed your exams, you just needed to remember stuff. So long as you could remember the dates Drake did all his robbing, and said he was great, you were fine.

When you think about it, America has a whole machine selling its fantasy. The old empires had to carve their stories on tablets of stone or write it out long-hand with some quill and ink, but America has a machine. Just watch a Hollywood movie and you'll see. They all end up telling how America saves the world. All of them, just making out how great America is. When I go to the pictures and see audiences lapping up all this crap, it does my head in. I watch them clapping and cheering and all sorts of crap when they see America save the world. It makes me puke. When I watch films like that, I just walk out to make sure I don't throw up.

But then they have their crappy music industry too. All these songs, telling you about all these places in America. Like Gene Pitney on his way to Tulsa. 24 hours from Tulsa, but no mention of 1921 and a white mob attacking the blacks. 300 dead. 24 hours. Then more sweet stuff about San Francisco and wearing flowers in your hair.

See, the UK never got that sort of crap going. 'When you're going to Kingston-on Hull, be sure to take your hat, scarf, and cagoul.' I reckon that's what Gandhi figured out when he brought down the British Empire. I reckon he'd worked out he was only up against George Formby, leaning on a lamppost, strumming away on his ukulele watching all the little ladies go by. That and a Fred Rose map, with John Bull looking down his nose at everyone who didn't have the sense to be born British. I reckon when the next Empire comes along and kicks America's arse, it's gonna need a massive, mega-media industry. Lots of bullshit on non-stop media. It won't matter that it's bullshit, it's just got to be non-stop, tick-tock. 24/7 squared. Maybe America has confused 'great' with 'big'. See, I'm telling you America ain't as great as it makes out. It is big, though. You can't argue with that; it's big. To get across the mid-west and out past the prairies, you need to be Lewis and Clark, I'm telling you, you need to cover a lot of miles.

So, that's what I did. Just hitch rides and cover some miles. A long line slicing a map, drawn in seconds, eating away days of my life. Magnificent days. Adventurous days. Eternity on my breath. Luck in my pocket. Just after I crossed into Indiana, I thought I had got lucky too. I met this trucker who was heading for San Francisco. It was still over 2,000 miles away, but he was going all the way. He planned to drive it in about three days flat. I guess he was on speed like lots of the truckers; that's how they cover the long distances quick. When he picked me up, his eyes were wide, and he couldn't stop talking. You know, as if his belly was full of words, and he couldn't get to heaven unless he told me everything. He was buzzing. Arteries full of glitter. He picked me up near Indianapolis and told me I could have a ride all the way to the west coast with him. He spilled from this to that and promised me we'd never stop. Aim at the red glare of the west and crank it up to 80 during the inky night, only slowing in the morning mist in case of cops. Then on and on until the purple evening cloaked us, then staring into blackness, on and on and on. It never happened, though. See, he started coming down and got all creaky, then pulled up at a roadhouse on the interstate near Champaign, Illinois, where we both got out. When I got back to his truck he'd gone. My bag was just lying there on the floor where his stinking truck had been. He didn't say anything, just chucked my bag out. Maybe he was still off his head and forgot I was with him. Maybe he just didn't like me. To be honest, I don't think he did, but I hadn't liked him much either; it just seemed tempting to slice America in one hit. To get to the west coast with one ride. Mainlining diesel. I thought it was gonna be the ride of my life. America in three days flat. But it wasn't. I just made a few lousy miles.

At least he didn't take my stuff, though. He'd chucked it out of his cab when he left, and it was lying on the dusty parking lot where his truck had been parked. I picked up my rucksack and looked at it. It was battered and worn now. When I first landed, it was brand new. Too new, too clean, too yellow. It was getting beaten and had a load of places I'd visited inked across the fading, worn fabric. It started to look as if it was full of fruit going off. Skin bruised and discoloured, soft, spilling out its heart and life. Passed its sell-by date. Overripe. Like a bag that had been places and needed to be eaten, quickly.

The truck stop was a dusty, desolate place. If I'd been in a movie, it would be the sort of place where tumbleweed would cut up the landscape. Dried egg-fried noodle balls of tumbleweed blowing in between the dusty trucks parked up outside the coffee house. There wasn't any tumbleweed, but it looked as if there should be. There was a coffee house, though, so I decided to step inside to see if I could meet some truckers and cadge a ride.

And that's where I met Annie.

It wasn't the sort of place I expected to meet anyone, let alone someone like Annie, but there she was. Sitting cross-legged on the dusty floor like a sphinx leaning against the coffee house. Sitting on the floor with her head bowed down. At first, I could only see her hair. The sun shone and streaked it with light. It was long and blonde. It had the look of sunlight, you know, as if it had been bleached by sunlight. She hadn't said a word, but her hair spoke. It said she would be miserable during autumn and would find winter unbearable. She may tolerate spring, but only because it marked the arrival of summer and sunlight. She had the look of summer about her, but not just one summer. A life of summers.

It was long too. Down her back and long enough to sit on. Each strand its own length. Not sheared straight by sober hands. Nature guided it as each strand chose its way.

With her head bowed, she looked preoccupied, deep in thought, but I couldn't really tell; maybe she was sleeping. I walked towards her slowly. I couldn't see much of her, couched down like that against the coffee house wall, but she was slim, skinny as me. She looked older, though, maybe twenty or something.

She was leaning against the wall, right next to the door, and I wasn't sure if she'd look up as I went in. I was kind of hoping she would and maybe say 'hi' or something. 'Don't have a southern drawl,' I thought.

She must have heard my footsteps, cos when I was real close, she looked up. I noticed her eyes. Beautiful eyes that sparkled like the Caribbean Sea. A turquoise aquamarine. The colour of the sea that hugs the coast of Antigua where the sun beats down and pierces the shallow water and bounces back off the pink, soft, coral sand.

I stopped. 'Hi,' I said.

The sun was behind me and cast a shadow over her. It cast a shadow on her hair too, but not enough so you would notice.

'Hey, stop blocking the sun,' she yelled. 'If I wanted to sit in the shade, I wouldn't be leaning against this goddam roadhouse wall, would I?'

It hadn't got off to a good start, but at least she didn't have a drawl. It wasn't one of those crappy whiney voices either.

'Sorry,' I said, 'didn't mean to—' I wasn't really sure what I didn't mean to do, but before I finished, she interrupted.

'You don't sound like you're from round these parts. You English?'

'Yeah,' I said. 'From a place called Birmingham,' I said.

'I like English accents.'

I thought about asking her if she would like to see my flag but thought better of it. 'Huh,' I said. I thought it was time for one of my 'huhs', so that's all I said.,

I smiled to myself. If I was in England, everyone would think I had a stupid accent, but she didn't have a clue. She liked it. All Americans liked it.

'You getting a drink?' she asked. It sounded more like an order. I think she was telling me I was.

'Yeah,' I said. Now really, I was going in to try and talk to a trucker about a lift, but I just said 'yeah'. She was the sort of girl you felt you had to say 'yeah' to.

'Great, you can buy me one.' She jumped to her feet and pushed open the roadhouse door. 'After you,' she said, and we went in.

The place was empty, but there were a few truckers playing pool and drinking coffee and stuff. They looked up. She was the sort of girl that made people look. She knew it too. She was pretty, but more than that she had something of the compelling about her. She drew people to her. I reckon if she walked into a place like this with Marilyn Monroe, people would have stared at Annie. Next to Annie, Marilyn would have looked like Danny La Rue on an off day.

We sat on some swivel stools by the counter and ordered coffees. We swivelled our chairs as we talked and drank coffee. We talked for a long time. I'm not sure why, but we did. In America, when you order a coffee, they will just keep topping it up for free, as if they have shares in the coffee company or something. Maybe we'd had too much caffeine, maybe we just got along, I didn't really think about it — all I know is we just kept swivelling our chairs and talking and drinking coffee.

She was banging on about all sorts of stuff, but I picked up that she was hitchhiking out west like me. She rattled on about some friends in LA who were in bands and stuff, and how she was thinking she may go out there sometime. She told me all sorts of stuff, but she kept coming back to a story about a commune in Oregon. She just kept telling me about this commune in Oregon she wanted to go to. She just kept talking about it and swivelling her chair.

We'd been talking for ages and it was getting late. I needed to look for a lift, so I got up to go. To tell you the truth, I didn't really feel like hitchhiking and could have stayed there chatting to her, but I told her I was gonna go and see if I could get a ride.

Then, right out of the blue, she said, 'Do you want to hitchhike with me?'

Her blue eyes sparkled. I was about to say yes. But she liked to talk.

'I get rides easy, but being a girl alone means I have to put up with some real creeps. You'd be doing me a favour hitching with me. Anyway, you'll get rides quicker if you're with a girl.'

I felt like telling her I had a Union Jack and I got rides okay, but I didn't. It sounded churlish. 'Yeah,' I said. 'Why not?' I said it as if I could take it or leave it. Inside I smiled.

And so that's what happened. For the next week, I just hitchhiked out west with Annie. We hitched across the green of Iowa and into Nebraska. Past homesteads and millions of acres of parade soldier rows of corn that had drilled the dust bowl of the '30s into farms of gold. We crashed out in cornfields and watched as the crop dusters circled. We'd run off, hide and find cover, and then I'd make out I was Cary Grant in *North by North-West* or something. We just horsed around and got along. I'm not sure why; we shouldn't have really, but we did. We just hitched and messed about and got along.

Really, we were as different as chalk and cheese. I shouldn't have liked her at all. I'm shy and don't say much. I don't like being around people much, especially if they are all outgoing and hectic and all. And that's exactly what she was most of the time. I'm telling you she was like a firecracker. I couldn't shut her up sometimes. She was always changing her mind and acting crazy and spontaneous and all, so I never knew what she was going to do next. Maybe I just put up with it, cos she was pretty and all, who knows? But maybe I just needed someone like that, there, in the mid-west, in the middle of nowhere. Maybe it's good to have someone like that around when you're in the middle of nowhere.

I tell you, though, she was crazy, proper crazy, you know, like a bottle of pop that had been shook up too much and was just spilling over. Whatever she did, she just spilled over. It was only trivial stuff and all, but she was always acting crazy. Like one time when I'd bought some apples in a deli. She said she didn't want one. 'I don't like apples,' she said.

But then, after I'd taken a couple of bites, she just grabbed it off me and started munching it. She ate it real fast, as if she was starving or something, right down to the core and all. She ate it all and then threw it and laughed.

'Bio-degradable.' Then laughter.

Now normally, if someone did that, it would do my head in. The first time she did something like that, I thought she was nuts, but she was always doing stuff like that so I kind of got used to it. I know she didn't mean anything by it, and in the end, I got so used to stuff like that I didn't even notice. That's the dangerous thing about some people. They start doing mad stuff and to start with, it freaks people, but then people say, 'Oh, it's just how they are, they don't mean nothing.' Then people get used to it and stop noticing. That's when it's dangerous. When what's crazy becomes normal. I didn't mind that much with Annie, though, it wasn't as though she was president or anything.

She'd always change the subject too. Sometimes you could be talking about something and she'd just jump up and start talking about something else. It was as if something had just popped into her head and she had to spit it out as if her life depended on it. I reckon Annie was on rocket fuel.

She was touchy-feely too. Sometimes, she'd just hug me or run her hands through my hair. She didn't mean anything by it, we were just friends and all, but she was just the type of person that did what she felt. I think too much. Analyse and think, that's my problem. Sometimes I wish I just felt stuff, but I don't. Like when something does my head in, I know I'm mad, but I don't feel mad. Knowing stuff ain't the same as feeling it. Sometimes I wish I felt stuff more, but I don't. I reckon Annie felt everything. Well, almost.

Usually, after a long day hitchhiking, we would crash out under the stars in a field or somewhere and she would just talk and talk. That's another reason why I liked her, cos she talked so much. Sometimes, people who talk a lot do my head in. If I'm not in the mood or I think they are just making out they are some big hotshot, then it does my head in, big style. But sometimes I like people to talk. I don't like talking much, so if I'm with someone for a while, I like them to talk a lot. I can just listen and don't have to think what to say. I like it that way.

Well, Annie could talk about anything. I'm telling you she could talk the hind legs off a donkey. Sometimes, she would rattle on and I would drift off for a couple of minutes. She'd still be going, and I wouldn't have a clue what she was on about. That's another reason why 'huh' is such a good word. If you ain't got a clue what someone is on about, you can always say 'huh'.

I don't know why I don't like talking. But I never have. Even worse when I was a kid. Remember, I told you about that girl I used to knock around with when I was thirteen. Well, I hated talking to her. I never knew what to say. I never used to speak to girls at all, except my sister, and she didn't count. What can you say to your sister? Well, I used to only see Jeanette on Fridays at that stupid kids' disco, and I never knew what to say. By Thursday, I used to start stressing out about seeing her, and then I started making lists of topics to talk about, just so I had something to say. I listed all sorts of crap, like 'I skipped PE', or 'we had a new teacher this week'. It was all crap, you know, all

111

really boring stuff that happened at school, but I had to list something just in case I couldn't think of anything to say. That's one of the reasons why I used to kiss her all the way through a record. I mean, part of it was because I really didn't know how long a kiss should last as I told you, but mostly, it was because that way, I didn't have to talk. I never knew what to say, so it was easier to keep kissing. Except between records.

A couple of local do-gooders used to run that crappy community hall disco. I think they thought it would keep kids off the streets. But the guy who played the records didn't have a clue, so he just fumbled around a bit after each record until the next one was cued up. Anxious waiting. Sometimes I tried to fill in the gaps with something off my list.

'I skipped PE this week,' I'd say.

'Did you?' she'd say.

'Did you,' I thought. Is that all you've got? I've been working on my conversation list and that's all you've got.

When that happened, I never knew whom I hated most. That stupid Jeanette, or that crappy do-gooder who couldn't cue up the records. Sometimes I hated myself just cos I hated talking.

I did have a conversation once, though. It was with this girl called Hilary Danforth. Everyone used to call her Hilary Dandruff, but that wasn't her name. Her name was Hilary Danforth. Kids can be real shitheads sometimes. Well, this Hilary was a bit of a loner. She just used to dance on her own in the corner. She always used to sit on her own too. Trouble was, she had eczema. Really bad it was. I've never seen anyone with eczema that bad. When you got near, you could see her skin was all torn up. Layers of her skin were just peeling off. You know, like flaky pastry. When she danced, she kept her hands by her side clenched in a fist shape. Fingers curled up so people couldn't see them, but when you got close, you could. They looked gnarled as if she was an old woman, you know, about a hundred or something. When you were real close you could even see blood. She was always scratching herself and making them bleed and you could see all the spots of dried-up blood on her skin.

The eczema was on her face and her neck too. She was only 12, but I tell you, she looked 100 or something. She used to cover herself up, hiding. Black long skirts and black long-sleeved blouses and stuff. I think she wanted to hide herself cos everyone gave her a bad time, but I think she also wore them because this crumby disco had ultra-violet fluorescent lights. The do-gooders who ran the place wanted to sparkle and installed UV lights. Trouble was, if you wore anything white under those UV lights, you stood out like a lighthouse. All the hotshots who wanted to stand out loved it. There was a load of lads who would wear white shirts every week just so they stood out. It looked stupid, but they thought they were the big 'I ams', so they wore white all the time. They had dark trousers and shoes, so when they danced all you could see was this white shirt flapping about. If you were real close, you could just about make out their shape, but from a distance, you would just see all these white shirts swirling around as if someone had left washing on a washing line on a moonlit windy night. Some of the girls liked to wear white too. White hot pants and white miniskirts, all swirling around on a moonlit night in the wind, like a washing powder advert. I never wore anything white to that place, I hated it. I tell you, you couldn't even smile in that place unless you wanted your teeth to light up. I hated those UV lights.

Hilary did too, that's why she wore black all the time. Black made you invisible. Trouble is UV light is persistent. It chases down white. When Hilary danced and moved around, some of the skin from her neck flaked and fell on to the shoulders of her black blouse. She couldn't see it, but after a couple of dances, her blouse was sprinkled with white flecks. Sometimes, it looked as if she'd just been out in a snowstorm. That's how she got the name Hilary Dandruff. She never had dandruff, just eczema, but kids can be shitheads.

Now this one time, she was dancing on her own in the corner and I brushed past her. I was going out to the toilets or something and I just bumped into her by accident. Anyway, a cotton reel fell out my pocket. I used to wear my school blazer to this disco cos it was black, and it made you invisible, but my pockets were always full of stuff, and as I passed her, it fell out. It rolled right in front of her and she slipped on it. She looked as if she was on roller skates the way she slipped, but I managed to catch her. I remember I grabbed her hand as she was falling. It was rough, like sandpaper. Like catching a bag of sandpaper.

She picked up the cotton reel and handed it to me. Now I bet if that had happened with one of the hot-pants girls, they'd have gone crazy with me. You know all hoity-toity and stuff, but she didn't. She just said, 'What's this?'

Now normally, the music was so loud in that place you couldn't hear yourself think. Sometimes it was so loud, you could have farted when you were kissing, and no one would have known. I reckon from the smell of that place, all those creeps in their white shirts did that all the time. But they were playing some slow smoochy ballad when all this happened, so I could just about hear her.

'Sorry,' I said. 'it's a cotton reel. I keep a load of crap in my pockets and it fell out. Sorry.'

'Why do you do that?' She asked as if she really wanted to know, as if she was really interested in me.

'Oh, I dunno,' I said, 'A while back I had some string in my pocket and I was with someone who snapped their shoelace. I gave them the string and they seemed real grateful. They seemed to like me, so since then I started keeping loads of stuff in my pockets. Just in case like.'

She smiled. 'It's nice when people like you.' She said it as if she didn't know what it felt like, you know for someone to really like you.

'I don't care so much any longer, but when I started carrying it all around with me, I thought if I was useful, people would like me.'

She smiled. 'Maybe I should start carrying stuff around to make people like me.' She smiled again. The UV light hit her teeth. I noticed they were straight and pretty; she had a pretty mouth when she smiled. Most people's lips never look that symmetrical to me, but her lips did. They curled up a little at the corners too and it looked nice. I reckon if she didn't have eczema, a whole load of people would have queued up to kiss that mouth. But she had eczema real bad, and so no one queued up. I didn't ever see anyone kiss her once.

But just as we were talking all quiet in the corner, this stupid gang of white shirts turned up and surrounded us. They started poking me and yelling, 'You love Hilary Dandruff. You love Hilary Dandruff.' They crowded in closer and closer and bumped into us and yelled louder and louder. A mad frenzy of white shirts screaming 'you love Hilary Dandruff' over and over. It was doing my head in, all the shouting and the jostling.

'Shut it, shut it, I don't love Hilary Dandruff.' It just came out.

I didn't mean to say it. I didn't want to call her dandruff, but they had been chanting and chanting and I was mad as hell, so it just came out like that. I didn't mean to say it, I swear to God I didn't, but I did. I said it.

Hilary ran off. I don't know where? Maybe she went and hid in the toilet or something, but she didn't come back. I went to that crappy disco every Friday for about three months after that, but I never saw Hilary again. I don't think she ever came back.

And that's the trouble with talking, it doesn't do you any good. It didn't do Hilary Danforth any good anyway.

It was weird, though, cos that was the first real conversation I'd had with a girl. You know, before all those white shirts turned up and wrecked it. We were just talking, just saying what was on our minds without trying to be anyone special, just ourselves. I never had a conversation like that with Jeanette. I knocked around with her for about six months or something, but never had a conversation, not one.

To be honest after that incident with Hilary and those bastard white shirts, I thought I'd never talk to a girl again, but Rusty changed all that. Yeah, Russell Timms taught me how to talk to girls. He had ginger hair and because of that, and his name and stuff, everyone called him Rusty. He always had loads of girls hanging around with him. He wasn't a great looker or anything. He had a squint in one eye and his hair was usually greasy, but he always had loads of girls hanging around. Hundreds, I'm telling you, hundreds.

He was a couple of years older than me and I don't really remember how I came to knock about with him, but I did. I bet we only hung out for a couple of weeks or something, but at that age it seemed as if it was forever. We used to hang around as if we were best buddies and stuff. Me and Rusty.

He made talking to girls look real easy, like as easy as breathing or something. I used to ask him how come he was so relaxed and all and whether he'd always been good at it. At first, he wouldn't tell me, he was playing his cards close to his chest, but one day he told me about this book he'd read. He couldn't remember the title now, but he told me it was all about getting people to like you and stuff. I tell you at 13, that was dynamite. I thought about Hilary Danforth and even thought I would tell her about it, but I never saw her again.

Anyway, once Rusty had spilled the beans about this book, he couldn't stop talking about it. It was as if he'd kept this big secret for so long, that now it was out, he had to tell me everything.

'Firstly,' he said, 'you just got to look at them, just look into their eyes. Don't stare, though, that'll spook them. Just gaze softly.'

Gaze softly, I thought. God, this is sounding difficult already. How do you gaze softly, for crying out loud?

He couldn't stop now, though; the secret was out — he had to tell me more.

'Next,' he said, 'you just keep looking at them and nod and say stuff like, ehm, yeah, ahah, huh. If you do this, you don't have to think of a thing to say, they just keep rattling on. It's easy. It don't matter if you drift off now and again, as long as you keep nodding and saying ahah and stuff, it's fine.' That's how I learnt about saying 'huh'. Rusty taught me that years ago and it works. I've used it for years and it works.

'Sounds neat,' I said, 'Is that it?'

'No,' he said rather impatiently as if I was a bit of an imbecile. 'Course that's not it. No, next, and this bit's ace,' he lowered his voice to a whisper as if this bit was the real secret he had been dying to reveal. There was nobody within a mile of us, but he whispered anyway. I hate it when people do that when there is no one in a mile of you, I hate it. But to be honest, I wanted to know this next bit if it was so ace, so I just let it slide.

'What you do now,' he looked as if he could hardly contain himself, he was getting real excited, 'you listen to bits of what they say, and then repeat stuff back to them. I am telling you this is a killer. You repeat bits back and they think you've been listening to them and you're interested and all. They love that. It's a killer, they love it.'

'So, you're saying, you reflect back some of the conversation to them, so they know you have been paying attention,' I went on, 'a bit like a mirror, reflecting back.' I was being a bit of a smart arse when I said that, but I think it was lost on him.

'Yeah, yeah, exactly, exactly,' he said. He lounged back in his seat with a big smile on his face, like a master who had passed on some great secret and was relieved of its heavy burden. I reckon if he'd had a big fat cigar, he'd have lit it right then. But he didn't, so he just leant back and grinned.

'See,' he said, 'a lot of those white shirt creeps ain't got a clue. They prance around with their muscles and their toothpaste smiles, banging on about how smart they are, but they don't know how to listen. I tell you, if they knew how to listen, ugly bastards like me and you wouldn't get a look in. But they ain't got a clue.'

I wasn't that chuffed that he referred to me as an ugly bastard, but I got the point, so I let it slide.

'Neat,' I said, 'but, it's better to paraphrase rather than just repeat what they say?' I was being a smart arse again, but I did want to check. This seemed powerful stuff.

He looked at me as if I was a bit of an imbecile again. 'Yeah, yeah, that's what I said, just repeat stuff back. Oh, and by the way, just chuck in a few questions now and again. That works magic.'

He looked exhausted and I didn't want to push my luck, but I had to ask.

'Just one more question,' I said, 'does this stuff work with everyone, you know, your mates, lads, teachers?'

'How the fuck should I know?' he said, 'I only want to talk to girls.' He looked as if he was exasperated. I thought it was best not to say any more.

It all sounded a bit crazy, but he said he'd read it in a book, and at thirteen I guessed it must be true. I hung around with him for a while after he'd told me about this stuff, and I watched him at work. He did everything he told me, and it worked. I tell you he was always surrounded by hundreds of girls.

And that's what I do all the time now. Not just with girls, but with anyone. If I spend time with people and I don't know what to say, I just ask lots of questions and do what Rusty told me to do.

So, that's what I did with Annie most of the time. I used to just let her gabble on, and I would listen or pretend to listen. It worked okay for both of us. Sometimes, she did ask me personal stuff, but I just used to dodge it. Like if it got too personal and I felt uncomfortable, I would just say something vague and then ask her a couple of questions. If I got lucky, she would then just bang on about herself again. I liked it when she did that, cos then I didn't have to say much about myself. I guess, I should be more willing to disclose stuff, but I usually don't like to. It's weird really cos I reckon after a week with Annie, I knew enough about her to write a book about the size of *War and Peace*. After a week, I reckon she would have struggled to fill in a postage stamp about me. Except one time, maybe.

One time, I did open up. She just kept asking me questions and I don't know why, but I just started telling her stuff. Maybe I was just starting to feel more comfortable around her, or maybe it was too much booze or maybe just one of those things, but I started to tell her about what had happened with my parents and all. We had crashed out under the stars after a long day, and she was just lying on the floor when I told her. I told her all the stuff about how they were out minding their own business when he hit them and how he just skipped the country. I told her what happened to me and how it left me afterwards, before I flew to the States.

I tried to explain to her how it made me feel. How everything went silent. How all I could hear was quiet. But it wasn't no sound, but a new sound. A new, peculiar, yawning, corrupted quiet. As quiet as the air in a balloon before it bursts. As quiet as the wave before it breaks. A quiet, full of fury. The fury of crashing waves that cannot find gravity or what it means to form and fall as exhausted foam. A stagnant, dull, low, hollow, despairing, quiet. A quiet that moved slowly. A grey quiet. A quiet that could not be heard, but screamed out, listen.

I told her how I tried to escape, hid in fields, listening. Days in fields, dazed in fields. How I could not escape the tormenting, stagnant, dull, low, hollow, despairing quiet twisting itself around trees and grasses. Twisting through skin and flesh and bone.

And how I got myself through. Saved myself. Saved by the sugar stealers blown on the breeze. Small, soft, white planets. Strands of angel's hair held in sphere. Perfect planets, floating, swirling, rising, falling, drifting, hiding. Hiding in silence. Not grey, ugly quiet, but silence. Perfect silence. I told her how I imagined myself as small as these planets. Gliding, clinging, tied to angel hair. Amongst the angel hair and floating. Floating in silence. Soft, luxurious silence. Escaping, hiding. Hiding with the sugar stealers.

She was quiet and listened. Listened. Then, she just sat up straight, as if she was on a spring or something.

'Holy shit,' she said, 'holy shit.'

It was the only time I saw shock on her face. She was serious and started asking questions. Loads of questions about the guy who did it, and where he was from in the States and where he was now.

'Holy shit.' She just kept saying it over and over.

'You should track the bastard down,' she said. 'Track him down and shoot the bastard or something.' She was serious too. It was the only time I saw her serious. But she was. Real serious.

'You should track him down,' she said it again. 'I would.'

I think she would have too. She acted real crazy sometimes and I reckon she really would have tracked him down. 'Track the bastard down and shoot him.'

I felt I needed to reply. 'Huh,' I said.

'You thinking about it?' she said.

'Huh,' I said.

Chapter Eleven

I love the sky in America. During the day, you look up and see a wondrous expanse, spreading. In the city, sometimes you look up and can only see a crumby little patch, you know, as if all the people and all the buildings have worn out the scenery. But out west, outside the cities, you see inside your veins. The guts of everything, the bottom of the world, returning from forever. Some days the sky is just an ocean of blue spilling into tomorrow. Some days it is shape. Complicated caverns of cloud curling, unfurling, whirling into ghost face. Mountains of cloud looking for climbers. Clouds clinging, changing shape. Clouds turned inside-out, swelling, shrinking, swooping. At night too. An endless pool of black. Ink and the underbelly of a forest floor, blink and explore the touch of piercing. A billion pinpricks of eternity. Sometimes, I think the best thing about America is the sky. We slept out under the stars almost every night. Sometimes, we'd be by the train tracks and listen as the box cars rumbled by. Trains a mile long with a thousand boxcars full of their own stories. We pictured ourselves jumping the trains like 50s hobos. We imagined ourselves laying out in an open-topped boxcar, guzzling gut rot from the bauble ball at the base of each bottle and looking at the stars as the sky slid by. Sometimes we'd wander off towards some vast unbroken horizon, across some farmland or prairie where there was nothing to see except sky. No railings, no creeks, no people. Nada. Just sky. We'd crash out, looking up at the stars. That's how I found out so much about her. She'd talk about herself until she drifted to another unnamed place. Sometimes, I didn't say much for hours, just listened. I just listened and I looked up at the sky. At the yawning, incorruptible sky. She had as many stories as stars.

She talked about how she had left home when she was just fifteen and how she had drifted about, travelling around the States. See, her parents had split up when she was just a kid after her mum had cheated on her dad. He found out and walked out on them both, and she'd never seen him since. Never seen him since she was about seven or something. She told me her dad found a new girlfriend after he left, and this new girl didn't want anything to do with her. Annie always said she was okay with that, and she understood why he couldn't come back to see her, but I don't think she was okay with it really. She said she was, but the way she used to tell it didn't ring true. I don't think she was okay with it at all.

After her dad left, Annie said she blamed her mum and things got bad between them. The smooth routine of childhood turned upside down and shook until the bones fell out. She told me that she'd run away from home loads as a kid and was always in trouble at school. Then at fifteen, she blew and left for good. Just like her dad, she walked out and had never been back since. Since then, she'd been travelling, working in bars, and hustling just to get by. 'I've even turned tricks when I have to,' she said. I hate it, when people say 'turn tricks'; it's almost as bad as that 'friendly-fire' bullshit. But that's what she said. She used to tell me about some of the creeps she'd met and how she hated men now. 'Men are bastards,' she used to say. I was never sure who she meant. Her dad maybe, all those creeps, me? Who knows? I don't think she knew herself; she just said it. I don't think she meant me, though, because I reckon, she just thought I was a kid. You know, as if I was her kid brother and she was looking out for me and all.

Sometimes she'd tell me about the crappy things that had happened to her, as if talking about them made it better. You know, like Catholics do when they confess all the shit they do to priests and stuff. She'd tell me about how she coped and how she would just completely switch off sometimes.

'I can lie there and not see a thing, not feel anything,' she said. 'Sometimes, I can see myself from a corner of the room. It's like I leave my body and just watch myself, like I'm a stranger just watching myself, but it's kind of not me, I'm just watching someone. Someone I don't know. That way, I don't feel a thing,' she said. 'I learnt to do that when I was kid after my dad left.' She looked kind of sad and angry at the same time when she used to tell me that. 'Yeah, that's what I learnt when he left,' she'd say.

Now, maybe Bandler would say it was just disassociation and stuff, and Leary would probably tell you it was all that astral projection crap, but I'm telling you, when she used to talk like that, she looked as if she was in a bad way. You know, someone who is in a bad way, but wants to make out everything is okay. She was always making out she could cope, but it sounded as if she couldn't. Maybe she could, I don't know, I'm not Milton Erickson.

Maybe she coped by escaping, you know, just running away. See, she never stayed in one place for too long. Jesus, she'd been all over the States. Out west, New Mexico, all down the east coast, she'd even lived in New Orleans for a while.

'Everyone is crazy in New Orleans,' she said, 'It's a party town. I don't think I could live there for long, but it would be a good place to die.'

Then she'd talk about the funeral processions, right there through the streets, with the music and dancing. And the voodoo and twisted people high on jazz and the steamboats churning up the Mississippi river. I never knew whether I'd get there, but I dreamt of how it would be. To meet people as twisted as the wrought-iron fretwork on French quarter balconies. To lean against the ancient, bone-dry walls of jazz halls, with creaking floorboards the colour of Mississippi mud that throbbed with a thousand tapping feet. And feeling the sweet vibrations of the double bass cut me in half, and to smell the rickety piano with its chipped and yellow keys, like the chipped and yellow teeth of the trumpet player who blew so hard his lips turned blue.

'Is it close by Texas?' I asked.

'As near or far as you want it to be. Like everything. As near or far as you want it to be.' But the place she talked about most was this commune in Oregon. She told me about it the day we met in that coffee house when we drank a hundred gallons of coffee, and she had banged on about it every day since. She told me about how when she was eighteen, she'd found herself in Oregon and had come across this commune where she stayed for a year or so. When she talked about it, she always seemed to calm down. Annie was never calm except for when she talked about that commune. She told me all about the place and the people she had met there. She said it was the only time she had been happy since she was a kid. When she talked about it, she looked happy too. Usually, she was all upbeat and acting crazy and stuff, but it always felt as if when she did that she was having to try. You know, as if she was trying to be upbeat and stuff even though, deep down, she didn't really feel like that. But when she spoke about that commune, it sounded as if she really meant it. As if it really meant something to her. So that's where she was heading. She had missed the place, the people, the calm. She missed just being herself. How she was before she got messed up.

125

'I've got to get back there,' she used to tell me, as if her life depended on it.

And so, we kept heading west. Sometimes north and then further west, but slowly always in the direction of Oregon. And we moved with the insanity and beauty of youth, believing nothing could touch us and we would live forever, thinking we held luck in our hands like a five-card trick.

We hitched rides north through Nebraska and into South Dakota and stopped in the Badlands, making out we'd landed on the moon. And we'd tear up the rocks with our hands and some of them were so soft that they'd crumble in our hands and our fingers got covered in the dust of the landscape. The dust was pink and lemon and looked like sherbet and we'd lick our fingers and then pull faces, cos it tasted like history and the bones of sea creatures that lived in an ocean before America was America.

We stopped in Wall and went to the stores and talked about how only Americans can make out nothing is something. We walked around the old, brown, wooden saloons making out we were cowboys, and we filled our bellies with their free coffee because we didn't have much money.

We got rides to Rapid City and then out to Mt Rushmore. Four white American Presidents carved into immortality right there where once the Native American Indians lived. We rode with a family in a pick-up truck just outside Hayward and they took us back to their homestead and let us camp out on their land. It was a nowhere place in the middle of nowhere. An old shack, right in the middle of nowhere. They had about a hundred kids who ran around in the fields as if they were the Waltons, and they cooked pancakes for breakfast before we left. About a thousand pancakes with a gallon of maple syrup in this hillbilly wooden shack in the middle of nowhere. And I reckon they were just about the happiest family I ever met.

It was in that shack that in her crazy spontaneous way she suddenly came out with, 'Why don't you come with me? Come with me to the commune in Oregon.'

She said it as if it had suddenly struck her that there might be somewhere. An angel's womb to reinvent her. A pure place that on her transition between birth and death, was not just the indigestible fruit of a toxic forest. That she could halt each bleak, gasping breath that sucked her closer to a pointless end and for a moment pause. Pause and find the indescribable taste of magic. A peach-blown heaven.

I don't know why she suddenly said it there; maybe the Waltons thing had got to her, but I remember she jolted upright as if the thought had struck her like lightning. It probably had too. Annie never really thought much through, she just said what came into her head. It didn't matter whether it was just some half-baked idea or if she would think something different five minutes later. That's what she was like. I usually hate that, you know, people not thinking stuff through, but in a crazy sort of way, I liked it in her. You know, never knowing. 'You'll like it, I know you will. Yeah, come with me,' she said.

'I dunno,' I said, 'It's tempting.' It was too. Annie made everything sound tempting. She kept telling me how beautiful it was, and how I'd like the people and all. I grinned and said 'huh' a few times, but I knew I would never go. I don't like being around groups of people much, and a commune would do my head in big style. Trouble is, I think that people are fine when they're on their own. They're just fine then but put people together and they change. People, together, act differently. I can't stand it. I know a commune would do my head in. I didn't say that to her, though, I just let her rattle on about it. She was so full of it, so excited; it was easier to just let her rattle on. Chances are, by tomorrow, she'd have forgotten all about it and some new crazy idea would have come into her head. That's what Annie was like. Normally, I would hate stuff like that, but that's what she was like.

So, we kept heading west, across into Wyoming. We were still about nine hundred miles away from this commune in Oregon, when everything changed. So, in the end I never had to tell her I wasn't going to go to the commune. I just didn't get there, cos everything changed. See, when you're hitchhiking, things can change just like that. You wait, someone stops, you exchange words and you get in. When you think about it, anything could happen, that's why a lot of people tell you not to do it. 'It's too risky,' they tell you. I know that's what Brooksey would have said.

Maybe, it is, but if you're lucky, things work out okay. You just need to be lucky and I reckoned I was.

See, I found out I was lucky when I was a kid. In that crappy department store called Henrys. Remember, that's where I got that book about Jesus. Well one day, my mum and dad were just shopping and my sister and me were just tailing them. It was boring as hell. I tell you, being a kid, tailing your mum and dad in Henrys was worse than school. But then, we came across this 'lucky dip' stand. I don't even know why it was there; maybe it was some holiday or promotion or something, but there it was, this great big barrel full of tiny keys. It cost about sixpence or something a go. To pick out a key and see if it would open a chest. Now even at five years old, I wasn't too excited by a crappy lucky dip like this, but it seemed better than just wandering around, so I was kind of glad we stopped. My legs were aching, so I was glad we stopped.

Everyone stared. You know, as if everyone thought it was better than wandering around Henrys.

'You'd have to be damn lucky to pick out the right key,' my mum said. 'Look, there must be thousands of keys in that barrel.'

'It's probably all a con,' my dad said, 'I bet there ain't a single key in there that will open that chest.' He said it in the way he said a lot of stuff. As if life had taught him how everyone lies. As if he'd found out that everyone was full of bullshit.

'Can we have a go, can we, can we?' My sister was a few years older than me, but not old enough to have learnt about the lies. 'Can we?'

'It's a waste of time,' my dad chimed in again, but it's not easy to win an argument with a nine-year-old.

'Oh, it won't hurt, let's have a go.' My mum and sister ganged up.

I kind of remember my dad looking at me for support, but I was only five. I think I abstained. Anyway, in the end, we all had a go.

My dad went first. Nothing. Then my sister. Nothing. Then, my mum. Nothing.

'I told you it was a bloody waste of time and money.' My dad seemed pleased. I think he thought being right was better than winning a prize.

I've noticed people do that a lot. You know, think winning an argument is more important than getting what you really want. I reckon some people get so caught up in winning an argument that they end up getting what they don't want, but they do it anyway, just to win. I reckon, one day a whole country will do something really crazy, not cos it's a good idea, but just to win an argument. Like everyone will see this crazy car crash unfolding in slow motion before their eyes, but because they said they were gonna drive off the edge of the cliff, they just keep driving. I reckon people are weird like that. Some don't even notice when they're doing it. You know, a bit like when they swivel on chairs.

'It'll only be some crumby voucher anyway.' My dad was building his case.

'My turn,' I said. I was smaller than that fat barrel full of keys. I was five, I was smaller than everything. My dad lifted me up so I could reach. I was kind of hoping I didn't win so my dad was right. My dad was a good man and I wanted him to be right. Maybe he was still hoping he was right too, but he still picked me up and looked as if he wanted me to win. As if he was hoping he wasn't right, just for me.

'Good luck,' he said, and he meant it too. 'Good luck,' he said it twice.

I dipped my hand and wriggled it around. The keys were metal, and they made my hand cold. I started to wish we hadn't stopped.

'Hurry up,' my sister said. She had already had her go and was lost between boredom and disillusion. I took my time, to annoy her. The metal was cold on my hands, but I took my time anyway.

There must have been a million keys in that barrel, but I tried mine and it opened the chest. 'Bloody hell, I wasn't expecting that.' My dad was gutted and delighted.

'He's always lucky,' my mum said. 'You're so lucky, you're so lucky.' She looked at me and kept repeating it. 'You're always lucky.'

My sister just stood there, angry. She sneered, as if she was thinking, 'I'll give him, he's so lucky.' I reckon if my mum and dad hadn't been there, she would have punched my lights out.

Right there in Henrys in front of the lucky dip. I pictured myself lying on the floor with a bloody nose and her standing over me saying 'who's lucky now?' But she didn't. I know she would have, but she couldn't because my mum and dad were standing there.

I don't even remember what prize we won. It was probably just some crappy voucher for less than the money we spent, but from that day on, I've always thought I was lucky. See, my mum told me.

Anyway, as I got older, I guess I knew it was all bull, but I don't know why, stuff like that sticks. When I'm in tight spots, things always seem to work out, and I think maybe I am lucky. I really don't know, but that's why I never worried much about hitchhiking. Chances are it will all work out okay.

And it usually did. Just not today.

We took this ride, see, Annie and me. Just outside Sheridan, Wyoming it was, when the guy stopped. Annie and me looked at each other. You know, looked at each other as if we were thinking the same thing. We didn't say anything, but we knew we were both thinking the same thing. The guy looked as if he might be a bit of a weirdo, you know, sometimes you just get a feeling. When you are accepting a ride, you have a second to make up your mind if you are going to get in, so you kind of develop a sixth sense. You have to. We should have listened to it, but the guy said he was going all the way to Portland, Oregon. It was about nine hundred miles away and Annie was desperate to get to that commune. She would have given anything to be there, at that commune, just outside Portland, so she didn't think straight. She was a bottle of pop spilling over.

'Great,' she said, 'Great, great, great.' She jumped in.

I looked at her, with a 'what you doing?' face, but she

ignored me. 'Get in,' she said, 'get in.'

The guy looked as if he might have been a war vet or something. Vietnam was still raging and a lot of vets who had been shot up real bad came home. Some of them were nuts. I guess dropping napalm on people and getting shot at all day and night ain't too good for the mind. I'm not surprised they came back nuts, but a lot of them did. They came back nuts.

He had short cropped hair, you know all crew-cut like in the army and he was stick thin. Not skinny thin like me, though, no, he was wiry. It looked as if bullets bounced off him and he still had the scars. Not on his face, though. He was almost good looking with high cheekbones and clear, tight skin that gave him a look between sinister and charming. He was wearing black. If he had worn a cowboy hat and leant up against Grafton's, chances are people would have thought it was Wilson. Wilson from the movie *Shane*. He had the same sneer as Wilson.

He was drinking heavily too. He kept opening bottles of beer. There were loads of bottles all over the car. He drank them fast, as if it was a race. A race to empty America of all its beer, and maybe its sorrow too. He wound down the window and chucked them out. I hated him for that. But he just chucked stuff out, as if there was some magic cleaning fairy waiting to pick it all up. He drove like a madman and the car zoomed on. Past the flat wasteland and debris and broken dreams and into the fumes of the traffic ahead. And the smell of fumes climbed in through the windows and filled the car with the stench of beer and petrol and hating and murder. But the car zoomed on and overtook recklessly and bounced off the soft shoulders and zigged and zagged like a desperate prey, chased and clinging to its last living moments.

Annie realised he was a whacko and tried to get a bit of a

conversation going with him, hoping he might lighten up, but he wasn't much of a talker. He liked drinking. Drinking and racing. Maybe he would pull over for petrol or something and I could tell Annie to get out, but he just kept driving. Driving and drinking. He hadn't said anything for miles, and it felt awkward. Awkward as midnight in a graveyard.

Then he looked at Annie. 'You got any dope with you?'

We didn't have much money, so we never bought any. We cadged loads from our rides, but never bought any.

'No, sorry,' I said, 'we ain't got too much money, we ain't bought any.'

'What about beers? You gotta have some beers in your packs.' He slurred and chucked more bottles out the window.

He still had loads of beers in the car, so I guessed he was baiting. It felt like trouble. 'No, sorry, we're a bit broke just now. That's why we're hitching.' I smiled trying not to wind him up, but he didn't respond. There was a silence. Alone in the graveyard, silence. Then he spoke. Almost a whisper.

'Well, if you ain't got nothing for me, I don't see why I should give you a ride.'

'I could give you a couple of dollars for fuel, if that helps,' I said, 'We don't have much.'

He sneered. 'A couple of dollars. I don't need a couple of dollars.'

He turned to look at Annie, who was sitting in the front next to him. 'What about you? You ain't saying much, what about you, what you got for me?'

He kept looking at Annie. 'What you got for me?'

I wanted to kill him. I was shit scared, but mad. Mad as hell. I was sitting in the back seat, next to his stinking bottles of beer. I grabbed the neck of a bottle ready to bring it down on his skull.

I squeezed it tight and thought about how I could bring it right down on his lousy stinking skull. Smash the sneer off his face. Beat his brains out. Bury his tormenting, tormented soul in a roadside ditch. Annie glanced at me and saw me holding the bottle. I think she wanted me to do it. Just hit the bastard over the head, just hit him. I told you I hate men; hit the bastard. I thought that's what she must be thinking. Maybe she was, maybe she wasn't, I never found out. I guess I didn't have the nerve to do it. I mean that guy deserved it, he deserved it big style. Annie could have grabbed the wheel if I'd knocked him out cold, but I just didn't have the nerve. I just didn't.

All I did was yell. 'No one's giving you nothing.'

He didn't say anything for about a minute, but then whispered again, 'Don't push it.' You know, he said it just how Wilson said it to Shane.

Now if I'd have been Shane, I would have told him he was a no-good yellow belly, but I just yelled, 'You ain't getting nothing.'

'Well in that case you're getting out.' He rammed on the brakes and we skidded to a halt. Right in the middle of nowhere, we skidded to a halt. The stink of burnt hot rubber filled my nose.

Thank God, I thought, we're out. We were in the middle of nowhere, but anywhere seemed better than his car, and his sneering face, and his belly full of beer.

'We're going,' I yelled. I grabbed my pack, pushed open the back door and started to jump out.

Annie hadn't moved. 'Come on,' I said to her, 'come on.'

'You don't have to go anywhere, if you don't want to.' He looked at Annie. 'I'll take you all the way to Portland, if you want.'

'Come on, get out.' I looked at her again, right in her

sparkling blue eyes and yelled, 'Get out.'

But she didn't move. She just looked at me. 'I want to get to Oregon,' she said, 'I've got to get there.'

I looked back at her sitting in that seat next to him. I was half out of the car.

'But I thought we...' I stopped. I realised that I didn't know what I thought we would do. We'd never talked about what we would really do. Late at night under the stars, she talked a lot about herself and her dreams and stuff, but right there, then, on the side of the road in the middle of nowhere, I realised we'd never really talked about anything. Nothing real anyway. I had no idea what we were going to do.

'You going to be all right?' I asked.

'I'll be okay. I have guys like this for breakfast. I told you what I think of men. One more ain't going to change anything.'

I wasn't sure if she had really wanted me to hit him over the head with that bottle. Maybe I had let her down, as her dad had all that time ago. Maybe I was the kind of man she hated, you know, a coward who couldn't even look out for her. Someone who couldn't even hit a no-good yellow belly like Wilson over the head when he was asking for it. Maybe the sleazebag next to her, was just a shit head, but it was me who had let her down. I never found out. I just knew I was the one who didn't have the guts to take him on. To do what he deserved. 'You heard what she said, now fuck off.' He chucked my bag at me. It hit my head, just about where I would have brought that bottle down on his. He had more nerve than me.

They drove off. And that was the last time I saw Annie. She was looking back at me out of the window of Wilson's car. I don't know if she ever got to Portland. To that commune. I hope she did, though.

Chapter Twelve

It was my birthday too. You know, the day Wilson chucked me out of that ride on the side of the interstate. Not that I'd mentioned it to Annie. I don't like birthdays and I knew she'd make a big deal out of it. We didn't have any money and stuff, so she couldn't have done much, but I know she would have got all excited and made a song and dance of it. 'Eighteen,' she would have said and rubbed her hands through my hair and hugged me and stuff. That's why I hadn't said anything. I don't like any of those days that get marked out in the calendar. You know, birthdays, Christmas, anniversaries and all. People always try to turn them into something special and then nothing special much happens so everyone ends up disappointed. But no one wants to admit they're disappointed, so then everyone plays this game of looking all excited and stuff. That kind of thing does my head in. See, trouble is, I reckon most people spend their lives making out everything is all hunky-dory and wine and roses and stuff. It's like when people have kids. They end up wiping the kids' puke and stuff off their best clothes or getting up at two in the morning, but they tell everyone it's the best thing they've ever done. It's changed our lives, they say. Yeah, it's changed their lives all right, cos they now spend all day wiping up puke and stuff. See, trouble is, after you've had a kid, who's going to say, I hate the ugly little bastard, I'd get rid of it if I had the nerve. See, that's the problem, people make out everything is hunky-dory and a bed of roses when really it ain't. And that's why I don't like fancy days. I just like ordinary days, where no one expects too much and ordinary is okay.

But anyway, my birthday ended in the pitch dark on the side of the interstate in the middle of nowhere. Not the ordinary I had counted on. To be honest, I had been a bit spooked by that nut-job and so I just sat down on the grass in a field by the side of the interstate. It was unnerving; I felt alone. It felt like the sort of place that if you screamed no one would hear. I felt like screaming. Not just cos I was scared either, but just because. Just because of that ride, and Wilson and my big mouth. I started to wonder whether I should have offered the guy more money for petrol or done more to persuade Annie to get out or maybe just shut my mouth when I told him we weren't giving him nothing. Trouble is, I'm not great at holding my tongue. I'm a real skinny wimp, but I never hold my tongue. It used to get me into trouble loads at school and it got me into trouble again tonight. You'd think I would learn, but I don't.

I had no idea where I was, but I didn't want to stand in the dark trying to get a ride. You ain't supposed to stand on the interstate anyway, not that that bothered me. But I was feeling spooked, I wanted to get away from this spot, so I started walking. I wished I had a horse so I could ride out just like Shane. I wished I had someone like little Joey chasing after me yelling he loved me, but I didn't, so I just started walking. I walked for quite a way across these fields and stuff. After a while, I saw some lights in the distance, so I headed for them. They were a long way off, though, and I kept tripping up as I walked in the dark. I walked for ages, but in the dark it was hard to tell how far off they were and I kept stumbling over chunks of mud and stones and stuff, so I decided it might be better just to crash in this field and then walk the rest in the morning. It was quiet in this field. I could just about see some lights in the distance and heard a faint rumble of cars on the interstate, but I'd calmed down a bit after walking so far, and it started to feel peaceful. Peaceful was what I needed, so I got my sleeping bag and lay down under the stars.

I lay there looking up at the dark patch of sky above me; it was full of blazing stars. When you're in the middle of nowhere, away from the light of cities, the sky is filled with light. Sometimes, the light of the stars blurs, and together swirls like cream dropped across the surface of black coffee. I like moments like this, you know, when I'm halfway between sleep and any alertness left. I look up at the endless, magical tract of space and wonder if there is someone looking straight back at me. You know, like a zillion light years away, someone, maybe God even, looking right back across this vast, dark space. I wonder if, looking towards me, they see a swirl of cream on black coffee too. Maybe that's all I am, just some froth in space. I thought back to New York and all those people rushing around squeezing a living. I thought of some fat-arsed, trumped-up president strutting and believing he was someone, when really, he's no more than some lousy froth in space. Maybe, that's all we all are. Just froth. It always makes me feel better, when I see the sky like that. When I remember that nothing, no one really matters, cos we are all just froth.

I stared at them until I felt sleepy. It didn't feel unnerving anymore, it felt peaceful. It ended up being a better birthday than I thought. An ordinary sky that happened to be extraordinary. An extraordinary day that turned out to be ordinary. Ordinary, just the way I like it.

I awoke when it was light. I took a while to come around, but when I did, I realised that the lights I had seen last night were from a roadhouse service station. The interstate curled and wound around the fields I had walked across and there was a station a couple of miles away. I reckoned I would be able to get a ride there, so I started walking. In the light I realised a small patch of the field had been ploughed. The brown mud had dried hard in the summer heat, but the plough tracks still stood out in their distinct lines. It looked as if someone had draped corduroy over the shallow slopes of the fields. A few stones and pieces of rubble had been churned up and tried to trip me as I walked.

As I walked, I wondered if Annie might be there. Maybe the nut-job did stop for some fuel or something and she decided to get out. Maybe she was waiting there for me, sitting cross-legged leaning against the side of the coffee house, like when I met her a week ago. I guess I knew she wouldn't really be there, though. She was desperate to get to Oregon and she thought that Wilson was her ticket. Anyway, she only used to see me as her kid brother, she didn't even know I'd turned eighteen. Why would she have waited? I walked that last few hundred yards to that station real slowly, though. I knew she wouldn't be there, but until I got there I could pretend. Until I got there, I had anticipation.

That's the sad thing about travelling, though; you never see a face you know. Like sometimes, I just wanted to walk around the corner and bump into someone I knew. Maybe Jim from school or even Brooksey. Even one of the thickos would have been fine. Anyone, just someone who would smile at me and remember yesterday. When you are travelling everyone is a stranger, everything is temporary. I suppose really, everything is temporary.

The station was empty. She wasn't there. I kind of knew she wouldn't be, but it still made me feel sad. It was stupid really, but it made me feel sad. I was feeling cold. Cold all over, but my hands were really cold, freezing cold. I went inside to buy a

139

coffee. I drank it slowly, staring into the cup as I drank. It looked a bit like last night's sky. I held the cup in my hands to try to warm them, but I couldn't get them warm. It felt cold without Annie. I missed her. And that's how I felt for the next couple of days. Cold. I got rides where I could get them and went in the direction they took me. Struggling across the miles. I was heading west, slowly, and meeting good people again. Kind people. People who wanted to help people. People who seemed to have good hearts. It started to revive my faith in people, and I started to feel warmer.

I found out that Wilson had kicked me out just near the Montana stateline, so I managed to get rides through the Crow Indian reservation and stopped by the Bighorn battlefields. I thought about the Native American Indians and how it must have been before they were chucked off their land. Chucked off their lands by arseholes, just like Wilson. It didn't make sense; there was so much space. Space for everyone. See, the best thing about America this far out west is the space. There is so much space. Tremendous, beautiful space.

Chapter Thirteen

Livingstone is about 60 miles from Yellowstone. It was dusk when I got there, and I'd been travelling all day. It seemed a good place to stay. It seemed to be a bit of a nothing place, but I didn't feel like hitchhiking in the dark. I don't like hitching in the dark and anyway, I guessed there wouldn't be much traffic heading out to Yellowstone this late.

I didn't have a clue where I was; it just looked like the outskirts of town. I kind of liked it, though, so I started wandering around. I was hoping I might come across a cheap hotel or a sign to a campground or something. Usually I like sleeping outdoors, especially on warm, clear nights under the stars, but I just didn't feel like it tonight. I don't know why, but I just didn't feel like it. I kept wandering.

It seemed like a quiet place, and there weren't many people about, but I quite liked it. I felt safe. After a while, I came across this old guy walking towards me; he had his dog with him. He was walking proper slow, as if he had all the time in the world. Livingstone felt like that sort of place. It made you feel as if you had all the time in the world. His dog was scurrying around in the gutter as dogs do. It kept sniffing around, you know, as dogs do. The old man kept pace with the dog, so he had to keep stopping while his dog sniffed about. He had the dog on one of those retractable leads, though, so, sometimes the dog was right next to him, cosying up against his legs. But sometimes he wandered off, right across to the other gutter and stuff. Sometimes, it looked as if the old guy wanted to pretend he was in charge, so he yanked on the lead and gave a shrill whistle. The dog usually took no notice, but sometimes it looked up and would scurry back, then they walked on a bit further. It looked slow progress, but it was Livingstone. They had all the time in the world.

I watched them as I walked towards them and I thought about crossing over the road. See, I don't like dogs. It was on a lead, but it was one of those stretchy ones and I don't like dogs. See, when I was small, I was almost bitten by a dog. It was one of the care-free days you only get when you're a tiny kid and I was out in the street on my bike. I was just minding my own business riding my bike. When I was growing up, there were never many cars driving up and down the street where I lived, so I just used to mess about on my bike, doing wheelies and stuff. Sometimes, I just rode round and round, in circles. Care-free circles. Well, that day, I remember Mrs Gwilliams was standing in the street and she was watching me. You know, watching me all the time like a real nosey parker. She was making out she wasn't, but she was. Just straining to look at me out the corner of her eye. Maisy Gwilliams it was. She lived about ten doors down from me. She was a right busybody, and there she was that day, gossiping away with Mrs Stevens. They were both looking at me out of the corner of their eyes, and I knew they were gossiping about me and my bike. I couldn't hear them, cos I was too far away, but I know they were gossiping about me, I could just tell they were.

To get away from their rotten snooping, I would ride up this cul-de-sac which was like a turning off my road. The cul-de-sac was on a bit of a hill, so I used to ride up to the top, then whizz down on my bike as if I was Evel Knievel or someone. I think that really spooked Maisy Gwilliams, cos that's when she'd turn her head to stare at me, as if she was the speed police or something. Mrs Stevens did too. They both stared. They didn't say anything, though, they just stared, as if I was doing their head in. I bet I was too.

Now while all this staring was going on, I noticed this stinking dog sniffing around in the gutter, not ten yards from me. I don't know whose dog it was, cos I hadn't seen it before. I didn't like the look of it, though; it was some really scruffy looking mut of a dog. Like a dog that no one cares about. Its fur was all rough and dirty and knotted up and it had long droopy ears that dangled in the gutter when it was sniffing around. When dogs do stuff like that it turns my stomach. It really started to spoil my day seeing that stinking mut scurrying about in the gutter and knowing all that gossiping was going on, so I was thinking about going home. I didn't want to ride my bike by that stinking mut. But just as I started to ride home, it stopped sniffing about, looked up and started to chase me. It started barking and yapping and snapping right at my heels. I just kept pedalling, but he kept snapping at me and was barking and yelping and yapping.

Yap, yap, yap. I can still hear it now. Yap, yap, yap.

Maisy Gwilliams started looking at me out the corner of her eye, but I just kept on pedalling. And that's when it bit me. I fell off my bike and started screaming, 'he's bit me', 'he's bit me'. I was lying on the floor shit scared while this crazy stinking dog pawed all over me. He just kept on yapping too. Yap, yap, yap. My bike was lying on the floor next to me and the front wheel was still spinning around. I could hear the whizzing of the wheel as it spun around and it got all blurred-up with that yap, yap, yapping. My head started spinning too and I thought I was going to throw up.

But then Maisy Gwilliams ran across to me. She chased the dog away and started to stroke my forehead and stuff. All gentle

143

like, as if she was wiping away all that yapping and whizzing that was ringing in my ears.

'Everything will be okay,' she said. 'Everything will be okay.' She repeated it about a thousand times as if saying it more than once made it truer. It kind of did too, cos, the more she said it, the more I calmed down. She was real friendly and smiled a lot and she rubbed my ankle, just above my socks where I thought that stinking dog had bitten me.

'You're okay,' she said, after rubbing my ankle. 'He's not bit you, you're all right.'

'But it felt like he bit me,' I said, 'I'm sure he did. Maybe you've rubbed away the mark where he bit me.'

'You're okay now.' She said it as soothing as she could and carried on rubbing my ankle. I remember thinking how her hands were quite soft for an old woman and I started to feel a bit guilty for thinking she was just this old busybody. She was like, but she was looking out for me, and so I started to feel guilty. She had soft hands too.

Anyway, she picked up my bike and helped me push it all the way home, past all ten doors. I didn't have it in me to ride my bike, so she pushed all the way home. All ten doors. I still don't know whether that dog bit me or not. When I was scared, I thought it did, but Maisy Gwilliams said it didn't. She was a lot older than me, you know, ancient like and she said it didn't, so I guess she was right. When you're a tiny kid, you always think what old people say is right.

And that's why I don't like dogs. For a while, after that, I was really scared of dogs, but now I just don't like them. Sometimes I don't like their owners much either. Boy, I'm telling you, there were some really shitty dog owners in New York.

One day, I was just sitting in Central Park. Remember, I told you I used to walk all over New York. Well, one day I'd walked about a hundred miles around Manhattan, so when I got to Central Park I just wanted to crash out. I'd bought myself a crappy sandwich and thought I'd flop down on the grass in Central Park, mind my own business and have this crappy sandwich. I'd spent so much money on crumby hotels and stuff that I didn't have money for food, but I was starving, so I bought some bread and some crappy meat. So, that's what I was eating. Some pink, crappy, processed meat on some dry bread. It was shitty really, but I was that tired and hungry, I was kind of enjoying myself sitting on the grass in the sun.

But then this hoity-toity type struts up and sits on a bench right close to me. She had the whole of Central Park and she decided to sit down, right next to me. She was about forty or something, real ancient anyway, but she was all dolled up as if she was off to a banquet. All dolled up as if she was just twenty or something when she was at least forty, maybe even forty-five. Anyway, she looked all la di da she did, real la di da. But what made it worse was that she had two rotten dogs with her. Great big massive things they were, I don't know, maybe Great Danes or something. All I know is that they came up to her waist. Even in her la di da, high heels, they still came up to her waist. Maybe higher. She had them on leads, one on either side, as if she was Cruella de Vil. I'm telling you, she pranced in as if she was the Queen of Central Park and plonked herself and these stinking dogs down on the bench, no more than ten yards from me. For crying out loud, you've got the whole of Central Park, why did you have to come so close to me? I hate it when people sit near me, when there is plenty of space. It really did my head in. It almost ruined my day.

But then she let these dogs off their leads, and they started wandering and sniffing around. They came right up near me sniffing around. I hate that, I really hate that. To try and take my mind of the dogs, I just watched her sitting on this bench for a while. She was fumbling around in this expensive bag she had with her. Some designer bag or something that looked as if it cost a million bucks. After a couple of minutes, she pulled out this massive sandwich about the size of a submarine. It was stuffed full of pastrami and it was overflowing with salad and pickles and coleslaw and everything. All the coleslaw was dripping out of the side of the rye bread, and it was massive and looked juicy and tasty and delicious. I looked at my crappy sandwich. I tell you it really ruined my day.

I didn't want to keep staring, but that sandwich looked so good I couldn't help myself. She kept taking all these mincy little bites, so it lasted forever, you know, as if she was wanted to tease me. The coleslaw was dripping out the side, but she kept taking these mincy little bites as if she was a princess or something and not one bit dropped on to her. I couldn't believe it. I'm telling you, if you eat a sandwich like that, it ain't natural for nothing to drop on to you. When I'm eating, I always drop stuff down my T-shirt. After about two days, sometimes you wouldn't even know what colour my T-shirt was supposed to be, because there is so much stuff down it. It don't matter what it is, I always drop something, but she didn't drop anything, not one lousy pickle or anything. I was willing her to, big style. You know, just hoping for a whole load of coleslaw to fall on to her fancy pants outfit, but it didn't. It got me real mad.

Now while I was watching her tuck into her sandwich, these stinking dogs were getting closer and closer, so I started looking at them again. Then, one of them, the dirty bastard, crouched down to do its business. Right there a couple of yards away from me while I'm trying to enjoy my sandwich. Now that is what really does my head in about dogs and dog owners. Now, I'm pretty sure that if I had gone up to Cruella and dropped my trousers and done my business, she'd have had something to say about it, but if it's a stinking Great Dane, it's okay. It does my head in big style. And that's one reason I hate dog owners; a lot of them don't give a shit.

Now, for some reason dogs seem to love sniffing shit, so the other Great Dane came over to stick his nose in. I mean literally, stick his nose in. I thought I was going to puke.

Now, the Queen of New York, cos I reckon she'd promoted herself by now, had been too busy stuffing herself full of this sandwich, the size of the Empire State Building, to notice what was happening, but suddenly she called over to them.

'Romeo, Juliette, come on boy, come on girl.'

Romeo and Juliette. Who calls their dogs Romeo and Juliette? You'd have to be a real la di da to call dogs that. Anyway, the dogs dashed straight back to her and jumped up on to the bench next to her. One on either side. She looked so la di da, I bet she'd paid someone to train them to do that. They curled up real close to her and she started getting all coo che coo with them.

'Oh, good boy', 'Oh, good girl' she kept saying in a stupid voice as if she was talking to some moron.

She was rubbing their coats and their heads and putting her face right close to their heads. They were panting and slobbering and rubbing their noses right by her and then started licking her face and all. I almost puked. I'm telling you they had just stuck their noses in some shit and were now licking her face. I was just ready to throw up big style, but then she started feeding them some of her pastrami sandwich. Jesus, they lapped it up, even the coleslaw. She was getting more coo che coo all the time and I was feeling as if I was ready to puke. I couldn't eat my crappy sandwich after that. I hated it. I hate dog owners sometimes.

So, when I was close by this guy walking his dog, I was thinking of crossing the road, but the guy looked okay, not at all like that la di da in New York, and the dog did too, so I just kept walking. When I got alongside him, he had paused again to let his dog sniff around.

'Hi,' I said.

'Hi,' he said, 'Nice night.'

'Beautiful,' I said. It did feel beautiful too. I don't know why, but I felt safe and even the dog didn't bother me, so it felt beautiful.

'Sky looks beautiful,' I said.

We both looked up. There were a lot of stars. The dog kept sniffing around in the gutter. I thought about Oscar Wilde and wondered whether he'd written an alternative version for dogs. 'We're all living in the stars, but some of us are looking at the gutter.' I bet if he had written something for dogs, Mrs La di da from Central Park had read it to Romeo and Juliette.

'I'm heading out to Yellowstone tomorrow,' I said. 'I'm guessing the skies and the stars are amazing there.'

'Magical,' he said, 'Yellowstone is magical, you'll love it.'

'Can't wait,' I said, 'I'm going to stay here tonight, if I can find somewhere. I have a small tent. Do you know of any campgrounds nearby?'

'Nothing here,' he said, 'Most people just pass through on their way to Yellowstone.'

'Pity,' I said, 'It seems a nice place.' Now normally I would have said something like this to pile on the flannel, but I actually meant it. I'm not sure why, but I liked Livingstone. It felt safe, a nice place to spend some time.

'Sometimes I've stayed in people's gardens when I've been travelling about. I've got a small tent. Do you know anyone around here who might have a small bit of land I could use?'

He paused. 'Not sure,' he said. The dog tugged at his lead. 'I've got a garage, though, if you want to sleep in there?'

'Are you sure?' I said. 'That would be great.'

I was hoping he was sure, but I thought it sounded polite, so I just said, 'Are you sure?'

'Yeah, for sure, come and meet my wife.'

And so that's where I stayed in Livingstone. His lovely wife made us coffee and soup and we sat in their kitchen and chewed the fat. They were both nice.

So, I slept on a camp bed in that garage and slept real well too.

Next morning, I had breakfast with them. Pancakes and bacon and syrup and then when I was about to leave, they offered to drive me all the way to Yellowstone.

'Are you sure?' I said. It sounded polite.

'Yeah, for sure.'

Yellowstone is about 60 miles from Livingstone.

Chapter Fourteen

I have a crazy way of deciding how much I like something. See, I like things to be 'just so', and I have this mad way of working out how perfect something is. I do it with everything, all the time. It's mad really, I know it is, but I do it anyway.

What I do is I kind of set up whatever I'm looking at against this perfect picture in my mind. I imagine I'm Michelangelo or Da Vinci or someone like that, then I think how they would draw what I'm looking at. It could be a landscape, a face, a building, a sky, it doesn't matter.

I just think how they would design it, lay it out and paint it, you know, if they were making this perfect masterpiece. Then, when they're done, I compare what they paint in my mind with what I'm looking at. If it kind of looks the same, then I know it's perfect. Most of the time, stuff doesn't even get close. That's what happened when I arrived in New York and I looked up at the buildings. Now, in my mind Da Vinci had painted these really neat buildings that reached right up into the clouds, but the real stuff was pretty shabby and too small. Old busted-up buildings in shadows. That's why it wasn't perfect, see, it wasn't how it should have been, how Da Vinci would have painted it. Sometimes, though, a place is perfect. Yellowstone is perfect.

I don't know why I picture myself as an artist, though, cos I'm crap at art. I didn't even pass my 'O' level, and all you need to do is draw a crumby picture. That's the trouble with exams, though. See, that day I didn't feel like drawing. To tell you the truth, I didn't feel like doing much at all that day, but I had to do this crappy art exam. We were told to draw a still life and they gave us a couple of choices. One was a vase and some fruit or that sort of crap on a tablecloth, draped over this old school desk. The other was a hand whisk. Now I'm crap at art, but even I could have drawn a crappy vase and some fruit, but I decided to draw the whisk. I don't know why I chose it, maybe it was cos I didn't want to do anything that day, so I wasn't really thinking, but I must have been nuts.

As soon as I started drawing, I realised I'd messed up big style. If you don't believe it, you try drawing a hand whisk. I'm telling you it's impossible. I bet even Da Vinci never tried a hand whisk. Everything on a hand whisk is nuts. There are all these little teeth on this little cog. And then, that cog interlocks with an even smaller cog that has even smaller tiny teeth.

Then there's the whisk blades. All the blades interlock in weird shapes and are all at different angles to the cogs. Then there's the handle and stuff. I'm telling you a hand whisk is just about the craziest thing in the world. I'd like to know which crazy bastard decided to get stupid people like me to try and draw a whisk. I reckon he must have been a real sadistic bastard.

I just kept drawing. I don't know why, I could see it was shit, but I just kept drawing. I bet you that was the worst drawing of a whisk ever. I reckon whoever had to mark those papers bust a gut laughing at my whisk. I bet they're still laughing now; it was that crap. I bet they didn't even know it was supposed to be a whisk. Now, if I had been in the mood that day, I might have come up with one of my smart-arsed plans and gone all cubist or something. I could have made out I was Picasso or someone and drawn everything at different angles on purpose. But I didn't. I wished I had when I thought about it afterwards, but I didn't think about it at the time. Sometimes you don't have a good idea until it's too late. I hate it when that happens. I tell you I'd rather not have a good idea at all than have it when it's too late. After the papers were marked, they posted the results on this great big noticeboard in the school. Just by the hall they used to post them, on this great big noticeboard. The noticeboard was about the size of a house and I reckon they posted them there just to humiliate everyone who had failed. See, everyone's results were there for everyone to see. All your failure on a notice board, the size of a house. I really didn't care too much about whether I passed or not. I thought who's going to give a toss whether or not I can draw a whisk after I leave school. But trouble was, everybody used to crowd round this noticeboard to see their results and take the piss out of anyone who'd failed. When I was standing there, there was a big crowd hanging around, jostling to have a look for their results. I don't remember who was there, except Jim. I remember Jim was there. Remember, I told you about him; he was that real bright kid from Canada.

Well, we all looked across the various subjects and found our names and grades and stuff. Now I knew I'd drawn this crumby whisk, so I knew I wouldn't pass, but when Jim saw my 'fail' grade he almost bust a gut. He couldn't stop laughing.

'You ain't even passed art,' he scorned. 'Look, everyone has passed except you.' He just kept laughing, as if it was the funniest thing he'd ever seen.

'Look, even Nick Bleak has passed. Nick Bleak has passed and you ain't.'

Now, Nick Bleak was the class jerk, he was crap at everything. He used to wear glasses that didn't fit properly and kept sliding off his nose. He was always touching his glasses to slide them back up on to the bridge of his nose, but it was a waste of time, because they didn't fit properly. He sweated a lot too and then they'd slide down even more. He was a jerk and couldn't see properly, but even he passed. Everyone passed, even Nick Bleak. I tell you Jim took the piss out of me for ages after that. I used to tell Jim that I reckon the markers must have mixed up my paper with that crumby Nick Bleak kid, but he never bought it. Jim passed all his exams. I told you he was smart. I think he got more out of me screwing up my art exam than all his passes, though. Sometimes, that happens a lot. You know, where people get more out of people's misery than from their own satisfaction. I don't know why people do that, but I've noticed people do. I've noticed it a lot.

I reckon I could have made a better job of drawing Yellowstone than that whisk, though. Yellowstone is majestic. 'The land of the burning ground' the native American Indians called it, and it is too. Even if you can't draw, I reckon if you drew it, it would still turn out okay. Yellowstone goes on forever. I reckon you could get most of Wales or something in Yellowstone and still have space left over. But, despite its size, it's all genius. Mountains, lakes, lodge pole pine forests, geysers. There are places in Yellowstone where the ground could eat you up. You could fall into a boiling cauldron and boil like a lobster. But it's genius. In places it's as if all the colours and all the elements in the universe have spilled out of the ground. It's genius, genius.

That's the weird thing about America, a lot of it is real shitty. Especially some of their crumby towns and trailer parks full of guns and confederate flags, but then you see stuff like Yellowstone. America is probably the best place in the world when you see Yellowstone.

I spent a few days there. I managed to get myself a pitch on a campground. The pitch was massive, so I put my tent in one

153

corner of it under a couple of pine trees. It was good to pitch under the shade of the trees and you could store your food in bags tied to the branches. Brown bears sometimes came down by the campgrounds looking for food, so you needed to stick your food in the trees. In the early days, the crazy Americans used to drive their open-top cars through Yellowstone and feed the bears. Feed the bears, leaning out their open top cars. See, that's Americans for you. Then you give them the vote and say democracy is great. Then they get a nuclear bomb.

The rangers put a stop to that, though, and now you probably won't see a bear, but you still got to be careful. So, I pitched my tent close enough to get some shade, but far enough away to avoid the bears.

It was mid-summer, though, and the park was getting full. Lots of tents and RVs too. And it was because it was pretty full that I met Bob and Angie Wolgar.

They arrived in their RV quite late, as the evening turned crimson. They were looking around for somewhere to park their RV and hook it up to the electricity and everything. Now, I wasn't using the electricity and you could have played a game of baseball on the pitch I was on, it was so big, so they came across and asked me if they could park up next to my tent. I like space to myself, so sometimes I might have been a bit pissed about them asking me, but they seemed nice and, as I said, my pitch could have swallowed an ocean.

'No problem,' I said, 'You can fit London in here, help yourself.'

They smiled and were real grateful and after they settled in, invited me for some food. Bob lit a campfire and we sat around and toasted 'some mores' in the flames. They told me about San Francisco and the mist that rolls in and the fishing boats on the wharf that look as if they're floating on clouds. And the mad twisting, Everest, roller-coaster of Lombard Street and the dust and noise and ghostly meaning of life on Mission Street. And of the joy of eating in Chinatown, listening to the hum of a hundred launderettes and ten thousand birds. I was in Yellowstone and I had no need to be anywhere else, but I yearned. Yearned for San Francisco. And the wood on the fire crackled and the flames licked the marshmallow and we ate and ate. Ate the toasted marshmallows and soft melted chocolate dripping over crackers. I think I ate too many cos I felt as if I might throw up. I didn't mind, though. I didn't mind anything thinking about what awaited. Dreaming in Yellowstone.

Hitching around Yellowstone isn't easy. Everyone is a tourist and a lot of people don't want to drive you around while they're on holiday, but I got to see a lot. Bob and Angie seemed to take to me after I'd let them use my pitch and took me all around Yellowstone in their RV. They took me up by 'Old Faithful' and up to 'Prismatic Spring', where it looks as if the earth has invented new colours. And we drove by all the rivers and lakes and watched the pronghorns outrunning extinct cheetahs and we saw the bison grazing. And the bison came right up to the cars, and nosed around, just as the bears used to do, but it was okay, cos the windows were up.

And they took me everywhere cos they were grateful, even though all I'd done was let them stay on some ground that I didn't own, and I wasn't using anyway. I thought about how big the world is and how much space there is in so many places that ain't really being used by anyone. And how people still build walls. Walls to protect land they stole from someone in the first place.

Chapter Fifteen

I think Freud would say I live in a state of expectant anxiety. Maybe I'm just overanxious or pessimistic or something, but a lot of the time I just feel down about things. Maybe everyone does, who knows? Anyway, I don't know why, but after I left Yellowstone, I felt down. No one should feel down after Yellowstone; it is too big for that. Maybe that's why I felt down, though; maybe, after Yellowstone, everything just feels too small.

I was heading south. I didn't much care where I headed that day, to be honest, but someone I'd met in Yellowstone offered me a lift south, so I took it. He told me his name, but to be honest, I didn't even bother to listen. I didn't forget it like, I just didn't bother to listen. He was heading down the Memorial Highway through the Grand Teton National Park towards Jackson. The way I felt that day meant it sounded as good as anywhere. After about five minutes with me, though, I bet he wished he hadn't offered me a ride. I was feeling down. When you get a ride, you got to try and be all upbeat and have all your best stories ready. Have all your best stories so the guy who picks you up thinks he's having the time of his life. Either that or listen to all his stories as if it's the best stuff you've ever heard. That day, I didn't tell him any stories. Not one. I didn't listen either, not even that phoney listening stuff. I wasn't counting, but I reckon I only said 'huh' once. I bet after five minutes he was feeling down too.

Although Yellowstone National Park has a boundary, nature doesn't pay much attention. Everywhere still looks beautiful and what was Yellowstone soon merges with what becomes the Grand Teton. I still wasn't feeling too great, though, so I asked the guy to drop me off. He looked at me as if I was nuts, asking to be dropped in the middle of nowhere, but that's what I did. He didn't say it, but I bet he was glad I did, though. The way I acted that day, I bet he thought I was Lord Snooty or someone. I bet it put him off picking up thumbers for life. I reckon he was real glad I got out.

I didn't really know where I was, but the scenery was delicious, so I just wandered around for a while. I looked across the meadows and could see the snow-capped silver granite mountain peaks in the distance. It's pretty high up in these parts, so the air was thin and clear. I could see forever. The moon was still out in the sky. You know how sometimes it is, even though the sun's out and it's the middle of the day. But the air was so thin and clear I could see it against the deep blue sky. Right there, just above the snow-capped peaks and the air was so clear I reckon I could have reached out and touched it.

I walked a little way away from the road and crossed into a beautiful meadow. There were pine trees sprung up everywhere, and between the trees, a valley, filled with wild grasses and flowers. Full of delicious yellow glacier lilies and purple fireweed risen from the ashes being blown in the breeze. A bit further on, I came to a lake. The water was clear and serene and still, just like the air, and the snow-capped mountains reflected on the surface of the plate-glass water. Upside-down mountains mirrored on water. The reflection played tricks. Looked as if it wanted to be a mountain. I thought maybe I should let it and so crouched down and tilted my head, so I was almost upside-down. I wasn't sure what was real and what was a reflection. I liked it, not being sure. Maybe the reflection did too. Not being sure.

The blood rushed to my head, though, and I felt dizzy, so I just lay down on the meadow grasses for a while. I lay down and looked at the snow-capped mountains hugging the lake and the purple flowers bending their heads gently amongst the grasses. I felt a warm breeze on my face. It seemed to start here. To blow from behind those grasses and purple flowers as if it had come into life to find me. I thought about the breeze and how the wind blows and how that breeze that was kissing my face had probably just been a heartbeat. A fluttering breath of chill way up in Banff or Jasper that flew down the Rockies and into the big blue sky of Montana and blasted across the glory of Yellowstone. And how after it paused by me, it would go on its way. Go on to Jackson and then twist west to the good folks of Salt Lake City, and the flat salt pans and across the bodies of long-haired lovers. Then across the dry, hot dust of the Nevada desert, warming all the way until its baking breath heated the wine of California, singing through Fresno and San Fran and then on and on, to who knows where until it dived in an ocean. I thought about the distance it had crossed and how long it might take me to travel so far. I wondered if I'd make it out to the ocean. I thought about how soft and gentle it felt on my skin and wondered if I travelled as far, I would still be soft and gentle. I wondered about life and the paths we follow and the paths that carve themselves before us. I wondered whether life would ever be so soft and gentle.

I listened to birds' wings fluttering through the grasses and the pines and the sound of the breeze singing its history. I did my Da Vinci comparison trick and decided it was perfect. I reckon if Da Vinci could draw sound, his birds would have sounded like this.

Lying there, I was kind of glad I jumped out of my ride, and I started to forget about feeling down.

I don't know how long I lay in that field. It felt like a week, but I guess it was just an hour or something. But then I started to think about what I should do next. I started to think about Annie and whether she had made it to Oregon and what that commune was like and whether maybe it was surrounded by meadows and flowers and the same breeze had brushed against her. I wanted to see a face I knew. I started to wonder whether I should head back that way myself.

And so, I never made it to Jackson. When I got back to the highway, I decided to head back towards Yellowstone. I mulled over whether I could head west across Montana and Idaho and past Crater Lake on my way to that commune near Portland in Oregon. I started thinking about the look on Annie's face when I turned up out the blue. Thought about how she wouldn't believe it, and would jump up and hug me and run her hands through my hair and make me drink too much coffee while she talked and talked and told me about everything that had happened to her. I couldn't stop thinking about it. I couldn't wait to see the look on her face. A face that I knew.

I was lucky and I got a ride pretty quickly, considering I was in the park. It was from a family who were on holiday. Benny and Freda and their three kids. There wasn't much room in the car, but they let the smallest kid squeeze in up front with them on the bench seat and I jumped in the back with the two older kids. They'd driven out from St Louis, Missouri, and the kids argued with each other over who would tell me about the Gateway Arch. They talked about that silver arch for most of that ride, and argued about who was scared of heights, and who had been up to the top the most times, and how tall it was, and whether it was higher than the moon. And we laughed a lot and shared some soda pop that they'd packed in an icebox, and it was so cold, it made our teeth tingle and we all pulled faces and it all went by real quick. It all went by too quick, like when you meet up with a long-lost buddy who can only stay an hour.

So, by dusk, I was back. Back, pretty much where I'd left that morning. When I got out, I showed them the Union Jack on my pack and the kids said they thought it was prettier than the Stars and Stripes and that when they were old enough, maybe twelve or something, they'd come to see me in England and maybe visit the Queen. Benny and Freda laughed, and we said our goodbyes and we swopped addresses and said we'd all meet up again some time and all knew we wouldn't.

I felt better now. Yellowstone was just the same as when I had left, but things were different. I was expecting to be holed up in Jackson by now but was back in Yellowstone instead. I'd been somewhere but got nowhere. But getting nowhere felt like somewhere. Nowhere had never felt so good.

But I never did end up in that commune in Oregon. After I left Yellowstone for the second time, I got a lot of good rides. Mainly farmer types in their pick-up trucks, but also businessmen who told me stories of when they were younger and hitched out west themselves, before they settled down and passed their days in meetings and on the road between them. One even bought me lunch at this fancy restaurant. We pigged out for an hour and I filled my empty, grumbling belly to bursting. At the end I offered to chip in some money, but he said no, and I was glad he did, cos I couldn't really have given any.

I wound my way out of Wyoming and up to Montana. I hitched across the seemingly endless plains of Montana, beneath its big sky. I felt like Steinbeck and even kind of got why he thought it was his favourite state and why he thought small boys would think it was like Texas.

I didn't know about that, cos I hadn't got to Texas yet. But I knew I would find out. It made me think about how far away from Texas I was, and how I needed to get there. It made me think about why I had come to the States, but for the time being, I was heading west.

I stopped in Bozeman and strolled down the tree-lined streets, thinking of what it would have been like when it was still a sacred Sioux Indian hunting ground. It made me kind of wish that all the American army colonels had been as crappy as Custer.

I crossed into Idaho and saw the Sawtooth Mountains from the shores of Redfish Lake. I ate lots of potatoes. Platefuls of potatoes. Potatoes shaped like Idaho. Big potatoes, small potatoes and every other size of potato in between. I tell you, if you hitch in Idaho, you'll smell of potato.

And then I got rides across Oregon. First from a war vet and then from an old hippy named Saturn, who said he moved up from California, cos it had all sold out down there and Oregon was where it was at. And he wore a bandana and kept saying 'man' and smelled of petunia. At first, I was stuck on the idea of finding that commune Annie had talked about, but as I got nearer to Portland, I couldn't face it. I kept thinking about how it would be full of people just the same as any town or city. How it would be full of people like Saturn, with stupid names, telling me where it was at. I mean they might have all gone off-grid and stuff and carved out some alternative lifestyle and all, but I reckoned it would still be people and their petty ways. I mean, to start with, maybe everyone is all lovey-dovey and stuff, but I reckon before long, it's full of all the same bullshit you always get when you stick people together. You know, people trying to outdo each other or getting all uptight about who's done what to whom. See, that's the trouble with people. One on one, people are fine, it's as if they don't have so much to prove, so much to pretend. But you stick people together and they all start acting crappy, worrying about who's the top dog and all that crap.

So, when I got a ride to Portland and the guy said he was heading across to the coast, I just stayed in the car. It was early afternoon when I passed by Portland. I was probably only about thirty miles away from that commune and Annie. I pictured her sitting cross-legged in the sun somewhere, just about thirty miles away. I didn't even know if she had made it there, but I hoped she had. I hoped she had found what she wanted, what she was looking for. I hoped she was happy. I hoped I might be.

Chapter Sixteen

The spray on my face was colder than I thought it would be, much colder. Saltier too. I ran my tongue across the surface of my lips and tasted the salt. It felt good. It was good to have reached the Pacific Ocean, good to feel the spray of the Pacific Ocean on my face. I thought back to those crazy nights in New York and of how shit scared I'd been. It seemed a long time ago as I stared out across the ocean. But I'd made it across America, I could feel the spray of the Pacific on my skin; it almost made me drool.

Parts of the Oregon coastline are wild and rugged. The Pacific Ocean rolls in and waves crash on to the sandy bays and coves. As you head south along the coastline, you don't see the lifeguard, bikini, beach-boy beaches of southern California. Oregon beaches haven't been tamed, they've grown up in their own way, on their own terms. The Oregon coast looks as if it has experienced things that it would rather not talk about. Dark, craggy sea-stacks barricade the shorelines and dense forest of pine crowds around to protect them. When the weather is bad, the wind whistles off the Pacific and the ocean rages with surf. The Oregon coastline rages back.

On a sunlit day, the blue sky lightens the colour of the ocean and softens the face of the craggy rock formations rising from the sea. The wind-sculpted shapes that on bleaker days have a sinister form take on a new and kinder look. Sea lions and grey whales swim offshore.

It looks like the kind of place you want to stay for a while.

When I first arrived at the Oregon coast, I thought about

heading north to Seattle, just cos Hendrix was from there, and maybe back into Canada, but I liked Oregon, so I headed south along the 101 and hugged the coastline. I decided to stay a while, so when I got near Cape Perpetua, found a youth hostel a couple of miles from the beach. Beaches are delicious, but hostels are cheap, and give me a chance to shower and get breakfast. I checked in.

I had stayed in a few hostels, mainly because they were cheap. Sometimes the rules were crappy, but they are clean and sometimes it's better than sleeping rough. There was this real neat one in Ottawa. It was an old, converted prison and everyone got their own cell. It had just enough room for a single bed and the only light came from a small window the size of a book, high up on the wall. It must have been hell. They used to have hangings there too. I wondered what it must be like, locked up in some crappy cell like that waiting to be hanged. You know, just counting down the hours.

Anyway, the hostel in Oregon was just a regular place, nothing fancy, not a prison or anything, but it was somewhere to stay, and I ended up holing up there for a few days.

Some hostels split up the boys and girls. The Oregon hostel split people. I was used to all that sort of crap, because I went to that crumby all-boys school, I told you about. It wasn't a fancy school, but there were only boys. It was crazy really, because the girls' school was right next door. I mean right next door. It even had the same name. When we were out in the playground kicking footballs around, we could see the girls in their playground through the fence. We could watch them play tennis and tried to look up their skirts. We were eleven, so we tried to look up their skirts. It was mad really, cos we couldn't study English together, but we could try and look up their skirts.

Mr Fox always used to show up when we were standing by that fence, though. He taught Science and everyone hated science. We used to mess about big style during his class, just to pass the time. We'd set stuff alight with Bunsen burners and burn holes in each other's bags with sulphuric acid and things. It passed the time, but no one liked Mr Fox. That's why no one called him Foxy. See, his name was made just perfect for adding a Y, but no one ever did. See, if he had been Foxy, it would have been as if he was a buddy or something, but no one wanted to be his buddy, so he was always just plain Mr Fox. Mr Fox in his stinking brown corduroy jacket.

See, he always used to wear this crappy, old, brown corduroy jacket. It was real shabby, except for the leather patches on the elbows. The leather patches were all shiny and smooth and they stood out against the worn fabric of the jacket, like a couple of lily pads in a swamp. Sometimes he wore brown corduroy trousers too. Brown matching corduroy trousers. They were always dirty looking too and had stains down the front as if he'd spilled custard down him or something. Sometimes, I'd watch him at lunch just to see if he did, but I never saw him eating a pudding with custard, not once. I don't even reckon he liked custard, but that's what those stains looked like, though, like little custard stains down the front of his trousers. But when we were hanging around by the fence, trying to look up the girls' skirts, he'd always show up. He'd come across and tell us to move along. One time, when I was in a bad mood and wanted to wind him up, I asked him if he thought the girls could play tennis better than the boys, cos they wore skirts and we wore shorts. See, they always looked as if they could play better than us and looked more elegant too. He just stared at me as if I was a bit of an imbecile and looked as if he was about to twist my sideburns.

See, that was his thing. He would just walk up beside you and grab your sideburns between his fingers, then yank your head. If you didn't have any sideburns, he'd just grab the skin and yank your head anyway. It used to hurt real bad, but he did it all the time. Sometimes he did it for no reason at all, but just because. Just because he liked doing it, you know, just for the sake of it. Well, when I asked him about who could play tennis best, I thought he was gonna yank my sideburns, but he didn't. He just said, 'Don't be stupid, it don't make a jot of difference to how well you play.'

He always used to say 'jot' all the time. 'It won't make a jot of difference', 'there's not a jot of difference between…' He was always saying jot and he said it then.

'That's what I thought,' I said, 'So why do the girls have to wear skirts then? And why do we have to wear shorts?' I looked puzzled and went on, 'You know, why do the schools have different rules, if it don't make a jot of difference to how you play?'

I emphasised 'jot' just to wind him up and all. I was hoping he wouldn't yank my sideburns, but I couldn't resist it and just wanted to wind him up. I hated him, see. We all did.

He looked at me as if my lights had gone out. 'You, stupid boy,' he yelled, 'it's the rules, girls have to wear skirts.'

I reckon I was real close to getting one of his sideburn specials, so I stepped back a bit. 'Thank you, Mr Fox,' I grovelled. 'I've always wondered, but that makes sense now.'

It didn't make any sense at all, you know, him saying it was a rule because it was a rule, but I reckoned I was too close to one of those sideburn yanks, so I backed off.

He stared right through me and started to yell at all of us. 'Move on, boys, move yourselves along. Right now, before I lose my temper.'

Now if it had been Brooksey, we could have had a bit of banter. We could have said something like, 'Mr Brooks, will you just do a couple of lines from Chaucer first, then we'll go.' He would have too. He would have done a couple of lines from some crumby tale in his crazy middle English and we would have moved on, no trouble at all. We'd have been so busy listening to his crazy language, we'd have forgotten all about the girls and looking up their skirts, no problem. See, Brooksey was clever like that, he knew how to get stuff done without twisting your sideburns.

But we moved off anyway, cos Mr Fox made us. It was funny, though, cos even after we left, Mr Fox would just hang around that fence for ages. Sometimes, he would look over his shoulder to see if anyone was watching, but most of the time he would just be looking over the fence. Sometimes, I reckon he was there for half an hour or more. One time it was about an hour and a half. I know it was, because I watched him from the second floor when I was in a German class. I could see the girls' playground way off in the distance from my seat in that class, and I saw him stay by the fence for the whole of the German lesson. It was double German too. I don't remember anything we did in the German lesson that day, not a jot. I just remember Mr Fox looking over the fence.

When we were about eleven, we used to go over to that fence loads, but we weren't tall enough and it was a waste of time; you couldn't see anything. That whole school was a waste of time; you couldn't see anything and never learnt anything, not even how to talk to girls. I went to that stupid school from age eleven until I quit after my exams about age fifteen. In all that time we weren't allowed to meet any of the girls, just watch them playing tennis. I reckon that's why I was so screwed up trying to speak to that Jeanette and all at that crappy disco. I don't know which mad arsehole dreamt up the idea of segregating boys and girls.

Probably some moron like Mr Fox. I don't know, maybe the same moron who called Britain, great.

Anyway, it didn't bother me that the dorms were split up like that in this Oregon hostel. In fact, it did me a favour cos when I stayed there, our dorm was almost empty and that suited me fine. I was only planning on staying one night, but things changed when I met Dave and 'porcelain' Pete.

The one guy staying in the hostel with me was called Pete. In the end, I quite liked him, but at first, he was a bit of a spook. Now, I'm all scrawny and pale, but I looked as if I'd been grilled on gas mark 8 for a couple of hours compared to Pete. I tell you he had the whitest, palest skin I'd ever seen. It was smooth too. Marble arms. Skin like glass. I was real spooked when we first met, but he was just pale, so what? I got used to him. That's when I christened him 'porcelain' Pete. I never said it to his face at first, I just used to think it, but one day it just came out.

'Porcelain Pete,' I said right to his face one day. He hated it, but I just kept saying it anyway. To start with I didn't like him much and I kind of said it to wind him up, but in the end, we got along, and I didn't want to annoy him anymore. I still said it, though.

I don't know why I give people these stupid nicknames, but I do it all the time. Normally, I don't tell them, unless it just slips out as it did with Pete. No, normally I just think it in my head. Usually, they never know. I did it loads when I was hitchhiking. I can remember loads of people who gave me lifts and know their nickname. But even if you paid me, I wouldn't be able to tell you their real name. It's crazy really, but that's what I do. Like there was Wilson, you know that nut-job that chucked me out in Wyoming. But there were loads of others too.

I remember this one guy; 'the Colonel' I called him. He was a real ancient guy who picked me up near Livingstone. He was about seventy or something and had this silver hair brushed back off his forehead. He has a silver goatee beard too, as if he was hoping it would make him look distinguished and all. You know, he looked like a southern dandy who had come up with a spicy breadcrumb recipe for chickens and shit like that. He was a bit of a weirdo, though. When we were driving along, he started telling me why he'd given me a ride. 'I liked the way you were standing,' he said.

'You looked like you meant business, like you were putting effort into getting a lift. You were standing up straight. I liked that.' He kept banging on about it and telling me that if I hadn't been standing up straight how he wouldn't have stopped.

Now I kind of got what he meant. Sometimes, I saw people hitching and they just sat by the side of the road, leaning on a bag or something. Sometimes, it looked as if they couldn't even be bothered to put their thumb out. That always did my head in, when I saw people hitch like that, but I saw it a lot. Maybe if they had known Mr Bagshot, they would have turned out different, I don't know. All I know is I got this ride from 'the Colonel' because of how I stood.

Then there was 'Captain Cadillac'. Boy, was he a headcase? I couldn't believe he even stopped to give me a ride. He was driving this great big flashy Cadillac and pulled over to give me a lift. I'd never been in a Cadillac before and I swear it was huge. You could have played tennis on the backseat. It had these fancy white leather seats that gleamed like an ice rink. I reckon he must have polished those leather seats for about a hundred hours every week for them to gleam as they did. There were tons of fancy gadgets too and chrome everywhere. And all the chrome was gleaming, just like the leather seats. To be honest, I think the only reason he picked me up was to show off and bang on about how bloody great he was because he owned this Cadillac.

I reckon he went around giving people rides just to talk about this crazy car. He knew everything you could know about Cadillacs and didn't stop talking about them the whole way. 'This is a '62 Cadillac Coupe Deville but it's in mint condition. I've got a '58 Cadillac too, but the difference is, the '58 has white walled wheels and different fins. I used to have an 8.2 litre Eldorado. Boy, did that Eldorado go. Blah, blah blah blah.'

I'm telling you, by the time I left him I knew everything about bloody Cadillacs. Everything. If you could take an exam in Cadillacs, I would walk it. It would be a breeze.

Anyway, I was always giving people names, so that's how come I christened 'porcelain' Pete.

See, I stayed at that hostel for about five days with Pete and that's how I got to know him. He had some strange ways, though. He was always tidying things, so everything was neat and in rows and stuff. He liked things in straight lines.

'Everything should be symmetrical,' he used to say, and then he'd start moving things and arranging them in rows. At first, I just used to say, 'huh', and ignore him, but after a while, I realised this stuff was really important to him. As if his life depended on it. Even his pack was organised to some crazy system. I just used to chuck my stuff in my pack, but Pete spent hours making sure everything was colour coordinated. Then, when he got out a pair of trousers or something, it would look as if it had just been pressed by the laundry department in the Ritz or somewhere. As if it had just come out a linen cupboard and been pressed by his private butler.

He always used to get up early too. He had this thing about getting up at exactly 5.55 every morning. For crying out loud, who gets up at 5.55? I used to ask him why 5.55, but he just used to say, 'One day I reckon I'll need to. You will, too.' He never really made any sense and I'm not even sure he knew why, but he said he had to and so that's what he'd do. Every day at 5.55. He had this stupid travel alarm clock with him. You know, one of those crumby little things that fold away into a small leather case, but that you can open to see the face of the clock at night. It had these crappy illuminous clock hands and numbers around the edge of the face that shone out at you in the dark. It did my head in that clock, with its stupid green fluorescent hands shining out at you all night. The alarm would go off at exactly 5.55 and he would get up and then go through all these crazy rituals. I didn't realise at first, but after a few days, I realised he always did everything in the same order. He was proper nuts.

The worst was listening to him wash, though. The shower room was right next to the sleeping dorms so you could just about hear everything. I'd lie in bed after he'd got up and try to go back to sleep, but I never could cos he made so much noise.

For a start, when he had a wash, he wouldn't fill the sink, but just let the water run. You could hear the water splashing out of the tap and rinsing around the sink. Then you'd hear the rhythmic gurgle every few seconds as the water dived down the plug hole. On and on it would go, it used to do my head in. I used to tell him that some poor kid in Africa is probably walking about a million miles with some crappy old bucket just to get some stinking water from a stream somewhere, but it never made any difference. He just used to tell me he didn't know any Africans and would just leave the tap running. Trouble is most Americans don't even have a clue where Africa is. They don't have a clue where anything is.

Weird thing was, he hated water. He'd splash it over his face, but as he was doing it, he'd make a load of noise. You could hear him puffing and sighing and gasping for breath. Then he'd start moaning and groaning and then more puffing and panting. The first time he did it, I thought he was having a heart attack or something, but that's just what he did. Every time he washed, that's just what he did. He used to make a song and dance of everything, he was crazy.

I asked him loads of times why he made so much noise and wouldn't fill the sink. To start with he wouldn't tell me. But one day he did. He told me this crazy story about how when he was a tiny kid, just a baby, someone had dropped him in a bath. He couldn't remember it, but his mum had told him about it when he got older. She told him that a few days after he was born the nurse in the hospital was bathing him and he slipped from her arms and into this bath of water. His mum told him that's why he didn't like water, because he'd been dropped in the bath by a nurse when he was born. Mrs Peters it was. That's why he was called Pete too, after Mrs Peters, the nurse who dropped him in a bath. I don't know whether he was ever dropped in that bath. Pete didn't really know either, but his mum had told him that's what happened and so that's why he didn't like water. He didn't know for sure, but I guess he believed it, and that's all that mattered. When you think about it, we all believe a load of stuff and we ain't got a clue if it's true or not. We still all act as if it is true, though, even though really, we haven't a clue.

Now, I would never have stayed at this hostel with crazy 'porcelain' Pete for so long, if I hadn't met Dave. But I met Dave the first day I got there, and he persuaded me to hang around for a couple of days and that's why I holed up there for so long and got to know Pete. Dave was a charmer. He was the sort of guy that would stab you in the ribs, but make you laugh so much, you'd never notice you were bleeding. He was gaunt and thin and looked as if he was about to die, but made you believe he would never die. He said everything was beautiful. He must have said beautiful about a hundred times a day. He had a beautiful car, a beautiful plan, a beautiful way of saying beautiful. If it had been the 50s, Dave would have been a hobo riding the trains. But the 70s was the age of the automobile in the US, and somehow, he'd managed to scrape enough money together to buy a car. It was a bit of a banger from the late 50s, a knock down, low-priced Plymouth. It was held together by rust and had lost more parts than those cars that I built in the factory in Birmingham, but it was his, and he lived in it. He had somewhere to crash out and could move like a gypsy. He was kind of an upwardly mobile hobo trying to scratch out a living.

He was up to all sorts of stuff. He was a mix of west-coast hippy drop-out, and American entrepreneur. In five years, if I met him again, I wasn't sure whether he'd be living in a ditch or running for president. Dave would have made a terrible president, but probably better than most. I'm guessing America will do a lot worse one day.

Anyway, Dave made a dollar or two however he could. He wasn't really a dealer, but there was so much dope and acid flying around the west coast in the 60s and 70s, he didn't mind pushing stuff and he had contacts. With so many travellers passing through, he made plenty of money that way. When he wasn't doing that, he was just hustling and when he wasn't doing that he was begging.

That's how I met him on that first day I arrived. He was

sitting on the floor outside a deli, begging. Later, he told me how much money he made some days.

'It's just a numbers game. A beautiful numbers game,' he used to say. 'If you sit there long enough and enough people pass by, some will throw you a dime or a quarter and if you're lucky a beautiful dollar. A lot of people walk right past you like you're a piece of beautiful shit, but I don't mind that. It's just a numbers game.'

He used to put this top hat down in front of him when he begged. Upside down, like a bucket for people to chuck money in. 'It's better than a cap or something,' he told me, 'Encourages people,' he said, 'encourages, it's deeper, holds more beautiful dough.'

His top hat was pretty cool too. It was a bit battered and faded as if it was years old and all, but it was the craziest hat I'd ever seen. See, I guess it was from the circus or some magic act or something once, because it used to collapse down, right flat like a frisbee. When he wasn't wearing it, he used to press it against his chest, and it would compress dead flat. He'd put it under his arm and carry it about as if he had this black frisbee or something with him. Then, when he wanted to wear it again or use it for begging, he'd flip the rim of the hat against his palm or something and it would pop out into the shape of a top hat again. It was the craziest hat I'd ever seen, but he had it with him all the time. When he walked around in it, he strutted about as if he was Abraham Lincoln or the Mad Hatter or someone. Dave was crazy, he just hadn't met Alice.

But that's where I met him, right by the hostel where I was staying, and that's how we got talking, when he was begging outside the deli. And it was cos of Dave that I ended up staying at that hostel for a few days. You see, Dave told me about this car he owned, and started to bang on about a plan he had to get him down to San Francisco. He told me that he wanted to head down the coast but didn't want to pay for the fuel, so he was thinking about selling seats in his car and trying to get a few travellers to chip in for petrol and stuff in return for a ride to San Francisco. He figured in a couple of days, he could hustle enough to get maybe five or more travellers to head south with him in his car. All they had to do was chip in for fuel and pay for his grub on the way down.

'We can all crash on the beach and party, it'll be a trip, a beautiful, beautiful trip,' he said. Now at first, I thought the guy was crazy. Why would anyone want to pay for fuel, when getting rides for free, hitching was pretty easy? But the more I thought about it, the more it seemed like a good idea. Although hitching was easy, it's unpredictable and you might miss the coast road. Almost everyone who was heading south wanted to follow the ocean on the coast road and Dave's sales pitch was all about hugging the coast road and crashing on beaches. I figured, split between a few people, the fuel wouldn't cost much and so told him I'd think about it.

'Beautiful, I'll count you in,' he said.

'Maybe,' I said. 'How many people have you got?'

'You, so far, but give me a couple of beautiful days.'

And that's how come I stayed at the hostel for so long and got to buddy up with 'porcelain' Pete.

So, five days after I met Dave begging outside the deli, we were heading south together in his battered old banger. Dave, 'porcelain' Pete, Mikey, Bella, Cindy and me. All heading south down the 101 for San Francisco.

'It's going to be a crazy, beautiful trip,' Dave kept telling us. We had a feeling he was right.

Chapter Seventeen

A lot of old American cars have bench seats up front. I love bench seats. I don't know why they don't have bench seats anymore. Probably some Health and Safety crap or maybe it was some stupid designer who thought it would be better to split up all the seats and put gear sticks and control down the centre and all. But Dave's banger had a bench seat up front and I'd called dibs, so I sat up front with 'porcelain' Pete. Dave drove. Mikey piled in the back. He was a Canadian from Vancouver who was heading down to see some friends in LA. He had picked up with this girl from Ohio, named Bella. They seemed sweet on each other so cuddled up in the back most of the time. I bet they'd have loved it if they had the backseat to themselves, but Dave had also cajoled Cindy into coming along too. She sat next to them gabbling on most of the time about how Dave should slow down. All our tatty rucksacks were squeezed into the graveyard trunk. We travelled light, and Dave only had what he stood up in, and if he wasn't wearing it, his top hat. It was a squeeze, but we managed somehow. The car was probably white originally, but it had been patched up over the years. From certain angles, it looked as if it might have been grey. Go around the other side and it may have been cream. Patched together from loads of different cars. A door here, a bonnet there, some door handles from something else, chrome bumpers from a truck. Parts tied with rope. Only the dents were consistent. It was dented from every angle.

Its shape sang of horror and Dave's driving was dark, but the

101 saved us. The road runs into US1 and both hug the coast all the way from Oregon to San Francisco. Stunning roads with delicious views. Your favourite pudding drowning in cream.

Dave swung the car around as if we were on a roller-coaster. Frenetic, wild, uninhibited, eyes gleaming, swinging it around hairpin bends, sometimes on two wheels, sometimes on four and all the time the bottomless ocean waited. The brakes were shaved, so sometimes slowing down depended more on gravity than friction. If, after the bend there was an uphill incline, the car slowed. If it was a downhill slope, Cindy yelled. Cindy yelled a lot.

Dave laughed. 'I told you it was going to be a beautiful, crazy trip.' And then he laughed louder and kept on driving. And the laughter echoed, and the roads were uneven and the bends like curved air. Gravity reshaped our bodies and with re-sculptured minds we clung. Clung to hope, clung to each other, clung to dreams that came and went with every mile and all the time, wondered. Driver, where you taking us?

Trouble is, most of the time we were all off our heads on anything Dave had brought with him. He had been getting stuff for travellers when I met him and had a sack full of tea and dolly mixtures with him. It was another American dream, money-making scheme he had for the trip. So, most of the time we were out of our heads. That's one of the reasons why it took so long to get to San Francisco. That, and the fact that Dave was having the time of his life. Sometimes we'd only travel about fifty miles or something before we pulled off near some secluded beach.

We'd get a campfire going and drink and trip out watching the sun set into the Pacific. Mikey and Bella would go skinny-dipping in the ocean cos they were so sweet on each other and Cindy would moan about the mosquitos and yell at Dave to move and drive on. Then we'd hear the mosquitos zuzzing and Mikey and Bella splashing and the waves crashing. Dave would start to tell stories about how if you sang to mosquitos in Spanish they'd lie down and fall asleep and he was so off his head he'd believe it too. Then Cindy would get mad and throw shells at him and slap her legs and arms as the pesky little buggers landed on her. Then Mikey and Bella would surface only to start making out behind the dunes and then you'd hear their aahs and oohs. Then you'd hear Cindy and her ouches as more little buggers landed. And the mosquitos were zuzzing. And Dave would start singing in Spanish even though he didn't know a single damn word. Then I'd take another draw of grass and I wouldn't be sure who was aahing and oohing and ouching and zuzzing and *por favor*-ing. And Dave would carry on singing to the mosquitoes and the waves kept rolling in, and everyone went crazy, except for Pete.

Everyone except 'porcelain' Pete. He got real freaked out and left the second night we stopped. He told us we were all nuts. This was the guy who was trying to set his alarm clock on the beach for 5.55, when we'd been smoking the moon dry until 5.00. I felt sorry for him when he left, though. When he told me he was coming with Dave, back at the hostel in Oregon, I'd asked him if he thought he'd make it. He got really mad with me and told me to mind my own business.

'There's nothing wrong with me,' he yelled, 'It's you that's crazy.'

And maybe he was right. Maybe it was crazy to be tripping off our heads on the west coast of America driving the coast road in a car with no brakes, with the thin, gaunt ghost of Dave not knowing what tomorrow would bring. Maybe he was crazy, with his stupid alarm clock and smooth routines. Maybe we are all crazy.

I missed Pete, though. When I first met him, I thought he was doolally, but then I got to know him and got used to his ways. He was just trying to cope like all of us. Trying to cope and make sense of stuff in his own way. Maybe it looked crazy to some of us, but maybe everything looks crazy to someone. I don't know. I just know I missed him. Like sometime, one day, at 5.55, I'd wish he was there putting everything straight.

There was a bit more space in the car, after Pete left, not that it changed much. Dave still drove too fast and Cindy still yelled at him to slow down. I think Mikey and Bella were hoping that Cindy would move into the front bench seat now Pete had gone, but I kept telling her how scary it was up front. Scary and full of mosquitos. She stayed in the back. That suited me fine.

'Stay cool. Stay a beautiful cool,' Dave used to yell back when she yelled at him, and then, to drown out her screams, he'd play music. Loud. He played it loud. He had this crappy eight-track player wired into his car and had some tapes with him. He had loads of stuff, but mostly west coast acid bands, like the Doors and Jefferson Airplane. He had Country Joe and the Fish too and we'd all end up singing along with the tracks, just as if we all played in the band. I'm telling you, if someone had taken a picture of us on that trip, we'd have looked as if we'd just fallen off the cover of 'Fixing to Die'.

One, two, three, and we'd bust out the chorus. All that stuff about wondering what we were fighting for and how no one gave a damn. Vietnam, Vietnam and on and on and back to the chorus, cos we knew we're all gonna die.

Some days, we'd drop acid and sing it a million times over as we floated around bends, staring at the Pacific below us. Inside-out bends and curved air and gravity and sometimes the world looked wicked, and sometimes it sounded beautiful and sometimes it felt like cold, cold ice cream melting on your tongue. Dave drove down US1 like a madman and kept telling us everything was beautiful. I told you I thought he might be presidential material. And sometimes it was beautiful, but that didn't stop us singing about how we're gonna die, cos that's what it felt like most of the time, like we were gonna die. Sometimes, when we were singing along, we'd forget the words and just go, la, la la, or doo, wee, dowah and stuff, but we never forgot the bit about dying. I don't know why, but no one ever forgot that bit.

Funny thing with songs, though: it don't matter much if you go la, la, la, or na, na, na, na and stuff, cos lots of bands do it anyway. You know some bands do it deliberate to make up some anthemic outro, you know, stuff like Hey Jude when the Beatles did it, or T. Rex and Hot Love. But a lot of bands just do it in the middle and stuff, as if they can't be bothered to think of any more words. Like they write one verse and a chorus and then just repeat it and add a few, sha, la, las and stuff. You know, as if they've already bust a gut getting that much together and can't be arsed to think of any more words. When I hear that, it usually does my head in. I always think what would happen if some author like D.H. Lawrence or James Joyce had just got halfway through a chapter and because they couldn't be arsed to think of any more words, just wrote la, la, la or something for a couple of pages. See, when bands do that, no one bats an eyelid, but if an author did it, people would get freaked. Mind you, maybe Joyce should have tried it. Maybe he could have pushed the boundary of language further. He'd probably have made more sense.

Bands don't bother to finish songs either. That's another thing that does my head in. Like when you listen to some crappy pop songs on the radio, a lot of them just go to a fade. Why would anyone do that? It does my head in. See, when they play it live, they've got to finish it, so it must have a proper end, so why don't they end it when they record it for the radio? I reckon one time someone will just write some crappy pop song that just goes la, la, la, or yummy, yummy, yummy, or something all the way through and then just fades out. Someone who can't really be arsed to write anything, you know, like most crappy pop songs.

I think that's one reason why I liked the Doors and the Airplane and stuff. They didn't do too much of that sha, la, la stuff. Just proper words and trippy guitars. But anyway, that's what Dave had on his eight-track, so that's what we played.

I hadn't really thought too much about England since I'd left. After what happened with my mum and dad, I didn't have much to go back for, and I think I was trying to put it out my mind. But listening to the Airplane and HP Lovecraft and all this crazy 60s stuff reminded me of when I was listening to that stuff at home. See, I was a bit of a loner growing up. I mean, I knocked about with that kid named Jim at school whom I told you about, and I went to that crappy disco for a while, but most of the time it was just me. I did know one kid I got along with, though. His name was Paul. He went to my school too. We never spoke much at first, but then as we got a bit older, we realised we were reading the same books. Stuff like Kafka and Camus. We listened to the same music too, a lot of this west coast stuff.

Anyway, looking back, I reckon Paul was probably the only person I ever really liked, like really got to know. He used to come and see me at my house, and I would go to his. We'd often argue about stuff and get into deep conversations. I think we were just trying to work stuff out. Seeing if someone else had any answers. When you're fourteen, you spend a lot of time trying to figure stuff out.

Well, listening to the Doors and all made me think about

him. Sometimes, when his mum and dad were out, we'd drop acid and listen to music in his house. In his room, wax, flat cardboard, two-dimensional mats of Northern Lights, blue and green, psychedelic painted spirals dripping from the ceiling, crawling down walls and through our changing bodies. Skin wrapped up in tipped-up, tripped-up, tingle cream neutrinos and laser beam liquid, acid guitar and distorted far-off voices. Sometimes, he'd open the windows while playing the Doors full blast, just to make sure anyone who was passing got to hear. It was as if we had to get everyone to listen to the Doors. Nowadays, if I see some smart-arse in their car blasting out music at traffic lights or something, I usually think they are an arsehole. 'Yeah, so you've got windows and a cassette,' I think, 'big deal.' They usually look out to see who's noticing them, and when they do that, I deliberately look the other way, as if I ain't noticed a thing. I reckon that drives them nuts. I bet we used to drive people nuts too. I bet when we used to open the windows and play music full blast, people thought we were arseholes too, but we were fourteen and we did it anyway. Anyway, it was different, it was California melted on vinyl. It was the Doors.

We used to play stuff like 'The End'. 'The End', drifting out of the window and down the street. It would start off all quiet and gentle and haunting. But then it would build into these big storms. Morrison in Tornado alley.

'I want to…'

The smell of earth's herbs and off your face and a band about to explode. Then you believed in spontaneous combustion. Densmore's crash cymbals and Krieger and Manzarek stuttering trippy stuff. You know, as if mushrooms had kicked in and everything was charged. Then Morrison would scream, Oedipus and Freud… aghaaaahhh.

The sound of someone finding love torn up by hate, like passion turned dread. As if he was alive, but dying, as if he was breathing and suffocating. At fourteen, that's how we felt. Maybe that's why we opened the windows, just to try and breathe and tell everyone that's how we felt.

Looking back, I guess we were just arseholes too, but at fourteen we didn't know any better, and that's how it felt. But tripping out and listening to the Doors in Dave's car made me think about all that stuff. You know, about Paul and about growing up in Birmingham and opening the windows. But now I was here. On US1 in California. It felt the same. I was 6,000 miles away and four years older, but it still felt the same. And Dave left his windows down, but he had to — they wouldn't shut.

'What do you want on next?' Dave asked.

'Strange Days,' I said, 'Strange Days.'

Trouble is, with tripping out so much, it's hard to remember what really happened and what just blew up in our heads. What was dream, what was real. I remember fragments, lots of pieces, but it's hard to put it all together, you know, all together in one coherent piece. I remember the redwoods. Massive, primeval trees. Forests of massive trees, taller and better than any building in New York. Trees over a hundred metres tall and two thousand years old. And memories, pictures, ideas about Dave driving through an underground flood tunnel in the trunk of a massive redwood tree. A tree wide enough to drive a car through. Can a pill make you smaller? Weird dreams inside a young mind drive the highway south. We're here, the west. The west is the best. I remember sunsets and sunrises, waiting for the sun. And going to Mendocino and walking down the bed quilt streets past the pretty houses and down to the sea. And the colours, the colours in Mendocino and the crystal ships out on the ocean. And the bleached white bark of pines. Unnaturally white, from a hundred years of salt, blown in by the ocean and seeped so deep, it made them look old. Old as crooked men bent over and dying. And their jagged, dry, dry branches, stripped of green, hanging like wild, tangled hair. Stiff, petrified, tangled hair.

I remember having this crazy dream. Over and over, this crazy dream. Standing on the beach, looking out at the sea. It was summer and the sea glistened. My mum and dad were standing on the hill. They were happy. I was happy too.

Shells on the beach. Thousands of wonderful seashells lying on soft white sand. Shells don't move. Crawling. Crawl and change into creatures. Small creatures, I don't know, like crabs crawling. Crawling all around over my feet and toes. Creatures growing and bulging and twisting. New shapes, distortion. Forming twisted shapes and then heads, and hands and feet. People, a race of strangers.

I looked back for all I'd known, and it was gone. Empty space and strangers.

We play strange, unnatural games. Become desperate, hopeless. Live in the games of others, listen to their rules. More rules, more rules. Listen to them chanting, 'all rules apply to everyone, but no rules apply to us'.

Maybe it was a dream, maybe it was America. Maybe it was Darwin's next theory or just human nature. Or madness. Maybe it was madness.

I wasn't sure what was real or what just happened in my head. Maybe that's life. You're not really sure what's real and what just happens in your head.

Dave told us it would be crazy. Beautiful.

It was quiet on the Golden Gate Bridge, the quietest it had been since we left Oregon. 'When the music's over' ended as we left the Marin headlands, and Dave switched the tape off as we crossed the bridge. Beads of sweat and concentration and the view that signalled a new beginning but felt like the end.

Like a mountain pass, we saw all that was San Francisco below us. Traffic sprawled across six lanes outside, and boats bobbled across the water that wobbled out of its Pacific existence, but the car was silent. US1 had drained our bodies of blood and our haggard, pale remains in need of transfusion sensed the end. We were only about five miles from downtown San Francisco, only five miles.

It was a sunny day, but even on bright days, the tops of the red piers of the bridge are often shrouded in the mist that rolls off the Pacific. It drifts in and out moment by moment, so that the view of the bridge and of the city fades in and out, moment by moment. At times, the view was fuzzy. Everything was fuzzy.

When we got out of Dave's car no one knew what to say. Dave drove towards the centre of town and parked outside a church. Looking at signs plastered about, it seemed to be run by the Sally Army. The mist hadn't reached downtown and so we all piled out of his car and tumbled on to the sidewalk in the sunshine. Bedraggled and dirty, unkempt and shabby. Dusty, ripped bandaged mummies stepping out into sunshine. The bright sun blinded us. We looked at each other as if we should have something big to say. Something big and memorable. But we didn't.

Chapter Eighteen

'Is this Pacifica yet?' I yelled to the driver. Outside, the breathy Frisco fog billowed.

'Close,' came the reply, 'I'll let you off next stop.' The driver chewed on his gum, tremendously in time with the wipers as they slid back and to across the windscreen. The bus drove on into the grey-white empty rolls of nothing that surrounded us. Out there somewhere was San Francisco, a rolling ocean, an earthquake waiting to awake us all until we screamed, but for now we sat in silence. Silent strangers, sitting heads bowed, lost in lives lived behind shutters and the grey-white empty rolls of nothing. He slowed and changed down through the gears. I grabbed my rucksack and listened to the sound of the engine.

'Pacifica,' he said. Wrapped in sheets of white and the momentary silver tin glimpse of cloud, I took his word. A stranger's word. I got out.

Pacifica is only about ten miles south of downtown San Francisco and I doubt whether I would have come here if it wasn't for Bob and Angie. Remember, I told you about them sharing that pitch with me in Yellowstone. They were real friendly back there in Yellowstone and they gave me their phone number and address, before they left. They lived in Pacifica, so that's how I came to be here.

A lot of people gave me their phone number and told me to look them up if I passed by. At first, I thought it was all flannel, but when I called, people seemed genuine, so I thought about calling Bob. I didn't really like calling people, though. I usually wondered if they'd even remember me, or just be polite, while cursing to themselves that I'd called. But I was in the second most densely populated city in the US without a place to stay, what had I got to lose?

Mind you, I don't like using telephones much anyway. Back in England, most telephone boxes smell of piss. You know, as if some drunken loser thought it was good to use it for a leak. You know, just as I reckon old geezers do when they use those crappy sinks in cheap hotel rooms. So that's one reason why I didn't like to phone people. Normally, you come out stinking of piss, then the smell gets up your nose and stays with you all day.

I don't like talking to people when I can't see them either. You know, when you can't see their eyes and the expressions on their face and all. Like someone can say something on the phone and it can mean anything. Unless you can see their face and eyes and all; they can mean anything. When people look you in the eyes, it's harder to hide stuff. It's harder to be a real bastard too. I reckon when people are on the phone, they hide stuff or get mean or something just because they don't have to face you. You know, meaner than if they had to look you in the eyes. Sometimes I wonder what it would be like if people could just write messages to each other. You know, instead of meeting or phoning each other, if people could just send stupid little written messages to each other. I tell you, at first, everyone would think it was genius, but then, I reckon people would start sending a load of fake, touched-up bullshit and sending abuse. You know, real bad stuff that would really mess with people's heads. I reckon people would do it, just because they could. Knowing they could just hide. When you don't have to look someone in the eyes, you can say anything you want, and no one can do a thing. Some bigshot will probably be running a massive company making shed loads of money out of it too. A bigshot, so no one will be able to do a thing.

Most American public phones aren't hidden away in phone boxes, though. They are hooked on a wall, in the fresh air. They don't stink. Maybe Americans just don't piss by them. I don't know why, but they don't, so it wasn't so bad using American phones.

I looked at the number Bob had given me. I didn't feel like calling, though, so I put it back in my pocket and went into the deli to buy a coffee. The coffee machines behind the counter spluttered and I felt the unimaginable warmth of a steaming rainforest and the smell of boiling, bubbling, frothing milk pouring onto the seed of Colombia and Brazil. Hippies treading time, lounged on deep, soft-cushioned settees and meandered through overtold, oversold, bold, magnificent stories. 'That's how it was, man', and 'yeah, yeah, yeah' and words spilled out like poetry jam. And they dipped their small mouths and even smaller lives into cups the size of buckets as if all that the world had learnt, was how to drink coffee.

And I drank too and started thinking about being in this big city without money and nowhere to stay. The smell of the coffee. I had nothing to lose by calling. Light-headed, I remembered that the good thing about having nothing, is that you have nothing to lose. I swam deep into Colombia and called.

It rang a couple of times. 'Hi, Bob speaking.'

'Hello Bob, Hel, uh, Hello, It's D, Dy, Dylan, Dylan Bardell, remember we met in Yellowstone.'

'You betcha,' he said, 'How are you? Where are you?'

'I'm great, thanks, I've got to San Francisco. How are you? How's Angie?'

'She's great, I'm great. We're both great. Where are you?'

'I've caught a bus down to Pacifica, I'm by a deli on Ocean Drive,' I said, kind of embarrassed that I was on his doorstep. 'You said if I passed this way to give you a call.'

'You betcha, you betcha.'

When we were in Yellowstone, he used to say 'you betcha' a lot. 'You betcha' and 'for sure'. He used to say 'for sure' a lot too. It was all coming back to me.

'Just wait there by the deli, I'll come and get you in five mins, you betcha,' he said. He sounded excited. I felt a little anxious.

And so, I waited. And the mist lifted. And he came. And the alchemy of air and wind and the magnificent Pacific turned the tin silver clouds to gold. And I went back and met Angie again and stayed with them for about ten days. Ten days in San Francisco, California with Bob and Angie from Yellowstone.

I liked them both. They were both in their 50s. Difference was Angie acted it. Bob didn't. Angie was mumsy. They hadn't had kids and I think she quite liked looking after me, making sure I was all right and all that. Bob was like a big kid. She'd looked after him. He had long hair. Hair that had not been cut since the beatnik 50s and the hippy-dippy 60s. Pierced ears and fancy earrings and beads. You could tell he was 50 or something, the lines on his face betrayed him, but he was really fifteen. I reckon he still blasted music out of open windows, just because. I think he liked having me around. His excuse to act like a teenager. Maybe he didn't need an excuse, but either way, I felt old next to Bob.

His body had aged. He was carrying weight around his waist. The weight of eating for fifty years. He wasn't exactly fat but wouldn't be described as slim. His face was round. Round and plain without features. Apart from his long hair, beads and earrings, he had the look of the ordinary. In a crowd, I reckon no one would have looked at him twice. A mild, grey, cloudy day that would be wiped from the memory. But he turned out to be crazier than he looked. I sensed it in Yellowstone, but I didn't know him well enough there.

His life had touched everything. An amateur bullfighter when he was younger, he went to bullrings in Mexico. He had crazy videos of when he was about thirty or something, showing his time in the ring. Parading, dancing, taunting, the terror and theatrical glamour of bulls. He showed me some of the outfits he'd worn, you know, the skimpy jackets and tight calf-length leggings. And the capes he'd used. Some still stained with blood. We talked. I expressed concerns. The half-hearted feeble voice of a guest not seeking rejection. Softly, I hinted it wasn't a great idea to kill bulls. He mentioned hypocrites. He said he'd heard it before, and people were hypocrites. He didn't say I was a hypocrite, just people. We remained friends. 'A bull is reared for fights. Loved and cared for. Reared with respect for years, in good condition,' he used to tell me. 'A prize fighter being made ready for the fight of their life. Treated well, a whole life and famous for more than 15 minutes. What most humans would give for such a life, for their 15 minutes.' He pulled out pictures of starving people in India and Warhol and desperate, hopeless, craving-for-fame, idiotic guests on desperate, hopeless TV game shows.

'When it goes into the ring, it has the chance to duel. It's a duel with an uncertain outcome.' He pointed at the blood on his bull horn, torn jacket. 'That's where I was gored back in '53,' he'd say with pride. He lifted his T-shirt and revealed a scar across his ribs below his arm. It was a big scar and I felt queasy.

'See, a lot of people tell you bullfighting is cruel, but they don't give a shit about that when they're eating steak.' He said it in an absurd oversized way as if it was checkmate.

'See, people don't care about the meat they eat. Most cattle are treated like shit. Fattened up and pumped with all sorts of crap. Fattened up for a lousy, short, miserable life, before their throat is cut and they are butchered into tiny little pieces.' He had a piece of paper in his hand as he told me that and he ripped it up into tiny pieces. There were bits of paper all over the table.

'See, people are hypocrites. They're always telling you what's right and wrong, but they don't care about all the shit they do. Most people are hypocrites, just big bastard, hypocrites.' The lines of a play. An argument soaked in aspic. Well-rehearsed, unquestionable, like believing in God or unicorns or the lost city of Atlantis. Like all things sunk so deep, that the time to think, review had passed. As if there is only one place in time and space and it is here and now and nothing else exists, or could, or ever did. That's how he said it.

I wasn't sure what to say. I thought about saying 'huh'. That was usually safe. But I didn't. 'Maybe it would be better if people stopped eating meat too.'

He looked at me as if I was crazy. 'You must be crazy, absolutely crazy. No one's ever gonna stop eating meat. Texas would fall apart if we stopped eating meat.' He kind of laughed as he said it, as if it was the craziest thing he'd ever heard. I kind of laughed a little too. You know, one of those laughs where you don't really think it's funny, but you feel obliged to laugh.

I looked for a truce. 'Maybe, I should read *Death in the Afternoon*,' I said.

'You should, you should,' he said and then told me about his trips to Key West and the drunken, all-night bars and how he'd met Hemingway and lost three days of his life.

And then there were his guns. Handguns and rifles lying around the house. To tell the truth, guns freak me out big style. When I landed in New York, I saw a cop with a gun in the airport. I'd just got through immigration and saw this cop standing there with this gun on his hip in a holster. Remember, that's where I was dying for a leak and went in the ladies by mistake. I think that was one of the reasons why I was sweating so much, because I saw this cop with his gun. The first real gun I'd ever seen.

I was real spooked at first, but after travelling around the States, I saw them everywhere. Sometimes, I'd get a lift and there would be a rifle in the pick-up truck, or I'd be walking down some street, or stop at a dusty gas station and there'd be a shop just selling guns. You know, selling guns just as if it was selling vegetables or pizza or something. It took a while to get used to them, but after a while I stopped thinking about it so much. It still seemed crazy, though. In some places, I couldn't even buy alcohol. In some states, I had to be twenty-one to buy a drink. I couldn't drink, in case I got rowdy, but I could get a gun and blow someone's brains out. Bob used to give me all this 'guns don't kill, people do' gun lobby crap, but I still got freaked out. I used to think back to that ride I had with that mad guy Wilson who kicked me out on the interstate. I bet he had a gun in his glove box. I bet he would have used it too. That's why I was too scared to call him a yellow belly.

Well, Bob tried to convince me that guns were cool and even took me to a shooting range. It was full of little kids shooting at targets, as if they were at the fair trying to knock down a rubber duck with a make-believe pistol or something. Difference was these were all shooting live rounds and wondering about what gun Santa might bring them for Christmas. If they didn't get one, they could go and buy their own soon as they reached 16.

That's another reason why I think rules are made up by madmen. See, someone dreamt up all those school rules where I've gotta wear shorts to play tennis, but the girls have gotta wear skirts, and I can't wear my hat in church, but I can get myself a gun. And all that turns into a million mad rules about Levittown segregation and black folks not being allowed on buses or eating at lunch counters with white folks and who can run everything. Run everything with lies and share the bits of history they want you to believe. And most of the time we don't even know who dreamt it up and nobody gives it a second thought, cos we're too busy swivelling on chairs and drinking coffee.

I suppose I just ain't used to guns. I never saw a gun in England in my life. Apart from air rifles and stuff. A kid at my school did have a Gat air pistol, though. Des Burnham. God, he was a head case. His mum and dad had split up or something. I'm not sure really, but I know his parents were never around. I used to go around his house sometimes and I never saw his mum and dad once. Not ever, not even once. Sometimes, I reckoned he didn't even have any parents. He had these big sisters, though. They used to knock him about. I don't know why they did, but he always came to school with cuts and bruises and stuff. Not on his face or anything, but on his arms and legs. You couldn't see them most of the time, except when we did PE and he had to wear shorts and crap like that. That's when you could see them, clear as anything. Massive cuts and bruises.

Anyway, he was a head case and skipped classes and messed about like a madman. One day, he brought in this Gat and started shooting. We all hid so he couldn't get close, but when he caught you, if the pellets hit, it stung real bad. When you got one right on the skin, like your neck or something, you'd end up with this massive red lump that was sore all day. I reckon if someone had got one in the eye, it would have blinded them. I never got one in the eye, though, just the neck. Now I reckon if Des had a real gun, he'd have used that instead. I reckon Des would have killed us.

I used to ask him about all the cuts on his arms and legs and stuff, but he would just brush it off. I always wondered why some of the crappy teachers didn't ask him about it, though. Especially Palin. He was our crappy PE teacher and he must have seen them. Pervy Palin who wandered around the changing rooms after PE when we had to shower and stuff. He must have seen them, but he didn't ask Des about them once. Not once. He was too busy telling us not to talk and to keep quiet and all while he wandered around. If you didn't, he'd pick you out and then after you got dressed, he'd give you the slipper. See, he kept this plimsole in his desk and if you did something he didn't like, like talking and stuff, he'd make you bend over and hit you on the arse with this crappy plimsole. He had this creepy assistant named Travis who'd just stand around and watch. Real creeps. After I left school, I heard Palin had been done for nicking some school funds or something and ended up doing a stretch in jail. I'm not sure about Travis, but I hope he got done too. I hope they both had some great big creepy guys in prison give them a real hard time. Maybe Des was there with his Gat.

Anyway, I didn't really like being at that gun range with Bob all that much, with all those little kids firing guns and stuff, but it didn't take long to learn to shoot. Like I don't reckon I would ever be a Shane or anything, but I learnt to shoot. Yeah, by the time I left that range I reckon I knew my way around a gun and would know how to shoot someone, you know, if I wanted to.

Bob went on forever. Fishing, flamenco dancing, I'm telling you he never stopped. He grew marijuana plants in the garage and was usually stoned. Sometimes, we'd go to the beaches just south of Pacifica and fly kites. Watching the Pacific Ocean rolling on to the long sandy beaches of Pacifica, flying kites. I liked flying kites with Bob at the beach; it took me back to when I was a kid. I used to like flying kites then. I even wrote poems about them. I wrote one once for my English homework. If I still had it, I reckon I would have shown it to Bob, when we were flying kites on the beach. I reckon he would have liked it too. He was over fifty, so he must have figured stuff out by then. I reckon that's why he acted as if he was fifteen or something, you know, so he could remember what it was like before he'd figured it all out.

I got to see lots of San Francisco. Alcatraz, jailor keys and the look-back prisoner-tease views of the city. Inhaling snow crab and clam chowder and the louder roaring glory of a Ford Mustang Bullitt taking off down Taylor. Like a drunken sailor with a girl on each arm, staggering up every hill and down again. Snoozing on the grass in Union Square, swimming through oyster sauce in Chinatown, and tumbling, twisting, a sinking ship, listing down Lombard Street. When Bob and Angie were at work, I used to get the bus into town and wander. Back out to the Bridge and back to Fisherman's Wharf to watch the coloured fishing boats sail out across the bay and back again. And days came and went and came back again. The Greenpeace ship docked up in San Francisco, right down at the wharf. Getting ready for another voyage and stocking up and trying to raise money to keep everything going. The Jerry Garcia band played right in front of the ship and there were people selling 'save the whales' T-shirts. I had nothing better to do, so I helped on the stalls. Me and the Grateful Dead and Greenpeace in San Francisco. Against Galton and his madman eugenics and watching the never fading, persistent, resistant pecking order. White men ahead, over white women, over anything black and rich over poor, and humans over whales and seals and the rainforest and anything that can't pronounce the word efficiency and show a 10% return by next week. All over the world people outside San Francisco thought that it was just mad hippies and counterculture and they shouted, 'get your hair cut' and 'get a proper job.' All over the world, people unable to think about being human, about being a virus, feasting unnecessarily and horridly. Hedonistic cells chewing into cells and creation. All over the world, people didn't think. A reconstructed order, a virus to take us all out. 'Get your hair cut', 'bums should get a job'. And the powerful have loud voices and seductive tools. Use mouthwash, keep your mouth clean; wash the taste away. Questions cause blisters, use the latest sunscreen, a new car, a TV, update your CV, you want to go places, don't you? Hubris has a loud voice, and so, they shouted, 'get your hair cut' and 'get a proper job.' And Jerry Garcia played Smokestack Lightning and we sold T-shirts.

I took the cable cars up to Nob Hill and hoped the clickety-clack, Morse code of the tracks would reveal all I needed. I took in the high-point views and searched for justice, then descending, descending, picked through Haight-Ashbury for the truth. I looked behind flowers in Golden Gate Park and imagined what it must have been like a few years earlier, when everyone was tripping the summer of love. And wondered if it ever was so. If anything, ever was so.

I could have stayed in San Francisco. It isn't a city. The people aren't city dwellers. If I had to stay in America, I reckon it would be San Francisco. It was the closest I had got, but not close enough. I'd found nothing. I wasn't in the mood to stop anywhere. I knew I had to head back east soon. I thought about starting, maybe getting a Greyhound bus to Texas. Getting a Greyhound bus, just as I'd told everyone. But Bob and Angie kept saying how I had to travel south down the US1 coast road. 'It's the best coast road in the world, they kept telling me.' Americans tell you everything in America is the best in the world even though most of them have never left the country and don't even have a passport. But I liked Bob and Angie, even though he was crazy. I wanted to believe them. One more chance. That's how I found myself heading further south.

Chapter Nineteen

I was feeling a bit hazy. The whole trip down the west coast had been pretty crazy and I'd smoked too much. California had lived up to its name. I kept thinking I should start heading back east, but Bob and Angie said I needed to see the rest of the coast road down to LA and to the Mexican border, so I kept hitching south. My first ride out of Pacifica was with this old lady, driving an Edsar. I reckon she must have been forty-five or something, but she was chatty and said she'd take me down to Monterey. We started chewing the fat about this and that and she told me lots of stories about living in California and what she got up to when she was my age and all. Then she started banging on about this car she was driving and told me she'd only bought this Edsar cos it was so cheap.

'They used to be overpriced, but you can get them for a can of beans now.' She smiled. 'No one likes 'em. They say the grill looks like lady parts. But I don't mind that,' she said and smiled again.

I told her I hadn't seen many so really didn't want to comment.

'Edsars or lady parts?' She grinned at me, as if I should grin back or something. I felt myself going red and so just used one of my 'huhs'. I smiled, though, just to play along, just to let her know she was a bit feisty and all.

'Yeah,' she went on, 'guys like messing around in 'em, but won't commit.' She grinned again. 'Guys seem to like stuff that looks like it can poke you.'

I smiled and told her how I thought guys were crazy and we laughed about how it was a crazy world and someday there'd probably be some old fat bald bloke on telly banging on about cars and how fast they go, as if it really made any difference.

We laughed for a while and when we ran out of stuff to say, I told her about my Martian thing, and how I reckoned if aliens came down, they'd think we were all ga ga. You know, swivelling our chairs and worrying about the size of car bonnets and all. She went quiet on me after that.

'I don't believe in aliens,' she said. 'You ain't one of those Roswell space-boys, are you?' I did my best to reassure her I wasn't, but it was too late.

We didn't speak. I thought about whistling, but I ain't much good at it, so didn't bother. After about ten minutes, we got near Santa Cruz and she told me I'd got to get out cos she was turning off. I knew she wasn't, cos she'd told me she was going to Monterey, but she pulled over and I said, 'Thank you, mam.'

She slammed the door and sped off as fast as that crappy Edsar with its fancy lady parts would go.

I stood on the side of the road and waited. I was in a lousy place for hitching, though, so I just started walking. Most of the way through Santa Cruz too, just to get back out on the road south. I kept thinking how I should have just kept talking about lady parts. She seemed to like that. Lady parts and the Edsar. I thought about Rusty and how he used to have a way with the girls. I reckoned if I ever bumped into him again, I'd have something to tell him. Something to tell him about old ladies from Monterey.

I walked about five miles but got another ride with a sleepy guy who didn't want to talk much and was driving a car that didn't seem to have any parts relating to the anatomy. He dropped me by the Cannery in Monterey.

I needed a place to stay. Travelling south with Dave in his car hadn't cost much and Bob and Angie were real generous, so I hadn't spent much money for weeks. I decided to stay in a motel just outside Monterey. I reckon I'd got soft. Too many soft beds at Bob's place and so I just didn't fancy the beach. I wish I hadn't bothered, though. The motel was a dump. I didn't get much sleep.

I hadn't stayed in many motels, but everywhere I stayed had these crappy sinks. Creased up and dirty sheets too. You know, as if they just couldn't be arsed to change them when people checked out. During the night, stuff kicked off in the parking lot too. You know, screeching cars and banging doors. Arguments and yelling and stuff. I kept thinking about all the head cases with their guns who were staying in the rooms next door. Bob had banged on about, guns don't kill, but people do, but for all I knew Des Burnham was next door.

The new morning was sweeter. A ranger picked me up just south of Monterey in an open-top jeep. He was heading down to San Simeon with time on his hands, so took me down all the back roads and beach tracks. In the hot sun, the jeep bumped its way through the shimmering heat. He showed me Pebble Beach and neat-street Carmel, though we couldn't see much cos the mist had rolled in. Then we moved on and stopped at Bixby Creek bridge and Big Sur, where the mist had rolled out and we saw everything. 'Big Sur is the most beautiful stretch of coast road,' he told me. It was too.

When we arrived in San Simeon, he took me to a campground and being a ranger, got me in for free. It felt good to be in my tent, out in the open. I walked down to the beach and watched the sunset. The heat haze shimmered on the surface of the ocean and the sun melted like a candle.

200

I wanted to get down to LA, though. Suddenly I felt in a hurry. Next morning, I got up early and started thumbing. A guy named Stefan picked me up in this mad 'suped-up' two-seater Toyota sports car. You know, like a car that was made for driving in California down US1. I don't know why he gave me a lift, cos his car wasn't made for two people and bags, but he didn't speak much English and wanted company. He was a German on holiday, and I reckon he just wanted someone with him to help him out when he got to restaurants or gas stations and stuff. He drove through Santa Barbara at about 80. Past the palm trees and the long, sandy beach. I blinked and missed most of it, but I was okay with that, cos we were getting closer. Closer to LA, where I wanted to be.

LA is like frogspawn. A massive sprawling blob, you could drive across it for a week and never get anywhere. He was lost. He didn't know where he was gonna stay, so he just drove around. We circled back and found ourselves back on the same coast road. We pressed on. Past Malibu and on to Santa Monica pier, you know, where Route 66 ends and life changes.

He hung a left away from the ocean and drove past bars and liquor stores and tattoo parlours. Onwards down six-lane avenues and palm trees and advertising hoardings selling nothing that anyone needs, but everything that everyone wants. We found ourselves cruising around Beverly Hills. Even wider, greener avenues lined with palm trees. Past houses the size of a town. Houses with their water sprinklers keeping the grass green.

Stefan had money. He was dreaming he was a movie star on holiday in his rented, rocket- fuelled sports car. His dreams were bursting with Beverly Hills. So, when he got to the best part of town where he dreamt about staying, I bailed. He said bye and hugged me. I tried to remember some German and for that second, wished I'd bothered to listen to Miss Rupin. I tried 'Auf Wiedersehen'. He smiled.

I told him I might head to the youth hostel. He told me to jump back in. He could have just dumped me anywhere, but he didn't. He drove me to it. Right to the door, as if he was a taxi or something. We parted again, but without all the 'Auf Wiedersehen' stuff this time. Before I left, I asked him if it was living up to what he'd imagined. He said, 'Not quite.' I told him about shittungap; he explained *verschmeltz*. We laughed and in our broken tongues agreed it was all the fault of the deceitful. The marketeers and advertising mad men and our own, wanting-to-believe, hopeful, hoping, gullibility.

The Y was real laid back. You could come or go as you pleased, and it was cheap, so I checked in for a couple of days. It's hard to find the centre of LA and most people don't try. It's a cold grey rash of offices and crappy buildings hiding under smog that looks as if it wants to kill you. People kind of have different views about where the centre is anyway. You know, it's a bit like all that early solar system argument, when people thought the earth was at the centre. Then they found out it wasn't, but some kept denying it anyway, cos they didn't want to believe it wasn't. So different people say different things. See, a lot of people want Hollywood to be the centre. You know Hollywood with all its phoney movie crap. Hollywood is a dump. It has some crappy buildings and a pavement with handprints. Big deal. Stupid people ogling at the stupid handprints of stupid people. Like if it was a nurse or a doctor or someone who saved someone's life no one would show up, but because it's some phoney who danced in the rain or something, it's full of crowds. Try explaining that to one to my Martian buddies. I'm telling you Hollywood is nothing much. You know, a bit like Times Square in New York.

More selling bullshit.

If you go up a couple of flights of car park dirty stairs when you are by the handprints, you can look out and see the Hollywood sign on the hill. You get loads of people doing that and going all gooey and stuff cos they've seen a sign. See, that's what America is great at, selling bullshit. I'm telling you if you were in England and someone put some crappy letters up outside Wigan, no one would give a shit. But because it's Hollywood everyone goes all gooey. Then they have all these crumby tours of crumby studios and stuff, to keep all this flannel going. People sit on open-sided trams and have crappy tours of the studios. 'Glam Trams', they call them, just to make out that you're having the time of your life. Then some whiney, smiling hostess tries to whip everyone up into a frenzy as they drive past Lucille Ball's stage set and crap like that. I mean, Lucille Ball and a Glam Tram for six bucks, who they trying to kid? Then, just in case anyone is getting bored, the hostess tells everyone to look out for the stars who might be on set. There probably ain't no one here, but the hostess keeps everyone on the edge of their seat, by yelling how she's spotted someone in the distance. 'Wow, look back, quick, look back, there's Farrah Fawcett Majors. Try and turn around, driver, quick.'

Everyone cricks their necks to try and catch a glimpse of someone who is about two light years away. You see everyone grabbing their cameras and listen to the clicks. There's someone in the distance, so small it could be a cat. Maybe a kid with a mop. Who knows? But you can bet a million bucks it ain't Farrah Fawcett. No, the stars are back in their mansions in Beverly Hills watching their grass sprinklers. Then two minutes later, the hostess yells, 'Bill Bixby!' Bill Bixby. For crying out loud.

See, it don't matter, though. The stupid people on the

glamour tram want to believe they've seen the stars. Seen anyone. It don't matter if it ain't true. It don't even matter if they know it's not true. See, this way they don't have to lie. They can go and tell all their stupid friends and the grandkids about their wonderful day on the glamour tram and how they saw the stars. They don't even have to lie, cos the whiney hostess told them they did. And that's how most stuff works really. Just bullshit that people want to believe, cos they think it's better than not believing it.

After I left that pavement where all the crappy handprints are, I started walking down Hollywood Boulevard. Now, it ain't any great shakes by the handprints, and that's where all the tourists turn up in their taxis and stuff, but if you go down a couple of blocks it's crappy as hell. Shabby buildings selling crap and looking as if they ain't been painted for about a hundred years. I walked a mile or something and got near the intersection with Vine Street. A couple of bums were there. An old black guy and his missus. The old man looked about seventy or something and was wearing a tatty old trilby hat. It looked as if he'd had it all his life; it was as beat up as him. But he wore it slipped on the back of his head with the front tipped up, as cool as Sammy Davis Jr. He was gabbling on to the old woman with him. She was about seventy too, crotchety and bent over with dirty, loose stockings hanging down by her knees.

They looked like an old married couple, you know, just the way they clung on. The way they talked to each other too. You know, like moaning and sniping at each other, but sounding as if they couldn't get through the next minute without each other. They were staggering, talking nonsense and I watched them as I got closer. Then, the old guy started dropping his trousers. I don't know why he did it, but he did, right there on Hollywood and

Vine. The old lady started yelling and beating on him, and they kind of leant on each other and stumbled. She helped him pull his trousers up, and in the stumbling and falling about, and the cursing and swearing, his hat fell off. I picked it up and gave it to him, 'Here you are, sir.' They mumbled something, and the old guy tried to throw me a high five but missed. He tumbled and he fell on the pavement. He got up, laughed. He was fine, but there was no handprint. No handprints of real people. Hollywood and Vine, about ten blocks down from the taxis and the tourists and the handprints of phoneys.

I reckon all that LA smog got to me, cos I ended up going to this crazy frisbee championship in the Rose Bowl. I met this couple in the Y, Mark and Sloan who had hitched across from Greenwich Village in New York. They were about the same age as me and I bumped into them cos they were staying at the Y too. They were kind of big into all this frisbee stuff and told me they were going to the Rose Bowl and asked if I wanted to tag along. I'd never thrown a frisbee in my life and wasn't too fussed, but I thought it might be neat to see the Rose Bowl, so I went. I thought it would be empty, but there were massive queues and the wait took forever. They offered a free frisbee to the first two thousand who arrived, so there was this massive queue. People will do anything for something free. I've noticed that about people. I mean, you can probably buy a crappy frisbee for a dollar or something, so who cares if it's free? But I've noticed people do. I reckon people would queue up for the plague if someone said you can have it for free.

Anyway, it felt as if it went on longer than Christmas and I kind of wished I hadn't come, but Mark and Sloan seemed really into it, so I just made out it was the best thing ever. I said 'huh', a lot.

There were all these crazy different competitions just to drag it out. You know, like who could throw the frisbee the furthest and who was the most accurate. Then they had this mad free-style competition where people were dancing around like ice skaters and tossing and catching their frisbees and stuff. I'm telling you, I thought I might be stuck in LA forever. But then it got worse, cos they had frisbees with dogs. Dogs jumping about and catching them and stuff. I hated it. All the owners going coo che coo with their dogs just cos they'd caught a stupid frisbee and all. And then there was all the licking and stuff.

Mark and Sloan were cool, though, and after we left, took me to a Hot Tuna gig. Jorma Kaukonen. The Americans held up their lighters and clapped and went wild after his guitar breaks, but it wasn't the Airplane. The Airplane playing Surrealistic Pillow in LA. A decade passes and white rabbits turn into dogs and frisbees.

When they left, Mark and Sloan said I could stay with them in Greenwich Village if I got back to New York. They lived with Mark's mum in the Village, but said they had a spare apartment that I could use if I wanted. Maybe seeing New York from an apartment in Greenwich Village was what I should do. Maybe buy an acoustic guitar and write folk songs and settle down with a girl named Hope. But I just wasn't sure. I wasn't sure what to do, or if I would ever get back to New York.

Getting out of LA was crazy. Untangling the twisted, complicated wiring system of roads that wrap themselves around the throat of LA. I should have just taken the bus, but I was getting cocky and I thought I might be lucky. See, trouble is, LA is so massive, you've kind of got to travel forever on overgrown ten-lane motorways across the city before you get out. I tell you, if you look at a map of LA, sometimes it looks as if Mexico is a suburb. Anyway, I tried my luck, but I guess it had run out.

I was standing where I shouldn't have stood, by an on-ramp, and choked as the traffic zoomed by and kicked up dirt. A girl stopped and peered out the window. She was wearing a head scarf and shades and looked as if she should be in a Hitchcock movie.

'You better not stand here. The feds will pick you up. That's if you ain't killed first. I ain't going far, but I'll drop you a couple of exits down. It's safer there.'

She had nice cheekbones, so I was thinking about jumping in, but two exits didn't sound much, so I just said, 'Nah. Thanks, mam, I reckon I'll take my chances.'

'Please yourself,' she said, and zoomed off, and that was the last I saw of those cheekbones. About two minutes after that, a cop came by and pulled me.

'You shouldn't be standing here, boy. You can't hitch from on-ramps. I could book you if I wanted, but it's your lucky day. I'll take you down a couple of exits and drop you there. It's safer. Maybe you should take a bus.'

So, I climbed in and listened to him getting calls about serious stuff kicking off in LA and looked at his fat cheeks jabbering.

Two lousy exits. It was safer. Safe, cos there ain't no traffic. I waited. Waited a long time. I thought about quitting thumbing and getting a bus, but I wasn't on a route, so I waited. What else could I do?

Another lousy hour. I got a lift from a girl called Beth, who took me down towards Newport Beach, and told me it would be better to get a bus out of the sprawl. Buses, damn buses. Does everyone have shares in the bus system in LA? I knew she was right. I knew everyone was right, so I got out and waited for a bus to take me down as far as San Clemente. But I kept hitching while I was waiting. No bus came, but I got another ride. A ride with a whacko who told me he was driving down to the hospital in San Clemente, cos he needed some hospital reports from the doctors. He said he'd been busted for pushing and was facing a long jail term. His lawyers said he might get off if he could get the doctors to say he was schizophrenic or something. I tried to change the subject and told him I'd thought about being a lawyer once. He said, 'Far out, man. You should do it. They make big bucks for twisting the truth. If you're good at twisting the truth, just go for it, man. Yeah, far out man, far out.'

I wasn't sure if I was good at twisting the truth, but I did think about doing law once. I reckon I'd seen too much Perry Mason, but I even spoke about it to my careers' teacher. See, I had to go and see this careers teacher so he could talk to me about what I might wanna do when I grew up. It didn't get off to a good start.

'Ah, Bardell, sit down, laddie,' he said.

Sit down, laddie. I hate it when people call me laddie but I reckon he tried that adding a Y thing to make out we were best buddies. We weren't, though, so I didn't take to him from the start. I didn't much like how he looked either. He was skinny and had this undernourished look under his grey cardigan. To tell you the truth, if he'd had fingerless gloves, I might have thought he was Steptoe. You know, he had that gaunt, bad teeth, undernourished look. Now if he had worn fingerless gloves, I reckon I might have felt sorry for him and let it all slide, but he didn't, so I couldn't take to him.

'Well, laddie, my name is Mr Herbert. I'd like to find out about you and what you'd like to be.'

Now when I first went in, because I didn't much like the look of him, I lounged back in the chair, you know, as if I ran the

Mafia. But when he said he wanted to talk about what I wanted to be I sat up straight. I leant my elbows on the table, sat up and looked him right in the eyes. I reckon it spooked him a bit, us being so close and all, cos he sat back. He didn't look right like that, though, leaning back like a Mafia boss in a cardigan.

'Well, funny you should ask me that,' I said, 'cos I've been giving it some thought.'

'Good,' he said, 'good, I'm pleased you have been thinking about it.'

He said it as if he'd just seen water turn to wine in front of his eyes. 'Very good,' he repeated. 'What is it you would like to be?'

'When I'm older I'd like to be steve evets,' I said.

'Steve evets.' He looked puzzled.

'Yeah, I've been thinking about it, and I'd like to be a palindrome. Steve evets would work fine.'

'A palindrome, a palindrome, what do you mean, a palindrome?' he said.

'You know, a palindrome, where a word reads the same backwards and forwards, you know, like reviver or steve evets.'

He phuffed a bit and raised his voice. 'I know what a palindrome is, laddie, but you can't be serious. You can't just go changing your name.'

'Well, it don't have to be steve evets. I was thinking that might sound a bit too DJ. That's just one idea. I've got a whole list if you wanna hear them. I got some other options, I reckon robert trebor would be mint. Or maybe, the slippery, lee eel. Maybe I should just play it straight and stick with something simple like pat tap or burt trub. I kind of like burt trub, cos it sounds proper salt of the earth. I got some more complicated stuf—'

He interrupted me mid-flow. Just as I was gonna drop him some biggies. I thought that was rude, but he came in yelling and stopped me mid-flow.

'Shut up, boy. Shut up. You can't go changing your name.'

'I beg to differ,' I said. I said it that way too. You know, not I disagree, but I beg to differ. I like it when people say it that way, so that's what I said.

'Dylan changed names. I bet he thought you could call yourself whatever you wanted.' Try that for size, I thought. Then added, 'John Wayne ain't really John Wayne and he's done okay. And Elton John ain't Elton John and he's doing fine too, even though all his songs are crap except "your song". "Your song" is all right, but the rest of his songs are crap, and yet he's still doing fine.'

'But these are entertainers, laddie, it's not the real world.' He was irritated.

'I beg to differ.' I used it again, cos I like it so much. 'Take Queenie, that lot changed their name and they're doing all right. It's Windsor now, but way back it was Wettin. Until George V thought that sounded a bit too German, you know, when we were at war with them, not cosied up like best buddies. They changed their name and look, they're doing fine. Then they got rid of Battenburg too and changed it to Mountbatten. You know, in case people weren't too keen on waving flags at Germans.'

He didn't say anything but looked as if he was ready to burst. He had this pencil in his hands and was tapping the lead against some paper on the desk. He was tapping it in that agitated way, when you're full of nervous energy or stressed out of your brains or something.

'Look, we're getting off the subject.' He tried to compose himself, but he was still tapping away with that pencil. 'I'm not here to talk about name changes, I want to know what you would like to do, you know when you leave school.'

'Sorry,' I said. 'Sorry, Mr Herbert, I think there's been a misunderstanding. See, you asked what I wanted to be, and I want to be a palindrome, like steve evets. Sorry, I didn't realise you meant what do I want to do?'

'Yes, Yes. Yes, laddie, what do you want to do? I'm trying to find out what you want to do. When you leave school, what do you want to do?' He phuffed some more and looked as if he was getting agitated again.

'Well,' I said. 'If you're putting me on the spot. On the spot, right now, then I'd say I'd like to write poems. Yes, a poet. That's what I'd like to do, write poems.'

'A poet. Are you any good at poetry?' He smirked as he said it.

'Brooksey says I am. Brooksey says it ain't safe for exams, but I'm real good.'

'But does Brooksey, er I mean Mr Brooks, does Mr Brooks say you are exceptional? You would need to be most exceptional to make any money writing verses and that sort of nonsense.' He said it in that dismissive way, as if he was earning a million quid an hour or something.

'Have you thought about anything like this?' He handed me a few pamphlets of people working in factories on production lines and all. All the workers in the pictures were smiling as if they'd just won the pools even though they were only screwing on bumpers or something. They were smiling, though, as if putting on bumpers was the best decision they ever made.

I leant back and flicked through his lousy brochures. I went all Mafia boss again and would have lit a cigar if I'd had one. Even though you couldn't smoke in school except behind the bike sheds, I would have lit one right there.

'Look, laddie, I'm trying to help you. Help you think about your future.' He softened a bit and tried a different tack. 'Think about where you'll next go on holiday. You'd give that some thought, wouldn't you? Where you wanted to go and why?' He was trying to reason.

'No holidays planned,' I said. I imagined I was blowing cigar smoke in his face.

He was irritated again. 'That's not the point, I'm just using a metaphor, to illustrate the need to think ahead.'

'No, you ain't,' I said.

'Ain't what? Er, I'm not doing what?' He realised he'd said ain't and corrected himself real quick to make out he didn't say words like ain't. I bet you, if you asked him, he'd make out he didn't even wipe his arse.

'It ain't a metaphor. All that holiday stuff. It's an analogy. Not a metaphor, an analogy.' I said it as if I was king of the metaphors.

Well, after that we must have spent about an hour arguing about the difference between metaphors and analogies and similes and why everyone gets 'em mixed up. I enjoyed it, but he just seemed to get more agitated. I raised the topic of allegories, but he didn't bite.

His pencil was hammering down like a pneumatic drill now. There were these crazy pencil dots all over this paper. I reckon he'd done about a million by now. From my angle, upside down like, it looked as if he'd drawn the face of a smiling cat. He hadn't drawn anything, but that's what it looked like from my angle. All those dots, all random, had come together by chance and looked like a cat. I reckon I could have had a good chat about Rorschach and stuff, but after he didn't bite on the allegory stuff,

I didn't bother to mention it.

'Look, laddie, I don't think we've made the best use of this time. Before we finish, is there anything I can help you with? Is there anything you think you would like to do, a career, a job, anything?' He tried to stay calm, as if he remembered he was supposed to be in control. To be honest, I didn't think he could help me at all. I reckon if I'd been at the bottom of a well filling with water and he was at the top, with a rope, he wouldn't have been much use to me, but when he said that, I thought back to this one time when I wanted to be a lawyer. It was only for a couple of minutes like, after I'd just seen an episode of Perry Mason on the telly and thought I'd like arguing and getting people off hangings and the like.

I was just about to get all serious and tell him. Tell him I did think about studying law once. But then I pulled back. I thought he'd just say how hard it would be and how I'd have to be exceptional and then show me more pictures of his smiling factory workers.

I wasn't done, though, so I thought I'd just goof around with him a bit longer. 'Well, I did think about the law once. I'd like to start soliciting.'

His pencil snapped in two.

Poor kitty, I thought, no milk for you.

I don't remember much after that, just him calling me laddie a few times and then saying my time was up. I shook his hand and thanked him for his time and told him it had been very enlightening. He phuffed a bit. I looked at his undernourished frame and faded grey cardigan and walked out. I half expected to hear him shout 'Harold'.

I didn't bother telling the guy all about that, though, just that I wanted to be a lawyer. Anyway, he kept telling me it was 'far out' and that 'everything is just about twisting the truth', and him and Mr Herbert got me to San Clemente.

Things have a way of working out, though. After all those crumby rides, I got a lift from a guy named Donald who took me all the way to San Diego. He let me stay with him at his place near La Jolla. I met his girlfriend. We drank beers and smoked grass. Dusk turned the world indigo, and night came and turned it to Indian ink. The sky filled with stars. Blazing lights from a billion years before I was born. But they found me alive. Alive in California.

Chapter Twenty

Parts of San Diego are full of Spanish architecture. Large parts of California too. I guess it's because it was Spanish once. Part of Spain and then part of Mexico. Most of the west and south from Texas to California was.

Then populist journalists like John O'Sullivan came up with ten-cents phrases like 'America's manifest destiny', and everyone in America bought into the idea that America should just take all the land from one ocean to the other, just as if it was always meant to be. It didn't matter that a lot of the land was under the legal ownership of Spain or that Native Indian tribes had lived on the land for hundreds of years. It was 'America's manifest destiny', cos some crumby populist decided to say it was. See, that's the problem. Anyone can come up with some cheating ten-cents phrase and make out it's supposed to be, and so long as you have enough flag wavers you're sorted.

See, that's what does my head in about flag waving and stuff. People get all proud and patriotic and stuff as if the country they live in is pure as driven snow. Everyone else is the bad guy and their country will save the world and stuff. But really, it's just about who's got the biggest dad. Who's the biggest bully. See, the Spanish conquistadors came and nicked all that space in the first place, you know, when they needed a bit more gold and stuff. Then in the war with Mexico, about a hundred years ago or something, America decided they should have it. The poor bastard native Indians didn't get a look in. They were just kicked off their land. Kicked off their land all over America like when most of the Cherokee nation were forced to march off their lands along the Trail of Tears. Now, most of the old Indian tribes are stuck on crappy reservations on the poorest, most desolate lands. A lot of Americans have a go at them and say they are lazy, no-good, drunken, gambling, layabouts, just like how they slag off bums in bus stations, but then they put up a statue of Andrew Jackson. They just keep quiet about his 100 slaves and his Indian Removal Act. Now if those Indians had a nuke or something, instead of just bows and arrows, things might have been different. But they didn't, see; their dad wasn't big enough.

That's why the Americans get so uptight about other countries getting nukes and stuff. America has them, it's used them too, but it don't want anyone else to get one. They just want to be the biggest dad.

See, that's what gets me about American bullshit. Like when they nuked Japan and stuff, they made out they'd done everyone this big favour. As if they sorted out the bad guy and shortened the war and saved millions of lives and stuff. Then cos they're good at movies and stuff they've got everyone to lap it up. But see, they never mention that Russia and China were already getting it sorted. They don't want anyone to know that cos then it might look as if they were a bit hasty and all. I'm telling you the Americans are the only ones who could drop a nuke and make out they're doing everyone a favour.

I sometimes wish that you could just replay the past. You know, replay it and change the rules. I can just picture Standing Bear and Sitting Bull calling all the shots and sticking all those settlers on some crappy reservations. Reservations with no gold or oil or decent farming land or anything. They could call it their manifest destiny and stuff and maybe ask John O'Sullivan what he thought about it now. I sometimes think about that with that bastard Todd J. Rumplan. You know, sticking him or his kids or something in a car and letting some nut-job crash straight into him. I'd like to see his face then. See how he likes it, you know, when you change the rules.

I started to think about that a lot, you know about changing the rules.

I'm not sure what San Diego would have been like if it was still part of Mexico, but I liked it anyway. The beaches, the palm trees, the architecture. I didn't really bother to do much while I was there, cos I found this cool bench in a park. You know, it was one of those days when I didn't feel like doing much at all, so I just stayed in this park and sat on this bench for a while.

I say it was a park, but it wasn't really a proper park, it was just this open space with lots of grass and palm trees and all, but it had footpaths across it and a bench, so it kind of looked like a park even though it wasn't. I liked sitting on that bench, though. I ain't normally a bench type of person, not unless I got to be, especially those crappy hard ones in the bus depots, but I liked this one. It was real comfortable for a bench, and in this real neat spot too. See, at the back of this park, there were all these genius buildings that looked like Spanish castles. Not those great big stone castles with turrets and stuff, more like those Moorish buildings you see when they show you pictures of Andalucia and the Alhambra in Spain. Well, there was this one building at the back of the park that looked real neat, just like that. I reckon it must have been a hotel or something, but it was painted this soft shade of pink. A really nice light pink colour that looked real ace in the sunlight. The bench wasn't facing the building, but I liked it tons, so I just kept turning around and looking at it. I even cricked my neck cos I kept turning around so much, but I didn't mind cos it looked so ace with the sunlight shining on that pink.

I bet to stay in that hotel, you would probably need a million bucks or something. I'm guessing it was full of all those hoity-toity types too, you know like that Cruella De Vil type I saw in Central Park, but I wasn't planning on staying there, so I didn't mind. What made it look even better, though, were all these palm trees fringing the building and the park. All around were these great big massive palm trees. You know, the ones that have great long slender trunks that make them look as if they're giraffe necks. Except, they're much longer and taller and go right up into the sky. Then when your eyes reach the top, you see a fan of palm leaves swaying in the breeze and looking all special against the deep blue sky. They shouldn't work really. You'd kind of think the trunks are too long and the palm leaves are too small, but they do. They work real well.

Sometimes, though, to stop cricking my neck, I stopped looking around and just sat there on the bench. I didn't mind that, though, cos the bench faced the ocean and although the view was different, you can't knock down a view of an ocean. I watched the waves break on to the rocky coastline. A dark blue sea, churning up and creating waves. Turning white and changing to foam as they crashed on the rocks. The flecks of white foam looked like pieces of icing chopped up on the dark blue ocean, and so, I just watched them and wondered what they tasted of.

I stared out over the green grass of the park too. Through the palm trees, and across the green grass to the waves crashing and mixing up foam. The grass was as green as a snooker table. You know, like a brand-new snooker table, when the green felt baize is stretched tight and new. Water sprinklers were keeping it fed.

There, slowly rotating at different points across the lawn, the sunlight pierced the spray as the head of the sprinkler spun from side to side. Sometimes, the spray from the jet of water was caught by a breeze and, as it blew skywards, the sunlight burst through it and a rainbow formed. Then the head of the sprinkler would rotate back to its starting position and the water would evaporate and the rainbow too. Then it spun again, and a rainbow emerged. I must have watched a hundred rainbows. Maybe more than a hundred, I don't know, cos I didn't count. But it was a lot, cos I watched until the shadows lengthened.

Now normally, I would have sprawled out all along this bench and made my rucksack into a pillow and all, but because I was watching all these waves and the grass and the rainbows and cricking my neck to look at that building and stuff I just sat up. After I'd been there a while, though, this lady walked towards me. I thought she might be just walking through cos the footpath was right in front of my bench, but when she got to it, she sat down. I didn't expect it, but when she got to my bench, she smiled at me and she sat down.

Now, usually, I'd be real sore if someone came and sat down next to me, especially when I was having such a good day with my rainbows and all. But today, I didn't feel sore. I don't know why, but I didn't mind at all. See, it was a pretty long bench, so there was plenty of room. Plenty of room for her to sit up the other end. She did too, so I wasn't squashed at all. It's not so bad sitting near someone when you're not all squashed up, and anyway the park and the waves and the pink hotel were all delicious; I didn't mind at all.

She looked quite a nice lady too, you know, tidy and well dressed, as if she had enough money to stay in that fancy hotel if she wanted to.

She sat down and said, 'Hi.'

'Hello, mam,' I said.

When I say hello to people now, I always say mam or sir.

See, I'd been in the States so long I'd picked up that people often say 'mam' or 'sir' when they address someone. You know, like if you were lost, say in a shopping mall or something and you needed to go up to a stranger to ask for directions or something. Then I'd say, 'Excuse me, mam' or 'Excuse me, sir.' That's what people do in the States, and I'd picked it up. I liked it too, so I started doing it. I kind of liked it cos it seemed that it was about respect and all, you know, not status. See, back in England, that crap is all about status and class and stuff. As if people feel they have to say sir and mam to the queen and all her cronies. You know the upper-class mob who have all been to Eton and got themselves fancy titles, but if you work in a factory or you're a cleaner or a care-worker who wipes someone's arse or something crappy like that, no one will ever say mam or sir to you. See, in England it's all about being deferential and kowtowing and class and stuff. You know, sucking up to some arsehole that's got more money than sense. But in America, people say 'mam' or 'sir' to everyone. It don't matter if they're serving you a burger in a crappy fast-food place or if you're the president. See, in America it's just about respect.

That's one of the problems with monarchies, see, it all revolves around status. Republics don't have so much of that crap. Like the French greet everyone by saying, monsieur and madame and in America you get a sir or a mam. Don't matter who you are; you get one. Not in England, though. In England you only get that if you're some la di da with a silver spoon up your arse.

Anyway, that's why I said 'mam' to her when she sat down, cos I'd picked it up in America and I liked saying it. She smiled and sat down at the other end of the bench. She didn't look as if she wanted to talk much, though, cos she just pulled this newspaper out of her bag. She was proper elegant, though, you know, how she sat down and did it. She sat there with her legs crossed, but they weren't all tight and squashed together like how some people cross their legs. Sometimes when people cross their legs, they jiggle their feet or crush their legs together so tight it looks as if they want a leak or something and are trying to hold it, but she didn't do that. She crossed them elegant. It's hard to explain really, but if you'd been there, you'd know what I mean. I reckon you would have said she looked elegant too. I reckon everyone would.

She was wearing these high heels and a pencil skirt that came down just below the knee. It looked as if it was quite tight, but not too tight as if she'd bought something that was too small. A lot of people buy stuff that's too small cos they're trying to kid themselves they ain't got all porky and out of shape and stuff. Then it looks real crappy cos you can see all these bulges in all the wrong places. But she'd bought it just the right amount of tight, just elegant tight, as if she'd had it measured and all.

It made her stand out a bit too. In the 70s most people were wearing all this crappy flouncy tie-dyed crap and platform shoes and tank tops and bell bottoms and stuff, so she kind of stood out, as if she was Jayne Mansfield or Jackie Onassis or someone.

The way she read the newspaper was elegant too. The way she held it, so it didn't get all creased up and tatty. It looked as if when she'd finished reading it, you would think it was still fresh off the stand. I reckon after she had read it, she could put it back on the stand and sell it again and no one would notice, except maybe the perfume. Sometimes, she would glance across at me and smile. She wouldn't say anything, though, she'd just smile. Sometimes, she'd uncross her legs and then cross them the other way and then she'd read a bit more and glance and smile again.

When she crossed and uncrossed her legs and all, she moved a little bit more towards my end of the bench. Not too close or anything, but just enough to notice. I didn't mind, though, cos I was still watching the waves and enjoying the sunshine, so I just smiled at her and didn't mind at all.

I was a bit closer to her now, so I took a look at her hands. Her hands as she was holding her newspaper. I always look at people's hands, you know, since I had that book about Jesus and noticed his were all smooth and pale even though he was a carpenter. She had proper nice hands. She had these really long fingers. Probably the longest fingers I'd ever seen. But they looked right, all slender and elegant. I'm telling you she had the best fingers I'd ever seen. You know, as if they were made to play the piano. Something soothing and gentle like *Clair de Lune*.

Neat nails too. She wasn't wearing nail varnish as lots of girls do, but they were all smooth and shiny and you could see the little white moons above her cuticles. They were all even and symmetrical as if they'd been filed down to be perfect, and you could see at least half a moon on each finger. Even on the thumb. Half a moon showing out above the cuticle. I notice nails a lot, cos mine are so crappy. I bite them, so that makes them all uneven and messy. Sometimes I even bite them down to the quick and then they get all red and sore. Everything about my fingernails is crappy; maybe that's why I bite them. Sometimes you can't see any moon on my fingernails at all, and when you can, it's just this little crappy tiny bit of pale white, so it don't even look like a moon at all. It just looks like a thin white strip about the size of a cotton thread. I've always wanted moons, but I ain't never had them. I don't know why, maybe some people just ain't born to have stuff like that. The only white I've got on my fingernails are all these little white specs that take ages to grow out. I can see them in the nail, and want to wash them out, but I just have to wait. Wait while they grow out. I watch them as the nail grows and they creep up slowly towards the end of the finger. Then when they get right to the end, I bite my nails. Trouble is, then more appear, so it just goes on. Someone once told me they come because I don't have enough calcium. I don't know whether that's true or not, but that's what someone told me. It don't seem right to me, though, cos I drink a lot of milk. I love milk and when I get the chance, I drink as much milk as I can get my hands on. Sometimes when I was at school, I wouldn't eat all day, except maybe for some crappy jammie dodgers from the tuck shop, but I always drank milk. Every day I drank it, but it don't seem to have helped any.

Anyway, my hands are pretty crap, but next to hers they looked as if I'd just dug myself out of Alcatraz. I did my best to keep them hidden. I kind of tucked them under my legs a bit, you know, like when you sit on your hands to warm them up. I think it worked too, cos she didn't see my hands once in the whole time we sat on that bench together. Not that I think she was looking much. To be honest, apart from all that smiling and stuff, she seemed as if she was all wrapped up in reading this newspaper she was holding in her elegant hands. Except for the time she got out a pen and wrote something down on the front page. I couldn't see what it was, though, and didn't really feel as if I knew her well enough to ask, given we'd only known each other ten minutes and all.

Anyway, she sat reading, and I just watched the waves breaking onto the rocks and all. Sometimes, though, I'd get curious and would look over at the newspaper and see what she was reading. I wouldn't make it too obvious like, I'd just turn my head a little or squint out the corner of my eyes, but I'd do it enough so I could read bits. Now, when people do that to me, it does my head in big style. You know, when someone reads over your shoulder or something. You can feel them peering across and straining just to read the paper or magazine you've got. When people do that, I always make it as awkward as I can by turning away, so they got to strain even harder to see. Sometimes, I deliberately give them enough time to read a big chunk, just to get them interested and all, but then when I know it's getting to the juicy part, I turn the page. I don't even care if I finished reading or not, I just turn the page so they can't get to the juicy bit. It cracks me up inside when I do that, cos I know they can't say a thing. See, they don't want to admit they've been a nosey parker, reading your stinking paper, so they can't say a thing.

Anyway, I shouldn't have been snooping over her paper either, but I reckon I got away with it, cos she didn't shift away or anything. I don't think she noticed. To tell you the truth I don't think she cared who was next to her. I reckon she would have smiled at anyone.

Reason I started snooping, though, was because I saw a picture of this little kid and the headline saying she'd been shot dead by her little brother. She looked a cute little kid about six or something and in the picture, she was smiling and holding a doll. She had pigtails down to her shoulders and was wearing this cute little dress, the colour of the sea. I couldn't read it all properly, cos I didn't want to make it too obvious I was snooping, but it said that she'd found a gun in a drawer in her dad's bedroom and her brother and she started playing with it thinking it was a toy and all. I couldn't read it all properly cos the sunshine bounced off some of the print, but it seems that her little brother shot her dead. It wasn't intentional like, but because he was only four and he thought it was a toy.

That was about as far as I got, though, cos just then this lady put the paper down and picked up her bag and got up to go. She smiled at me as she left and said, 'Bye, have a nice day.'

I smiled back and said, 'Thanks, you too, mam.'

And then she walked off past the sprinklers and the rainbows.

Because I was watching her walking off down the footpath towards the ocean, I didn't notice that she'd left her paper on the seat next to me. I picked it up and thought about running after her, but she'd gone quite a way and I didn't want to leave this bench, to be honest. I was still wondering about that little kid too, you know, the one in the paper, so instead of chasing after her, I just picked up the paper.

I opened it up by the story about the little kid and read the bits I couldn't see when I was peering over her shoulder. It made me pretty sad, reading about this little kid who had been shot and all, especially when it said how wonderful she was. See, it ended with a bit of a tribute to her, saying how beautiful she was and how everyone in her class loved her. It said she loved dancing and was the best dancer in the school and how she had this really bright future. They even had a quote from her school principal, and he said she was destined for a wonderful future and was one of the kindest girls he'd ever met.

It's sad. You know, how when you read a newspaper, only wonderful people die. How newspapers and death make you a two-sentence somebody.

The paper was all so neat and tidy. I just folded it with the front page in place and all and thought I'd leave it on the bench. It was still neat, as if you could sell it again, just as I told you. Except for that number written on the front page. Like a phone number or something.

I didn't stay on that bench much longer, though. I walked into town thinking about what to do next. See, I was thinking I'd like to go to Mexico, but my crappy US visa had run out and I didn't fancy my chances of getting back into the country. I had enough trouble getting a visa in the first place and maybe I wouldn't be so lucky next time. That's the trouble, see. They can nick the country and then put walls up and decide who comes in. If I had a bigger dad, I'd nick it off them. Trouble is, thanks to Rumplan, I don't have a dad at all.

The west coast on US1 had been delicious but hitching over the last few days had been gruesome. I started to think about getting a Greyhound bus and heading back east. I'd told everyone I was gonna Greyhound around, so maybe it was time. I kind of wanted to head straight across Interstate 8 towards Phoenix, and then pick up the 10 East to Texas. I mulled over a map and reckoned if I took night buses I could be in Texas in a couple of days.

I was kind of excited but scared too. I had this plan to get to Texas all the time, a plan in the back of my head, but I'd sort of put it off by hitching around and thinking I could get to see some of America first. Maybe find peace or another way out. But nothing was resolved. It was getting closer; the only way out felt real. I was scared. Not scared like in New York, full-on, swirling engine scared. But it was the only way out.

I bought a ticket to Phoenix and waited in the bus station in San Diego. Another dump. I sat on the floor by the water fountain while I waited and scribbled on my rucksack. All the places I stopped at on the west coast were now scars on my rucksack. Swollen veins and place names on a faded rucksack. A lot of place names. My rucksack had faded. It was yellow once but had been scraped around on floors, on beaches, it was almost brown.

Crunched up too, a bit like a walnut. A dry, brown, crusty, gnarled walnut. Frayed, it wouldn't last too much longer. I thought about 'porcelain' Pete and what he would say if he saw it. I guessed his was still as neat and tidy as the gardens of Versailles. Immaculate. I wondered where he was, where Dave was. I wondered if Brad was still in Bar Harbor and if Marty and Dan were in Harrisburg. I thought about Annie and remembered what she'd said one night when I told her about my parents and all.

'Hunt the bastard down and kill him,' she said.

The bus station was full of bums and sad-eyed Mexicans emptied of history and of the land they'd once owned. The inflated-bellied, hollow-headed waiting people ignored them. It felt like New York, but it was San Diego. Things were the same, but they weren't. Things were different.

Chapter Twenty-One

The bus journey to Phoenix was boring as hell. I couldn't sleep, see. I should have been okay cos I bagged myself a double seat as soon as I got on and so had plenty of space. I even did that snoring trick when passengers got on during the night. You know, sprawling out across the two seats and pretending I was asleep so no one would sit next to me. Last thing I wanted was some old biddy sitting next to me. You know, some old biddy who peed her pants cos she couldn't hold it. You'd think it wouldn't happen, but it does. I know it does cos I've seen it with my own eyes.

See, I was on this bus once and I had to sit next to this real old guy. I thought he was about a hundred or something, he looked that old, but I got talking to him and he said he was only ninety-one. He looked as if he might be a hundred, but he said he was only ninety-one and so I believed him. See, old folks never say they're younger than they are. Like people who are thirty or forty or something are always lying about their age to make out they are still young and all. It's as if they don't want to get old, so they just tell people they're younger than they are. Old people don't do that, though. I reckon old people think their age is some stupid badge of honour or something. You know, as if they've just rescued a drowning cat from a river or something. They say things like 'I'm ninety-five, you know', and they always say it with this great big grin, as if they've just got to the top of Mount Everest. I never know what to say when old people tell me their age like that, like when they're beaming as if it's something brilliant, so I usually just say 'huh'. I bet most of them want me

228

to say something slushy, you know, like 'wow, you don't look it'. But I don't. See, I don't like it when people fish for compliments. Not even when old people do it.

It's kind of crazy really, cos kids like to make out they are older than they are. You know when you are thirteen or something, you try and make out you are fourteen and a half or something like that. And then old people tell you their age cos they're proud they're still breathing. But everyone in between makes out they're younger than they are. It's crazy really, cos no one seems to like what they've got, as if it's always better to be something else.

Anyway, this old guy who I got talking to was named Moe. That's what he told me anyway. At first, I didn't want to talk to him at all and I wished he hadn't sat by me, but in the end, I thought he was okay. Not brilliant or anything, but okay. He was pretty clued up for an old fellow, though, and started telling me all these stories about what he'd done when he was my age and stuff. He banged on about how he owned this boat and had sailed across the Atlantic and stuff when he was young. He told me he could play the saxophone too and went banging on about all these bands he had played in when he was about thirty. He was making out that he had been best buddies with Alan Freed and all, but I hadn't heard of any of his bands, so it might have all been bullshit, but I just went along with it anyway. To tell the truth, I reckon he was making most of it up, you know, as if he was looking back on his life and wanted to jazz it up a bit to make out it had all been worthwhile. As if he needed to be some treasure-box full of jewels. I didn't mind, though, cos he had some good stories and it stopped me getting bored. Trouble is, that bus didn't stop much and when we got off, he stood up and I could see wet all over the back of his trousers. His seat was all wet too. See, an old guy like that just couldn't hold it, so he'd just peed his pants. Right there while he was telling me all this crap about playing the saxophone and Alan Freed and stuff.

Anyway, cos I'd seen that with my own eyes, I just kept worrying in case someone got on the bus and sat next to me and peed their pants, so I reckon that's one reason why I didn't sleep. Because I couldn't sleep, I spent a lot of time just listening to the engine and looking out of the window. It was still light, so I watched San Diego dissolve into the sea behind me. I watched as the magnificent trinket, one square mile of all cities mutated into its labyrinth of disfigured, ragged, soot black streets filled with the heavy steps of the downtrodden. Hours before, in La Jolla looking at that pink hotel and the waves and all, San Diego was a blossom tree in bloom. But if you asked me now, driving through the debris, I'd tell you, you'd be better off getting the plague.

The bus was travelling east on IS 8, and that kind of tracks the Mexican border. I started to think about all that O'Sullivan 'manifest destiny' crap, and how this would still be Mexico if it wasn't for all that bull. Where the road skims the border, I pictured the Americans building a wall to stop Mexicans getting across. Great big steel pillars going on for mile after mile. Most of it rusty, and looking like the wasted, dead, brown trunks of tree. Thousands of dead, brown trees in a row. Without branches or leaves to make them pretty. Tall, straight trees. Too straight to look as if nature could want them. Sometimes, I saw a Mexican town just across the other side of the fence. You know, like if the bus stopped, I could have walked to it in five minutes flat. I could too, if they don't build a wall.

It made me think about how everyone is spooked by simple difference. You know, like if someone has a different colour skin

230

or believes something different. I noticed that at school. Like if someone had ginger hair or freckles or something, kids would get spooked. Anything, if it was different. It was fine if loads of people did it. You know, like you fitted in. If loads of people did it, no one seemed to get spooked. Like a load of kids used to pick their nose.

Right in the middle of a divinity class or something, most kids were bored as hell, so they'd just start picking their nose. They'd roll it up between their fingers and mess about with it and make it compact and then put it in their mouth. Now, loads of kids did that, especially in divinity, cos it was so boring, but nobody cared cos loads of kids did it. Some of the teachers did it too, though, they tried to hide it a bit and pretend. People do it in cars too. You know, people sitting at traffic lights, picking their nose, as if no one can see. If a kid did something different, though, say like getting into ballet or something, they were for it. In big trouble. I remember there was this one kid who played the violin. He could play it real good too, but no one else played the violin so that unnerved everyone. He got it in the neck big style cos he played that violin. The kids were always on his back. They'd nick his violin case and point it at him as if they were gangsters and all. You know, like when gangsters in crazy Mafia films and stuff carry their machine guns in their violin cases. When they did that, they'd make all these stupid noises like the sound of a machine gun. Brrrrrrrrrrrrrrrrrrr.Brrrrrrrrrrrrrrrrrr. Then they'd jump him and push him to the ground, just cos he played the violin. Now if he'd picked his nose in divinity instead, he would have been fine, but he didn't, he played the violin. Some of the people who jumped him would bring their Jethro Tull albums into school with them the next day. Then they'd bang on about Jethro Tull and worship Ian Anderson and everything.

It was as if they couldn't join the dots. If they'd gone to school with Ian Anderson when he was a kid, I bet they would have beat him up too.

The worst one, though, was what they did to Brian Holloway. See, I don't know why, but when you were at junior school, it was kind of a rule that boys wore short trousers. I don't know if someone had made it a rule or something or if it was just what people did, but if you were a boy, you wore short trousers. But when you got to eleven, you'd switch schools and start senior school. Now when you did that you could start wearing long trousers. I reckon it was like some rite of passage or something, but that's what everyone did.

I don't know if there was a rule written down somewhere, or if when mums went and bought the trousers, they just knew, like an instinct or something, but that's what happened. Anyway, when I switched to my senior school, I turned up on the first day wearing long trousers. Everyone did. Everyone except Brian Holloway. There were about a hundred new kids aged eleven, all in their brand-new long trousers, and then there was Brian Holloway. All the other older kids who were already at the school all knew what to wear, so they were all in long trousers too. About five hundred kids in long trousers and Brian Holloway in his shorts. I'm telling you he never lived that down. I don't know why, but it kind of twisted everyone cos he was different, and he never lived it down. After that, all the kids made his life hell. And not just for a week or two either. No, forever. See, the 'in-crowd' used to think it was a good idea to dunk kids heads down the toilet. It happened to everyone, unless you happened to be in the 'in-crowd'. It happened to me once, but see, it happened to Brian all the time. I reckon they must have put his head down the toilet a thousand times. I ain't kidding either, I reckon it must have been a thousand, maybe more. I don't know why, but kids would just pick on him for anything. Sometimes, for no reason at all. One time, a whole bunch of them knocked him to the floor and all and then just started laying into him. They were all putting the boot in. He was trying to shield himself with his hands and arms, but it was a waste of time; they just kept laying into him. Then this great big fat bastard who thought he was king of the 'in-crowd', Saul Roberts, landed this boot to Brian's head. Roberts was wearing these great big heavy boots and all. You know, leather boots with great big thick soles that looked as if they could kick down a wall. You didn't need to wear boots like that to school cos we just had to walk down tiled corridors and all, but I reckon he wanted to make out he could kick down a wall if he wanted. Well, he kicked Holloway right in the head. I don't know why he kicked him so hard; he didn't need to, but he did, he kicked him as if he wanted to kick his brains out, as if he wanted to kill him. I think he almost did too, cos Brian Holloway lay on the floor for about five minutes after they finished with him. He didn't move at all for a couple of minutes, he just shook and shuddered a bit with his hands still holding his head. He didn't cry, though, he just shuddered a bit. Shuddered and wriggled, a bit how a fish does when it's on the end of a line and is pulled out the water.

Trouble is, a lot of kids saw Roberts do it, you know, saw all this crazy mob, led by Roberts, kicking Brian's head in for no reason, but no one did a thing. I saw it, and I didn't do a thing. Now, I've never been very proud of that. You know, just standing by and not doing a thing. Looking back, I wished I'd have had the guts to go up and help Brian and all. You know, as if I was as brave as Diane Nash when she organised the lunch counter sit-ins. But I didn't. It made me think, though. Seeing stuff like that made me think about how the powerful always get immunity cos most people are too scared and just watch.

Crazy thing is the poor bastard Brian probably didn't have a clue about the long-trousers thing. Maybe his mum didn't know the rule, or maybe she was too poor to buy him some long trousers. All I knew was, it spooked everyone big style, just cos he was different and that was reason enough to make his life hell.

Now I reckon Brian never got off the hook, partly because of his name too. See, you can't do much with a name like Brian Holloway. Now, if he'd have had a name like James Smith, I reckon he may have got away with that short-trousers thing. See, the kids would have been able to mess with his name a bit and call him Jimmy or Smithy or something. They would have been able to do that adding a Y to the end of one-syllable names thing, and I reckon that would have calmed it all down. See, if you start calling someone Smithy, it's as if you're suddenly best buddies, you know, as if you've been muckers all your life. It's hard to kick someone in the head after you've called them Smithy or Jimmy. But no one could find a way of working a name like Brian Holloway. There ain't any rules for changing names like that, and I reckon that's another reason why no one could be his best buddy. That's why everyone clung on to that short trouser thing.

Thinking about all that stuff meant I didn't sleep too well, so I spent most of the night staring out the window. Just staring at black space most of the time. Staring at black space and wondering if I would have the bottle to save Brian now.

About two hours out of Phoenix, though, the bus made its last stop. I did that pretending to snore thing when the new passengers boarded, but the bus was pretty full, and so, the new passengers started nudging people to get them to make room. I was still sprawled out and hoping I would get away with it. I even thought about taking it up a gear and pretending to fart as people got near me. I thought maybe if I did that, it would work better than the snoring thing and everyone would steer clear and sit next to someone else.

I left it too late, though, cos just as I was about to make this great big farting noise, some old biddy came and sat down next to me. An old dear, wrapped in a grey overcoat that was belted tight around the waist. It was still dark, so I couldn't see her too well, but in the half light of the bus, I could just make out a few features. Her face was thin, and she had those sunken cheeks which made her look gaunt and all. Her lips were slither thin too and both pressed together so tightly; it looked as if she only had one. She had wrinkles around her mouth too, you know, like people who smoke too much and end up with a million spider trails around their mouths. She looked as if she smoked about a thousand woodbines before breakfast.

I moved my bag and shuffled over a bit to make some space for her. I didn't want to, but I didn't see how I had any choice. I started to regret that I hadn't made that farting noise. I even thought about trying to pull it out now just as she was sitting down, but the bus was getting crowded and probably I'd just get someone else. At least she was skinny. Maybe if I got shot of her, I might end up with some real fat bastard sitting next to me. I didn't want to sit next to anyone really, but if I had a choice, I'd take a wrinkly old biddy over a fat bastard any day.

See, America is full of fat bastards. I'm talking real fat too. You know, fat as if they've got a couple of cows stuffed down each trouser leg. You see them everywhere in America. I first saw it in New York. You know, I'd just be walking down 38th street or somewhere and I'd catch up with a couple of slobs shuffling along the sidewalk. They'd kind of wobble along, rocking from side to side as if they were a suspension bridge being blown in a hurricane. I'd get stuck behind them cos they'd walk so slow. You know, as if you got to have a week free just to walk one block. I'm telling you some of them had such fat arses, I reckon I could have smuggled myself through borders hidden up their cracks. Usually, the top of their crack was on show too, cos they'd always wear these crappy tracksuit bottoms that hung half-way down their arse. I bet most of them had given up on trying to get trousers big enough to fit them, but some of them looked as if they couldn't be arsed to pull them up anyway. As if getting dressed got in the way of eating. See, they'd always be eating. Eating and gasping for air. I'd wait for a gap in the traffic, then dash around them in the road to get by. I'd see them sucking away on a couple of hot dogs or turkey leg or something. They'd chomp away and then have a breather and gasp for air, as if they were half-way up Kilimanjaro. The first time I saw Americans as fat as that, I thought it would be the last, but it wasn't. America is full of fat bastards, all over the place. They're always eating too. Always eating stuff with cheese on it. It don't matter what it is, it has to have cheese on it. I reckon some of them put it on ice cream.

So, I settled for the old biddy.

'Hello, young man,' she said as she sat down. 'You don't mind me sitting here, do you?' She spoke quietly, but her voice had a rasping tone.

'No, mam,' I said. As if I have a choice, I thought. God, I'm a hypocrite. I blame Brooksey.

'My name is Betty and I'm going to see my grandson in Phoenix,' she went on. 'He's a lovely young man, just graduated, you know. He's very bright. He's going to be a doctor.' The rasping erupted.

'You seem very proud, mam. I guess you're looking forward

to seeing him.'

'Oh yes, he's such a lovely boy. His mother is too. They're both lovely.' She coughed a little as she spoke and tried to clear her throat. Then she coughed some more and cleared her throat again. She carried on rabbiting on about how wonderful her grandson was as if he put Mother Theresa in the shade and all, but every time she spoke, she coughed and cleared her throat. Then she started grappling with her coat pocket as if she was trying to pull something out. She had sat down awkward and the belt was so tight, she struggled to make any progress. But she just kept rabbiting on and grappling with her pocket and coughing and clearing her throat. She was doing my head in, but she managed to free a handkerchief from her pocket. She raised it to her thin lips and cleared her throat again. Then gobbed. Gobbed a load of crap into her hankie.

'That's better,' she said. Better for whom, I thought.

Now if I could have got away with it, I reckon I would have used my rucksack as a pillow and pushed it over her head until she stopped breathing. It was almost dark enough on that bus too, but I didn't have the nerve, so I just said 'huh'.

Those last two hours into Phoenix seemed to last forever and she just kept rabbiting on and on. To tell you the truth, I didn't listen to her much and just said 'huh', from time to time. But I watched the sun come up. I watched the darkness fade and the deep orange glow of the new sun transform the desert into deep yellow against the lapis blue of the vast new morning. I looked at the sage grass and, in the half-light, imagined madmen from an earlier history, crouching, ready to spring and remind us about all we have forgotten.

I saw the strange green of the saguaro cacti for the first time and the unnatural shadows they cast across the desert. I thought about the peace the desert suggested and all its dangers too. I thought about its possibilities and of what might lie ahead.

The sun was full up by the time the bus pulled in at Phoenix. The bus was full, so it took a while to unload, which meant I had to listen to the old biddy babbling on for a little while longer. I helped her down the step and listened to her coughing.

'Well, goodbye, young man,' she said to me as I helped her down the step. 'Enjoy the rest of your trip.'

She reached into her pocket, pulled out her handkerchief and spat into it. 'That's better,' she said.

I couldn't bring myself to say it was nice to meet you, even though habit, and the memory of Brooksey, forced it on to my tongue. I swallowed.

'Enjoy your visit to your son,' I said.

She pulled out a packet of cigarettes and lit one. 'Would you like one, young man?' she asked.

'No thanks, but thank you anyway, mam.'

She coughed, then took a drag, then coughed again. 'Bye,' I said. I'd seen enough of Phoenix.

Chapter Twenty-Two

Ford Thunderbirds have bench seats. That was one reason why I bought it, that and the fact that it was the cheapest car on the car lot. It was a bit of an old banger, but I figured it would get me a thousand miles or so to Texas and that's all I needed. I hadn't ever planned to buy a car, but I just didn't feel like hitching anymore and I couldn't face any more bus stations or the thought of sitting on buses next to some fat bastard snoring or some old biddy coughing her guts up. Getting a car had crossed my mind when I was with Dave, though, but it was just a mad idea then. At first, it seemed crazy, but I saw how his old Plymouth gave him a place to kip and, even though it was an old wreck, it got us all the way down the west coast. Petrol was cheaper than water in the States in the 70s too, and so the more I thought about it, the more I kind of liked the idea. Anyway, I hadn't been spending too much money, cos so many people had given me lifts and let me stay with them and all, so I had a few hundred dollars spare. I didn't have loads of money left, but enough to get me to Texas and I wasn't going to need any after that, so I bought this Thunderbird.

I didn't have a licence or anything, but I figured no one would ask me about that. People in America just want to sell you stuff, so I reckoned no one would ask, and if they did, I would just make up some crap like I'd left it with my relatives in Phoenix. You know with good old Aunt Betty. Then I'd tell them I needed the car desperate like, to drive her to hospital cos she was dying of lung cancer. 'She never smoked in her life, not one drag,' I'd say.

Then they'd reply, 'Life's not fair.'

And I'd say, 'What can you do?' I had it all planned.

I hadn't even passed my test in England, but I could drive fine. My dad took me out in the car a lot when I was a kid and when I'd turned 14, he let me have a go, you know, just down some quiet country lanes and stuff. Driving in America is a doddle anyway. Out west, there ain't no traffic on the roads, and in the cities the roads are that wide you could drive in circles and no one would notice. See, everything in England is about a million years old and as crooked as a bank robber, but America is all straight lines. Straight, wide, to the end of the universe lines. It ain't anything like England at all. Not one bit, even though England spends most of its time trying to be like America.

It wasn't much of a car, though. I bet when it was built it was a real head-turner, but it had done a lot of miles, and was beaten and torn up pretty bad. It still felt cool, though, you know, to be driving my own T-Bird with its bench seat. I thought about all the times back home when I told people I was going to Greyhound around. I wished I'd told them I was going to cruise around in my own Ford Thunderbird instead. God, they would have drooled then. Thing is, I didn't have a clue I was gonna buy one way back then. Crazy thing is, if you'd asked me when I was sitting on that bench in La Jolla a couple of days ago, I didn't have a clue then either. It was just after that crappy bus ride, I couldn't face it again, so I thought about buying this car. You know, on the spur of the moment and all.

See, I got into Phoenix real early and after I said bye to Betty, I just didn't want to hang around. The bus depot was the pits and even though it was early, it was hot. Baking hot. I couldn't face the city. It felt as if it was too big with too many people. Most of

Arizona is empty, you know, just the beautiful desert, the saguaro cacti, and sage grass. That's how I wanted to remember it, so I just decided to get out of town on the IS 17 north. I thought I would get to the IS 40 and then try to head east to Texas. I caught a local town bus towards Deer Valley and planned to hitch north to Flagstaff, but when I got near Deer Valley, I saw this car lot and I don't know why, but that's when I thought about getting this car.

There were about a hundred cars on this car lot and there were all these advertising hoardings plastered all over the place telling you all this bullshit about how you could get the deal of your life if you bought today and how there was this special reduction if you bought this car or that. See, the Ancients worked out how to build shrines to Gods, but America's Gods worked out how to sell stuff. It don't matter whether someone needs it or not, Americans like selling, you know, selling the idea of buying. Selling consumption. Selling everything. Selling.

The worst thing about buying the car was that I had to put up with this creepy sales guy giving me all this crap about how he loved my T-shirt and my accent and how he would love to visit England and stuff. I'm telling you, you could shoot someone right between the eyes in front of an American salesperson, and to get a sale, they'll tell you they love shooting people in the head too. Trouble is, in America, with all their guns and second amendment crap, a lot of them really do.

He was doing my head in big style, spouting out all this 'I bet you've always dreamt of' crap, as if he'd lived in slime and watched all those slimy ads when he was growing up. I was gonna tell him I'd always dreamed of pushing some arsehole like him under a bus, but I didn't. I just wound him up by asking him lots of questions to waste his time. You know, as I did when I bought my camera. See, I reckoned he was on the clock or something and had some crappy sales target that he had to hit. You know, like if he didn't sell ten cars by lunchtime, he'd have to lick the boss's arse or something. I could tell he was on the clock, cos when other people came into the sales lot, he got all twitchy and shaky and stuff as if he was worrying whether one of the other salespeople would get a sale and he wouldn't. Then he'd probably be at the bottom of this sales chart or something and he'd have to top himself, cos he wasn't salesman of the month. That's the kind of guy he was, and I didn't like him much, so I kept teasing him. I kept saying I just had a couple more questions then, I was definitely gonna buy. I was too, because I'd already seen this T-bird, but I just wanted to keep him hanging on and waste his time because he was giving me all this phoney sales bullshit. So, I just kept asking him loads more stupid questions. I just asked him any old crap that came into my head. You know, all that stupid stuff about how many miles per gallon each car did and when you had to change the oil filters and stuff. I didn't know anything about how cars worked, I'm the type who kicks the tyres to see if they've got air in them, but I just wanted to drag it out to waste his time. The longer it took, the twitchier he got, but he'd been programmed to keep telling me how much he loved me, so he was stuck with me.

Anyway, I must have dragged him around every car in his crappy sales lot for a couple of hours or something. I kept looking at all this new flashy stuff with the 2,000-dollar tags and made out I had loads of cash to splash about if I found the right car. I kept banging on about how Auntie Betty would lend me some money if I saw something I really liked. I wasted a ton of his time doing that, but in the end, I just bought this old T-bird for a few hundred dollars. The one I knew I was gonna buy all along. I bet he made about two bucks commission or something for that crappy sale and it took him about two hours. Maybe more than two hours. I reckon he had to lick his boss's arse big style that day just to keep his job. Just to keep his job at this crumby car lot.

Anyway, that's how come I ended up heading north on the IS 17 with my rucksack next to me on the bench seat of my Ford Thunderbird with its Arizona plate.

Flagstaff was closer than I thought, and I got there in three hours. I was enjoying cruising along, to be honest, so I can't say I really noticed the time. I was thinking about taking the 40 east and just pointing the bonnet east all night until I got to Texas, but I kind of liked just cruising through the deserts of Arizona with my arm out the windows as if I was James Dean. It sort of felt as if I was in the wild west; I just needed a gun. Maybe I should get one. Buying this car was a piece of cake, maybe buying a gun would be fun too and anyway, it would be a gas to wind up some crappy gun salesman. Maybe I could wind up some gun sales guy for an hour or two and waste a load of his time. I could make up all this bullshit about how I'd moved out here and was living in the wilderness near the Mexican border and how I needed a load of guns to protect myself from all the crazy Mexicans and stuff. I knew from the people I'd met along the way that this was the sort of bullshit that they'd lap up. You know, how everyone needed a gun to protect themselves from crazy foreigners.

Anyway, it was when I was cruising along with my arm out the window, thinking about all this crappy gun stuff, that I saw a sign to the Grand Canyon National Park. I hadn't paid too much attention to where I was, to be honest, but the sign said the entrance at the south rim was about 60 miles away. I reckon that was only about an hour in my fancy T-bird. I liked driving through the Arizona desert, so I followed the sign and headed for the south rim.

I don't get impressed by much, but American National Parks are something else. The Grand Canyon is something else. I was kind of expecting it just to be a big hole in the ground. That's what I used to say to people before I left England. Like everyone in the universe has heard of the Grand Canyon, so sometimes when people found out I was going to America they used to ask if I was going to the Grand Canyon. As I told you before, I never had a clue where I was heading, but I just used to say 'maybe'. You know, I said it all casual like. Like maybe I would or maybe I wouldn't. You know, as if I would be doing it a favour if I went to see it.

'It's probably just a big hole in the ground,' I used to tell people. I used to say it that way to let them know nothing impressed me much.

But it did. It was another Da Vinci or something. You know, he would have painted it just as it is. If he could paint so good, that is. I only ever went there, cos I saw the sign and wanted to spend a bit longer driving through the desert, but I ended up staying days. If you want, you can do all this crazy stuff like walking down to the river about a million miles below the rim. You can even go down on donkeys and stuff if you have loads of cash and don't mind getting some poor bleeding donkey to bust its back for you, but I just found a quiet spot, sat down and looked out. I sat there all day, all day for three days, just looking out and watching as the light and shadow changed. See, the sun moves around and paints it in all these pale pastel shades at noon. Sometimes, it's almost white. Then, red at sunset. Lots of different reds too. Bright red like holly berries, then red like a Bordeaux wine. In between it's a million shades of pink and purple and ochre and a lot of colours that ain't even got names.

I stared at that hole in the ground for days and thought about how life does that. You know, just wears you away and puts holes in you and that's when I decided to move on. At first, I thought about backtracking down to Flagstaff, and sticking on the interstates, but now I had this car, I didn't need to stick to the main roads.

Anyway, I thought there would be less chance of running into cops on the back roads. When you're hitching, it's easier to stick to the big roads, but now I had my own car, I could do what I wanted. I still wanted to get across to Texas but decided to stick to the smaller roads. I headed out towards Tuba City and towards Monument Valley. That way, I could drive this T-bird through some of the wilderness in Utah and New Mexico, before I got to Texas.

The idea of buying that gun came back to me as I was driving, though. Maybe it was the wild west landscape that got me thinking about it, but buying the car was easy and I thought it might be fun just to see if I could waste someone's time in a gun shop. When I was in San Francisco, Bob took me to that shooting range and told me anyone could buy a gun. I'd seen loads of gun shops all over the States. Sometimes, I'd even seen them in gas stations when rides stopped for fuel and stuff. I wasn't sure if they'd ask me a load of crazy questions about who I was and why I was buying it and stuff, but I thought if they did, it would be fun wasting a load of their time. I decided to do it anyway.

Really it was only a bit of a crazy idea at the back of my mind, just something to do if I got a bit bored or something. To be honest, I didn't even know if I'd come across a gun shop, but on the way to Monument Valley, I came across this creaky old gas station that had some rifles and handguns and stuff. So, I went in and browsed around for a while as if I was some hunting guy or something. After about five minutes, the assistant came over.

'What you after, buddy?'

Now to be honest, I had no idea. I'd only ever touched one gun and that was at that range with Bob. It was only this crappy handgun, but even that had freaked me out, so I really didn't know what to say.

'Just bought a place in Nogales,' I said. 'It's a bit isolated, you know, out in the sticks on its own. Wanna be able to defend myself if trouble comes my way.' I put on this phoney American accent, cos I didn't want him rabbiting on about me coming from England and all. I'm crap at accents, so it sounded real put-on and all, but he didn't say anything about it, so maybe he bought it.

'Handgun or rifle?' he asked.

'I'll probably bag a couple of rifles when I'm back next time,' I said. I thought if I said that it would get him all fired up as if I was gonna spend a million bucks with him sometime. 'But I reckon a handgun today. I ain't got all my cash with me today, cos I've just got myself a new car.' I tilted my head in the direction of the T-bird, parked outside his crappy store in the parking lot. 'Spent more than I thought on the car, so just a handgun today, I reckon. What d'you recommend?'

He glanced out the window at the car but didn't say anything. His casual glance gave me the impression that he wasn't impressed, but he shuffled across to open the gun cabinet anyway. It wasn't locked, so he just leant over and pulled out a couple of guns.

'You can't do better than this one.' He handed me a revolver, he handed it to me as if he was passing me a box of washing powder or something. You know, as if it wasn't anything special, as if I might just wash my clothes with it and no more. But when he talked about it, he was different. He talked about it as if he couldn't talk about anything else. You know, as Gaugin might talk about painting. As if he didn't really have any of the right words but made up for it with some deep irrepressible passion.

I didn't have a clue what he was on about and to tell you the truth, I was starting to get a bit freaked out by holding the gun. It wasn't even loaded, but I was still freaked out. I started to sweat, but I kind of felt I couldn't back out now. You know, it was like one of those slow motion car crash moments that I told you about before. You know, when you know what you are doing is crazy, but you just do it anyway. Because I was freaked out, though, I changed my mind about asking all my crazy questions and wasting his time. I just wanted to get out. 'Sounds just what I need,' I said, 'What about ammo?'

I felt stupid saying that, but I really had no idea what to say. I wasn't sure whether you had to ask for bullets or what, so for some reason I just said ammo.

He didn't say anything, but just grabbed a box. '100 rounds, that do you?'

I don't know how many Mexicans he wanted me to shoot, or if he was just up selling, but I just wanted to get out.

'That'll do me fine.' I said it in that crappy American accent again. It hadn't got any better. I sounded like the chimney sweep in *Mary Poppins*, but he didn't seem to care.

'40 bucks. I just need to see some I.D. and stuff,' he said.

I wasn't sure what I needed or what he wanted to see; it had all moved along faster than I had planned. I had to think fast.

'What d'you need? I got some papers in the car,' I thought that would get me off the hook. If I could get out the store, I'd just high tail it off the car lot, before he worked out, I wasn't coming back.

'Yeah, I'll go get stuff from my car.'

'Nah, you're okay. 40 bucks. Show me your papers when you come back for the rifles. I don't need to see any papers so long as you're only shooting Mexicans.' He laughed. One of those laughs that people use to cover up the shit they say and make out it's just banter.

I just said 'huh'. I felt like calling him an arsehole, but he was holding the gun, so I didn't, I just said 'huh'.

I rummaged in my pocket for the 40 bucks and picked up the gun and box of 100 rounds. 'Thanks, see you, see you again.'

I walked back to the car and dropped the handgun and rounds next to my rucksack on the seat. I kind of wanted to hold it. I didn't really like the idea of having a gun and kind of wished I'd never gone in that crazy gas station. But I kind of wanted to hold it at the same time. I can't really explain it, but I wanted to hold it and not hold it at the same time. You know, like Schrödinger's cat or something.

I was a bit spooked, though, so I started the car and drove off fast. It shuddered up to 40, but I cranked it up all the way to bursting as if I'd just pulled off a bank heist or something. America is crazy. A lot of the time I couldn't even get someone to serve me a beer, but buying a gun was a piece of cake. Buying everything in America is a piece of cake, except alcohol maybe.

I was near Monument Valley, so I kept driving on the narrow strip of black tar that cut through the dry, red dust like an arrow. The enormous presence of the west. I felt as if I was in a western.

Chapter Twenty-Three

Monument Valley isn't really a valley. In America most stuff ain't what they say it is. Monument Valley is still genius, though. I kind of felt as if I'd been there before cos I'd seen it in loads of westerns and stuff. I drove along this dirt track and stopped at John Ford's Point. I don't know who the hell John Ford is, but that's what the sign said, and I recognised the view. You know, it's the one used in about a million films with this ace view of all the buttes and mesas rising out of this flat red desert. Everything is red. Except the sky. The sky is thalo blue, but everything else is red.

The roads are lonely in this part of the States. That suited me fine. I like long empty roads, stretching into the horizon. Sometimes the only thing on the road is the line and sometimes there ain't even a line. I like it even better when there ain't a line. It was so quiet out here. Sometimes I just pulled up on the side of the road and sat on the bonnet or wandered off into the red sand and sage grass. Then wandered back with my trousers turned red with the dust as if I was a reddleman on Egdon Heath. Nothing much came past, and when it did, the roads are wide and silent enough, so no one cares much. Stopping gave me a chance to look at the gun. I opened the box of bullets and held one in my hand. It was smooth and shiny and perfectly symmetrical. I thought about that mad guy named 'porcelain' Pete I'd met in Oregon. He loved symmetrical. I bet he would love this. You know, cos it's so clean and smooth and symmetrical. I thought about how small it was and wondered how something so small and delicate could be so deadly. It didn't seem right. I can't really explain what I mean, you know, how little small things can change everything, but it just didn't seem right.

I picked up the gun and spun the barrel. It was empty and the chambers were shining and clean. It spun real smooth. I thought about when I was spinning that book stand in Henrys, you know, where I bought that book about Jesus, where everyone was happy. I span the barrel a few times and listened to the sound it made as it slowed and came to a stop. It kind of sounded how that book stand in Henrys did, but that book stand was more creaky, not smooth like this.

I took a bullet and loaded it into the chamber. I tried to remember what I did at that shooting range in San Francisco. It slid in easy, as if it was born there and had just come out to get some light or something. You know, how a desert mouse comes out to get warmth during the sunlight before burrowing back into the sand.

There was no one around, so I stood by the side of the road and pointed the gun at the horizon. I wasn't really aiming at anything, just the horizon. I wasn't fussed about hitting anything, I just wanted to see if I could shoot that gun. The gun I'd bought in a gas station near Tuba City.

I pulled the trigger and the shot rang in my ears. The gun jolted my hand and it rocked back a bit and I could feel a sensation in my fingers and into the wrist. You know, a bit like when you stand right next to a rail track and the engine whistles past you at a million miles an hour or something. You know, when you are standing so close and the engine whistles by only about a yard away and the wind takes your breath away. I tried it again, and again. Blood flooded my veins. It was kind of addictive, so I loaded it again. I loaded all six chambers and fired off each one. Bullets flew like shooting stars. Then I did it again and again. Then I did it again, but this time I took aim at rocks and stones and stuff. I wasn't bothered about being a Wilson or Shane or anything, maybe I wouldn't even be as good as Torrey, but it was addictive. I reckon in time, I could probably outdraw Torrey dead easy, you know, almost as easy as Wilson. It was getting easier. It was a bit like kissing or hitchhiking. You know, you spend all that time getting stressed out about it and then it's easy. Then you can do it without even thinking about it.

After all that shooting, I never worried much about guns anymore. I even kept it loaded, right there next to me on the bench seat of my car. Right there, whilst I was driving with my arm out the window.

I headed across into New Mexico with its soft coloured desert landscape full of the haunting voices of its ancestral Puebloan people. I could have gone to Albuquerque or Santa Fe in search of Spanish conquistadors. Any place I wanted. With this car and this gun, I felt as if I could have gone anywhere, but I didn't want to run into the cops and didn't feel like going back near the interstate. I kind of liked the smaller roads, the sound of native voices in the wind. The sound of no intruders, the sound of space.

The weather changes quick in America, especially around these parts. I staggered on eastwards as the rain came down. Hammering down and bouncing off the road with machine-gun madness. Bouncing off the roof of the car like kids going crazy with marbles. The wipers skidded across the screen like skaters who'd forgotten how to skate. The water swamped and flooded and filled my nostrils, and insane, delirious, black clouds swirled into the tarmac. I couldn't tell if I was driving on cloud or black tar or with Dorothy to Kansas, but the rain hammered down, and

251

blurred, astonished lights swam at me through water. I tried to hug the kerb or the line in the middle, but couldn't see either, just rain, then cloud, then ghosts, and continuous holy water rain.

I kept driving, but more holy water. The Red Sea had parted and was flooding back, and I steered in search of some promised land. Bony, swollen knuckles gripped to life and the whole mad world vibrated. It was getting late. I was getting tired. Exhausted. I decided to find a place to stay.

I came across a crumby roadhouse near Springer. It looked like the sort of place where they shot *Psycho*. The pouring, soaking rain bled down upon it, as if someone was about to plunge a blade into its belly. I parked and waited for the rain to ease. I wondered if it would ever ease. I waited.

Most motels in the States look the same. You know, those crappy one-storey buildings made from wood that look as if someone built them in about two hours flat. There's usually a crappy parking lot outside, half-filled with cars with out-of-state plates and some creaky neon sign. Live moths circle insanely, looking endlessly for something they'll never find. Mostly, there's a light out, so it usually says, OTEL, or MO EL, or something. The given-up moths seek peace as black, charred debris burnt into the hum of hot glass tubes. Some motels are two-storey places, with a creaky staircase up to the balcony, you know, like the place where they killed Martin Luther King. But they're all crappy. Inside they're all crappy. The sheets are never changed. Every time I stayed in a crappy hotel or motel, I noticed how they never change the sheets. I don't know why they don't change the sheets in America, I reckon all these places are run by lazy, dirty bastards. I bet they make out they are ace and run the best motels in the world, but they don't. I'm telling you most of them are run by lazy, dirty bastards. Lying bastards too, cos they say they are the best in the world.

Anyway, this place near Springer was a real dive, so I slept with my gun under the pillow. I kept it loaded too, you know, just in case. I fell asleep wondering how many other people were sleeping with a gun under their pillow. America. Everyone sleeping on dirty sheets, with a gun by the bed.

Next morning, I checked out early and headed for Texas. I crossed the state line at a place called Texline. Texline, Texas. I was here. About to do what had to be done. I should have felt something tremendous, but I didn't really feel anything. I should have, and I was expecting to, but I didn't. I'm not really sure how to explain how I felt, I don't even think I can, I just didn't feel much at all. I just knew nothing felt right.

See, I'd been thinking about coming to Texas since before I left England. Since I'd found out that bastard Todd J. Rumplan ran his lying, cheating, murdering politics out of Fort Worth. Fort Worth, it should be called Fort Worthless if scumbags like him live here, but now I was here, nothing felt right.

See, back in England, after my parents were killed, I tried to sort stuff out, but no one wanted to help. They just treated me like a kid and wanted me to go away. You know, go away and keep quiet as people do. You know, like how we all did when we saw that fat Roberts bastard at school kicking Brian Holloway's brains out. But I didn't want to go away. I couldn't. I'd heard about the likes of John Lewis and Bob Moses. 20-year-olds with the courage to sit up front on a Greyhound bus only a decade or so ago. The courage to say we just want to be treated as equals. The courage to challenge oppression without fear of the consequences. Stuff was going on in my head. I wasn't sure what, but I needed to do something. That's when I knew I wanted to get out to the States, but I didn't know much about how it all worked. I didn't know how they did their politics over here. That's one reason why I came, cos I wanted to find out how it all worked. I tried to find out about stuff when I was moving around, and I found out a lot. I'm scared, though, shit scared. I didn't even have the nerve to hit that sleazebag over the head. You know, that stinking sleazebag who chucked me out in Wyoming. I didn't have the nerve. Maybe I just don't have the nerve. Maybe that's the problem; I just don't have the nerve.

See, I reckon I'm a big coward deep down. I wished I wasn't, but I reckon I am. I remember reading some Shakespeare stuff once. You know, one of his fancy plays, full of fancy lines, and it banged on about how cowards die a thousand times, but brave men only once. That ain't the exact words or anything, but that's the gist of it. That's the gist of how I remember it anyway. Now my dad was a brave man and I'm glad he only died once, even if it was at the hands of that bastard Rumplan. But, I'm a coward and so maybe I don't have the nerve. I'm not sure. That's why I didn't rush here, see. Anticipating stuff is one thing, but I'm not sure. Thing is, travelling around meant I found out a lot. A lot about me, a lot about Todd, a lot about everything.

Texas is big. You could fit England into it easy, so after I crossed the state line, I just kept driving. Driving past all the Lone Star State flags. Past all the Confederate flags. Past all the 'don't mess with Texas' signs. I didn't like it from the start. It thinks it is bigger and better than everything, you know, as if it makes the rules, not follows them. It kind of strolls around with a swagger, all superior and all. You know, how some countries and cities do. As if they think they can do everything better on their own and would prefer not to join in. It's so far up its own arse. I reckon if it fell down a toilet, it thinks it would come up smelling of chocolate. It wouldn't, but it thinks it would. People fall for it, and so that's what it thinks.

I reckon it would take all day to drive across the whole of Texas and that would have done my head in, so I was glad I didn't have to. By the time I'd got near Fort Worth, I was already sick of all the oil fields and the gushers and the cattle ranches and Texans striding around in their ten-gallon hats. Fort Worth was only about 400 miles from the state line, though, so it didn't take so long. I was there at noon.

I looked for a cheap motel. I hadn't seen too many places to stay, cos Texas is mostly nothing, but I found a place not far from town. It looked crappy like all the others, but I checked in anyway. It was hot and the sheets were dirty. I chucked my rucksack on the bed. It was dirtier than the sheets, but I didn't care much cos I knew they wouldn't change them. I opened my bag and took out the gun. It was the only shiny thing in the room. I put it under the pillow.

Fort Worth and Dallas merge as a sprawling mass. If they were sisters, Fort Worth would be the quiet pretty one. Dallas would be the gobby one. The overdressed, overconfident, brasher loudmouth. If they ever made a TV show about the place, they'd call it Dallas, not Fort Worth. A lot of America is like that, a loudmouth, an overdressed loudmouth.

I looked around. Trying to get into bars around Sundance Square, making out I was Butch Cassidy or someone. I walked around the cobblestone streets of the Stockyard district and thought about all the cowboys and outlaw hustlers that passed their time in the saloons. Holing up here with the law on their tail, before heading south to cross the border into Mexico. Now, it is just full of tourists clicking cameras and bleached blonde hussies and ranchers and city oil slickers in oversized boots and oversized hats and all of them talking unnaturally loudly.

I went across to downtown Dallas and walked by the glass shiny office blocks with windows full of make-believe sun. And across to Elm Street and I stretched out by Dealey Plaza. I hated Dallas. About as much as Jackie Kennedy, but I had stuff to do, so I went anyway. I went and checked stuff out.

It was late when I got back to the motel where I was staying. I spoke to the girl on the desk and checked in for a couple of weeks. I gave her all this phoney shit about how much I wanted to see Texas. I didn't have enough money to pay for two weeks, so I fed her all this bull about how I was waiting for a big cheque from England, and I could settle up when I left. I worked up my English accent and stuff and laid on a load of flannel about how much I loved Texas and how much there was to see. I'm not sure if she bought it, or really didn't give a shit whether I paid or not. It wasn't her hotel, so maybe she just didn't give a shit.

I reckoned two weeks was enough. Enough time to get used to the place, to find out how stuff works, to get stuff done. I didn't have any money coming to pay for the stinking place, but I didn't need to worry about that. Not after I'd got all the stuff done. Not if I had the nerve. Not if I could figure out all that Shakespeare stuff.

Chapter Twenty-Four

I don't really want to bother to tell you how I tracked him down. To be honest, it wasn't that hard, and I reckon you'd be bored as hell if I did. It ain't as if I'm Sherlock Holmes or anything. There was loads of stuff in the libraries and Brad had filled me in more than he'd realised. He kept saying I used to ask him crazy questions, but he used to answer anyway, so he filled me in lots. To be honest, Todd made it easy as hell. A bigshot like him is so far up his own arse, he'd plastered pictures of his ugly face all over the place. All over Dallas and Fort Worth. All these creepy pictures of his bleached white teeth and his ten-gallon hat. He did all these rallies too. Standing on the stage as if he was Mr Perfect, making out he was gonna save the world if everyone gave him their vote.

I listened to him spouting all his bullshit. All this crap about how he loved America and his wife and his kids, and how he couldn't have done it all without his mum and dad and all that phoney crap. Sometimes, he'd have his wife and kids with him and hug and kiss them and stuff. It all looked real phoney, but he did it anyway. It was all part of his act. His wife always used to look real uncomfortable; the kids did too. You know, as if they really didn't want to be there. But he didn't give a shit, cos it was all part of the act.

I've got to admit, though, his wife really didn't look his type. Now, I ain't no oil painting, but she was downright plain. I really didn't care if she was plain or not, but she just didn't strike me as his type. Her clothes didn't seem to fit her right either, as if she'd bought them too big or had slimmed down or something and hadn't got around to getting any new ones yet. They made her look a bit comic. Like when clowns deliberately wear oversized trousers and jackets and stuff just to get laughs.

They were out of date too. As if she was the plain one next to Doris Day in a 50s movie. She wore dresses like the ones they wore in those movies. You know, those sleeveless ones that showed her arms, then clipped her upper body only to flare out a bit after the waist. Right to the knee, just below sometimes, they'd flare out like that. They always had flower patterns too. Bright coloured, large flowers so she looked like a garden in spring. I kind of liked them cos it reminded me of the sort of dresses my mum wore when I was a kid and we went shopping in Henrys and stuff. But on Rumplan's wife, the colours just served to make her look even plainer. You know, as if the gardener hadn't got around to her face yet.

She didn't smile much either. She tried to. I reckon he'd told her she had to, but she wasn't any good at it. She tried that phoney clenched teeth smile. The one where you part your lips a bit to show your teeth and try and curl the corners of your mouth up. Her eyes didn't smile, though. There was no light or those tiny changes of shape you get when people are really smiling. That's hard to fake and she couldn't do it, so she just did the phoney clenched teeth thing.

The kids clung to her as if she was Marie Antoinette being dragged to the guillotine. But they never smiled either. They hadn't even learnt the phoney clenched teeth bit and just stood there as if they were on strings. As if someone was working them with strings.

It didn't matter, though, cos he still whipped everyone up. Standing there in his oversized lapels, with a cornfield of blond hair mopped across his head. An avalanche of emotion hiding the facts. He got everyone waving all these stinking placards that his cronies had given to everyone when they showed up. You know, all these crumby ad slogans to make out he was some genius, some saviour or something. You know, shit like 'Texas ain't Texas without Todd' and 'Rumplan. The Man who Can'. They lapped it up big style and were all cheering and whooping every time he spouted some more of his phoney bullshit. I'm telling you he was spouting so much shit, his teeth should have been brown. They weren't, though, they were that stupid bleached white.

He was banging on about everything. You know, all that pro-life stuff and how America should be for Americans. He kept mentioning the Mexicans, as if there were about a million of them all queued up to come and take back Texas. Then, when he'd spooked everyone about what these Mexicans were gonna do to everyone, he went banging on about how he was gonna defend the second amendment and the right to bear arms and all. He went banging on about that for ages, as if Al Capone was in the audience and he wanted his vote. The crowd lapped it up big style, you know, as if they'd be happy to have their head blown off so long as they could carry a gun and wave a flag.

Thing is, that was the biggest load of bullshit of all. See, when you went into this rally, there were all these heavies searching you and all. You know the type, great big fat guys who look as if they ain't happy unless they've put an axe through someone's head. Well, these fat bastards were searching everyone and making sure no one had a gun or anything. They wouldn't let anyone take in a gun. After all that crap about the Mexicans, it didn't stop the chanting, though. They kept chanting crazy stuff like 'Defend our rights' and 'Free to carry guns', and all this crap, and Todd kept whipping them up. 'Yeah,' I thought, 'free to carry guns into diners and shoot up all the servers, just so long as you don't go near Todd lying J. Rumplan with one.' See, that's the sort of double speak Orwell used to bang on about. But people don't see it. Not even when it's right there in front of their eyes. They just don't see it. Not when someone's whipping them up.

Anyway, it all ended with this anthem and everyone singing 'God save America' while they put their arms across their chests and rested their hands on their hearts and all. I was ready to throw up. You know, seriously throw up, it made me feel that sick. You know, like when you were a little kid at school, and they made you eat stuff you couldn't stomach.

I hated eating most of the crap they gave us when I was a tiny kid at school. It was all this crappy boiled cabbage and crap you wouldn't even feed to pigs. But that's what they gave us anyway. I remember this one day, after I'd piled down a load of this soggy cabbage crap, they gave me this pudding too. I didn't want it, but they gave me it anyway. There it was right on the tray next to all this plate of cabbage. I don't know what it was, maybe spotted dick or something, but it looked real shitty anyway. Anything called spotted dick has got to be crappy. Anyway, it was all sludge, and the gooey sludge was full of these little black squelchy crappy things. I guess they were currants, looking back, but at five, they just looked like dead flies. You know, as if someone had just decided to drown a hundred flies in this sludge. I couldn't eat it to save my life, but this crappy teacher just sat there staring at me saying I had to eat it. Mrs Cauldwell it was. She was a mean bastard. She hit me around the head one day, just cos I ran on, after the bell. I was running real fast cos it was playtime, and I couldn't stop that quick when she rang the bell.

She didn't give a monkey about that, though, and just hit me round the head. I tell you she was a real mean bastard.

Anyway, this day I'm telling you about when I had to force this spotted dick shit down my neck, she was on dinner duty. She could tell I couldn't eat this crap. I know she could, but she just kept staring at me and telling me I couldn't leave until I ate it all. I kept spooning the sludge and all those things that looked like flies into my mouth, but I couldn't swallow them. I'm telling you after a couple of mouthfuls, I don't reckon I could have swallowed them even if someone had promised me a ride in Fireball XL5. She didn't care, though, and just kept staring. Sometimes a kid would make some noise on another table or start to fool around and stuff and that would distract her for a minute. She'd look over at them and start yelling and all. She was always yelling, to be honest. Yelling and hitting you around the head. Anyway, when she got distracted, I would get my handkerchief out my pocket. I always had a handkerchief, cos my mum made me carry one just in case and all. I was glad she did too, cos that day I don't know what I would have done if I didn't have that hankie. Anyway, while Cauldwell was distracted, I put that hankie right by my mouth and spat all that sludge and the flies and everything into it. It was all slimy and stinking, but I had to put it back into my pocket. It was full of all this crap, but I had no choice, see, I had to. I was wearing my shorts, you know, grey shorts as I always did when I was a little kid and there wasn't much room in the pockets, but I piled it in anyway. It was all slimy and stinking in my pockets, but I had no choice, see. Trouble was, because she yelled so loud, everyone would quieten down and she'd stare at me again

When she was staring, I'd just dip my spoon into the slop in the bowl, slowly as I could, helping them dead flies swim lengths.

I just kept dipping. Dipping and hoping someone would start messing and distract her again. When they did, I'd put the hankie to my mouth and spit more sludge for my pocket. I reckon I was stuck at that table for about a week, just trying to get rid of all those flies and stuff. I missed the whole of my playtime that lunch break, just cos it took so long to get all that sludge off my plate. I reckon she knew what I was doing, cos it was taking me so long to eat that crap and anyway, she could see all this slime and stuff on my trousers by the pockets. I reckon she knew all the time, but she just didn't care cos she was a stinking sadistic bastard.

When I got off the table, I went straight to the toilets and puked up big style. I reckon I must have puked up for an hour or something. Just puking up all this sludge and stuff that looked like dead flies. I don't reckon I've ever puked up like that since. I ain't felt as sick either. But when I saw all these phoneys cheering Rumplan and singing 'God save America', I felt that sick. Just like when I was at school. That's how bad it was. As if some sadistic bastard had forced a load of shit down everyone's throats.

I'd had enough, so I left and went back to the motel. I lay on the bed and thought about what to do next, you know, kind of weighed up my options.

I was always in and out of that motel and so I got to see the girl on the desk a lot. She started to get real friendly and would ask me about my day and everything. Then we'd chew the fat for five minutes, talking about this and that. I found out her name was Sissy, and she told me she'd moved here from Georgia, and I told her a bit about where I was from in Birmingham. Nothing about my folks or anything, but just stuff about England and where I'd been in the States.

To tell the truth, I didn't like her much. She had all these break out spots and her skin gushed out oil. It looked as if she'd rubbed Vaseline across her face, and it shone. Sometimes, it looked as if she was fed up of shining, so she'd grab a tissue or cloth and dab herself to dry it out. But it didn't make much difference and two minutes later she'd be all oily again. I reckon if she had produced petroleum oil, she'd have been worth a fortune, but it wasn't. It was just lousy teenage oily grease. I could have lived with that, I don't reckon she had oily skin on purpose, but she was a nosey parker too. Always asking questions. That got on my nerves, but I hadn't paid a cent and needed to keep her sweet. So, I just kept giving her all that flannel about this big cheque that I was gonna get from England. This great big fat cheque as if I was gonna ask her to marry me and it would pay for our wedding.

She used to just nod and smile and babble on in this southern drawl. 'Now, don't you all go worrying about nothing,' she used to say. 'We'll catch you, before you go,' and then she'd smile.

I didn't like her when she said stuff like that. It made her sound all creepy, but I needed to keep her sweet, so I just smiled and chewed the fat with her.

Rumplan was everywhere, though. There were loads of these crappy rallies and walkabouts giving him chance to talk to people and kiss babies and stuff. Election time means all these creeps want to get out and meet the people, so they can make out they give a shit. You know, so they can make out that they're normal and down to earth and wash their own cars and change babies' nappies and all that sort of stuff. So, tracking him was a piece of cake. I followed him back to his offices and then back to where he lived and saw his wife and kids. I saw her fill up with gas at the gas stations and leave the kids in the car while she went in to pay. I watched her drop them at school and go to the shops. I watched them drive out into the countryside and saw the kids playing in fields by an oak tree. I watched loads of stuff. You'd kind of think this stuff would be really tough to do, but it ain't.

Think about it, this stuff ain't hard to do at all. Like, not long before mobs used to roam these streets and lynch people. Almost 500 in Texas. 500. You know, some crazy white guys would just hunt down a black guy like Jesse Washington or Allen Brooks and string them up. A noose around their neck until they couldn't breathe. Right there in front of everyone on the streets of America. 'I can't breathe.' White guys wound up so tight with fear and hate by freaks like Rumplan who create 'them' so that a group called 'us' needs someone to save them. And Hollywood entertains us, and politicians say it's the greatest country on earth and 400 years of slavery and abuse gets buried beneath idle collusion and another cup of coffee.

I even walked down the street where Brooks was hanged. A street where you might walk with your kids, on sidewalks and stand under lampposts and do normal street stuff. Rumplan did too, not that he gave a shit, he was too busy kissing babies. I went down by where Kennedy was shot too. Just a few years earlier, the President of the US, gunned down just where I was walking. See, that's the thing about Dallas, the thing about America. You'd think all this sort of stuff would be really tough, but it ain't. And this ain't a hundred years ago, this is now. Anyway, after all that, I guess that's when I decided it was time. I couldn't just stand by. I thought about Annie and what she'd said, 'Why don't you hunt the bastard down and kill him?'

Chapter Twenty-Five

I don't really feel like talking about all the stuff that happened after that. I just got on with everything, then put it to the back of my mind. To tell you the truth, none of it worked out as I thought it would, but what does? I reckon most stuff don't run as sweet as you think it will. You just got to learn to live with it like that, you know, shittungap and not going quite to plan.

You'd probably like me to get into a load of detail and let you know how it all unfolded, but as I told you, I don't wanna talk about it, so that's that. Anyway, if you're that interested, you can read about it in the papers. Not that you should believe much of what they say. They had a field day, though, filling up page after page with pictures and sensational headlines and a load of phoney bullshit. I reckon the editors love it when something like this happens. They probably just lean back in some great big leather chair in their great big office with a great big fat cigar in their mouth. I bet most of them go to bed praying for some massive disaster or epidemic or shooting or something. See, the papers write themselves then and they don't need to worry about how they're gonna fill them. They don't even worry about if what they say is true, cos most of it ain't. Most of it's just mad, made-up bullshit to sell papers. Thing is people read it anyway, so why should they care? See, most people's lives are that dull, they got to find some way to spice it up. It don't matter how they do it so long as it don't embarrass them and they can do it sitting down.

I knew I'd never get away, though, you know, get out of Texas. To be honest, I'd never counted on it, didn't really want to. I wouldn't have minded getting out to see some more National Parks and that sort of stuff, though. That's when I was happiest, when I was just sleeping out under the stars and looking at the skies and wandering around in the beautiful open spaces. Looking back, I should have tried to get to Yosemite and some of the parks in Utah, like Arches and Bryce and stuff, when I was heading across to Texas. I should have taken more time, but I kind of just thought I was stalling and so I didn't. Looking back, I should have, but I didn't, and I can't change it now. I can't change anything now.

My lawyer says I shouldn't be so pessimistic and he's gonna check into this and that. He asked me loads of questions and stuff, but I couldn't explain it too well. That's when he asked me if it would be easier just to write stuff down. 'Anything you want to write,' he said. 'Don't worry if you don't know where to start, or what you want to say, just start writing and see what happens.'

I told him I liked writing poetry, and would it be okay to do that? He looked at me as if I was a bit crazy, but he smiled and said, if I wanted. I was just messing with him really. Like I do like writing poems, but really, I just wanted to see if he was like Brooksey. I just wanted to see if he was the type that thought we should play it safe. He didn't, though, he just said I could if I wanted to.

I liked him for that. I reckon if he'd have done that Brooksey, play it safe stuff, I'd have fired him on the spot, but he didn't, and I liked him for that.

Anyway, that's how come I wrote it all down. All this stuff you've just read about. I didn't do any poems, cos I didn't want to mess with him, so I just wrote down a load of stuff. Just as it came to me, without thinking about it much. Just so my lawyer would know how I felt and what I'd been up to before Texas.

I don't reckon it'll help much, though. I'm not sure if it even makes much sense, but he seems like a nice guy and I didn't want to offend him, so I said I would. I reckon he's a bit of a fool really and is just wasting his time. Not a fool like me, you know, a proper all-star gold-plated fool, but still a fool. I didn't say that to him though cos I quite like him and anyway, what else have I got to do?

Chapter Twenty-Six

Now, if I was you, I wouldn't read this next chapter. I'd skip to the last chapter and just read the last couple of pages. That's what I'd do if I was you, but I ain't, so I guess it's your call. See, I didn't want to write anything else down as I told you, I didn't even wanna think about it, but my lawyer got all uppity with me and in the end I caved.

See, he kept telling me I was letting Rumplan get away with it and the press were printing all this crap. He was getting all worked up about it too, saying he couldn't help me unless I told him exactly what happened at the end. Sometimes, he would give me a load of flannel about how everything I'd written had helped him understand how I was feeling and all, but really, he just wanted to open me up. Open me up about what I saw at the end.

I just used to smile at him and say stuff like, 'What's the point? It's just gonna be 50 plus 1'. He used to go nuts when I said stuff like that.

'I don't know what you're on about,' he'd say. 'Stop giving me all this 50 plus 1 crap and tell me what happened.' Sometimes he got mad and started shouting, as if he was all exasperated. Then sometimes, he'd even smash his fist down on the table as if he wanted to find out about things so much, help me so much, that he didn't know what else to do. I kind of liked it when he did that, cos then I sort of thought he'd got it. You know, felt a little bit like how we all feel sometimes when things aren't going our way.

Sometimes the guard would barge in and say, 'Shut it. Shut

it, or I'll kick your ass.'

He'd say it just like that, you know, 'ass', as Americans do. As if they can't pronounce the word arse and they invented language. When he said it, he'd stare straight at me. He wouldn't have kicked my lawyer's ass, just mine, but he was the guard and so he acted like a bigshot. He was a great big fat, black guy, with a face as round as a dinner plate. His uniform was too tight too and fat bulged out, pressing so tight against his shirt and stuff it looked as if it might burst. My lawyer looked as if he might burst; it was kind of funny to watch.

I don't know why the black guy was so uptight with me, though. His grandpa and great-grandpa would have had their arses kicked big style, maybe even his dad. And by people like Rumplan too. People like Rumplan running their plantations whipping the arses of black guys like him, cos they were black and cos they could.

He was working for Rumplan now, though, so he just told me to 'shut it'.

After that, my lawyer would quieten down a bit and say stuff like he was just trying to help me.

'I'm just trying to help you, honest I am, but you've got to help me to do that. If not, you're a dead man walking.'

'Dead man walking,' I said. 'We're all dead men walking,' I said. 'That's the tragedy, you're born and then from then on you're dying. We can't do a thing. We're all dead men walking, we just don't know when.'

He'd heard me out, but you could see him hold in a sigh and mutter under his breath, but he didn't want that guard coming in again calling the shots, so he held it in. I used to respect him for that, you know, being able to hold it in when he just wanted to burst.

'Look,' I said. 'Look. I know you're trying to help, but the cards are stacked. There's me and you. You're doing your best, I know you are, but it's just me and you. Maybe the British Government too, but they're so far up America's arse doing a trade deal, that they're worth diddly-squat. So, it's just me and you.'

I paused and quietened down a bit, cos the guard was hanging around.

'Then there's Rumplan, with the cops in his pocket and the press up his arse. And all his heavies and his flag-waving groupies and his ten-gallon hat and his bleached white teeth. You do the math.'

He kind of looked at me as if he was feeling sorry for me, as if he knew that's how it was, but he couldn't give up.

'But what about the truth?' he said. He said it as if it meant something, as if it wasn't just a word. A lousy, stinking word with too many consonants and no backbone.

'The truth. Yeah, the truth.' I said it slowly, as if I was thinking about what the word meant. You know, not the dictionary definition, but what it really meant.

'The truth.' I repeated it again. 'Like the truth about Drake and whether he's a pirate or a gentleman. The truth about Anne Boleyn and whether she's just some on-the-make hooker or the victim of a crazed, deranged madman. The truth about Macbeth, and if he was a noble king or the bastard Shakespeare painted.' I pulled up sharp, I could hear myself getting louder, and the pitch of my voice getting higher and shriller, which is how I speak when I'm getting all twisted. Like how everyone in Birmingham speaks when they're wound up.

I could see the guard waiting near the door looking for a chance to pounce. He was sweating and dark rings dripped from his armpits. Damp patches had formed where his fat, bulging flesh tried to burst through his shirt. I didn't want to smell him. I spoke more softly.

'There ain't no truth. Just what people believe. And mostly, I reckon people believe the stuff that guys like Rumplan tell them.' I leant back in my chair, as I did when I told that stupid teacher what assonance meant. It kind of felt appropriate. You know, how nothing really rhymed but we just made out it did.

He went quiet, as if he understood what I was telling him.

'I get what you're saying,' he said. 'I get why you feel like you do, why you think it's all a waste of time. But please, please for me, won't you just give it a shot, just let me know what happened. Please.'

I don't know why, but I kind of felt sorry for him. I shouldn't have really, I was locked up, not him, but I liked him. I knew he really did care and really did think he could make a difference. I didn't wanna be the one to kill that.

'Okay,' I said. 'I really don't wanna tell anyone anything, but I will, just for you. I like you, see, so I will, just for you.'

And so that's when I wrote down this next bit, just cos I felt sorry for him and didn't want to break his heart.

So, when I was lying on those dirty sheets in that crappy motel, I used to just mull over what I could do. I really just wanted Rumplan to go back to England and face the music for what he'd done. Maybe it was an accident, maybe he wasn't drunk when he smashed into my parents, but he never had to answer a single question. He just ran away. All I really wanted was for him to go back and talk about what had happened just as everybody else had to. You know, everyone who ain't in some special club.

I knew that weren't gonna happen, though. When I was back

in England, I tried all that stuff, got a lawyer and everything, but there was no way he was coming back. I used to ask my lawyer why we couldn't pull some strings to get him back. I used to tell him I thought Britain was supposed to have a 'special relationship' with the States. 'We do,' he used to say. 'They tell us what we are gonna do, and we do it. That's special.' He'd always smile when he said it, as if to say, 'What you gonna do?' I used to like that lawyer, though, cos at least he told me it straight. A lot of people used to give me all that phoney crap about how they wanted to help, but he just gave it me straight.

'You're wasting your time,' he'd say. 'Our government will say all the right things but behind the scenes will just lick arse cos we're in the middle of some deal. The Americans will hide behind some legal crap and Rumplan will carry on shafting Texas within an inch of its life. Try if you want, but you're wasting your time.'

I even thought about talking to Rumplan myself, but from what I'd seen, I reckon he would have just laughed in my face. I thought about my options. I wanted to hurt him bad. Maybe I should just run him down in my car. That's another reason why I'd bought it. Running someone down is easy. Just drive. If you know how to drive, you can just hit someone when you're going at 30 or 40 or something. They don't have a chance. You can run anyone down easy. Maybe I should run his wife down, or maybe his kids. They hadn't done a thing, so I kind of felt bad thinking that, but maybe losing them would hurt him more. Then he'd have to live with it, as I do. Maybe that's what I should do.

I still had this gun, though, and enough ammo to take them all out. I reckon I could shoot better than Torrey now. I don't know, though, maybe running them down is easier. I was angry. I was down. I was a kid alone in America. I lay on those dirty sheets and just kept thinking. Running through stuff in my head until I drifted into an uneasy sleep.

Next morning, something happened, though. Something I didn't see coming. I was trailing Rumplan as usual, when he walked out of this office with a girl. She looked about 20 or something and I watched her get in his car. I hadn't seen her before and thought she might be his PA or something. But I tailed them and that's when I got lucky. Since I'd picked out that key in Henrys and my mum told me I was lucky, I kind of always knew I was, but I didn't see this coming.

Anyway, I tailed them for about 20 miles until they pulled up in a hotel parking lot. It wasn't one of those crumby motel places I stayed in, but a swanky hotel. The sort of place you needed money to stay. I didn't pull into the parking lot, cos I thought my old banger would stand out amongst all the flash motors, but I was close enough to watch them go inside. Maybe they were just going to another meeting, maybe lunch, who knows? But it didn't feel right. You know the way they cosied up to each other and giggled when they walked.

I hung around outside that hotel for hours. I thought about going in, but I reckon I would have just attracted attention and anyway, I could see his car from where I was parked, so I just waited.

It must have been about three hours, but when he came out, that's when I got real lucky. They walked out together and were arm in arm. He had taken off his tie and was carrying his jacket over his shoulder, you know, as if he was advertising aftershave or something. Her hair was tied up in a bun when she went in, but now it hung loose over her shoulders. She shook her head and it blew in the wind as if she was in a hairspray ad. But it was the way they were all cosied up that struck me most. You know, interlocking arms and gazing at each other as they skipped back towards his car.

I grabbed my camera. I hadn't used it much, to be honest, but it was with me in the car, and so I grabbed it just in case. And that's when they kissed. Not a peck on the cheek, like with your sister or a close friend. Not how the French do when they kiss their buddies on both cheeks, but a kiss. A long kiss. A kiss that might have lasted all the way through a record at that crappy disco I used to go to.

I must have taken a whole reel of film. Well, almost. See, I'd already taken a couple of shots in Dallas at those crappy rallies, but I reckon there were still 20 shots or something. I reckon I could have taken more because that kiss lasted so long. But it didn't matter. I had plenty of shots. I watched as he got back into his car and wound down the window. She stood outside a little longer and there was more giggling. Then she bent down a bit so they could kiss again. It was shorter this time, but still a kiss that told me it wasn't his sister. He drove off and I watched her walk to a car. I guessed it was hers. Maybe she had left it there earlier. I looked at the plate and remembered the number. School had taught me to remember stuff, so I remembered it easy. But I wrote it down anyway. Just in case, I wrote it down. I didn't have any paper, but I had my hankie. So, that's where I wrote it down, on my hankie.

That night, I mulled over my next move. I didn't expect it, but I now had something on Rumplan. Something that could hurt him bad. Maybe I should just get the pictures developed and give them to his wife. Trouble is, she looked as if she'd been programmed. You know, programmed to put on a smile when she wasn't happy. Maybe, I could give them to the press and watch his campaign crumble. But maybe he had the press in his pocket and anyway, sleazebags like him usually just brush stuff like that aside. You know, I reckon a lot of politicians can do what they want with women. It can even be caught on tape and stuff, but they talk themselves out of it. Say it's just locker room banter and what lads do. People buy it too. People still go out and vote for them. Even women. I've never got that, but that's what happens. Diddly-squat.

I got my gun ready. I didn't reckon I would use it, but I wanted it with me anyway. I picked it up and got out the last of the ammo. I wasn't sure how much I had left, but I opened the box.

I thought I should have more. I hadn't been counting or anything when I was firing off all those shots in the desert, but I just reckoned I should have had more. Something didn't feel right, but to tell you the truth, I wasn't really planning on using it anyway, so I just chucked the gun and the ammo in my bag. My rucksack was almost black now. I'd scribbled so many place names over it in ink and dragged it across so many beaches and crappy motel floors it looked like decaying fruit. A dried out, wrinkled, putrefied piece of black prune.

Really, I decided I'd just spook him. Spook him bad, just enough so he'd know what it's like to feel as if everything has fallen apart. As if nothing's fair or working out as you wanted it to.

Trouble is, that's when I found out I ain't really lucky at all.

See, I followed him out that day, when he had his wife and kids with him. I had the gun with me, loaded too, and I had that roll of film. I reckoned on spooking him real bad, you know, getting him to understand what it felt like. I followed them out of town and onto some quiet roads. I'd followed them here before, and I knew they had a spot where they'd all get out and stretch and look at the view and all. It was a quiet spot where the kids used to run around. His wife would keep an eye on them and Rumplan would look through some papers and stuff as if he was always working, even when he wasn't. Well, this day they pulled up at this spot, but instead of me driving on as normal, I pulled up right behind them.

They got out and the kids ran about, shouting and messing about as kids do. As I used to do when I was their age. Like before you've worked out how bad things get. Mrs Rumplan shouted after them and urged them to be careful. You know how mothers do. The kids took no notice. You know how kids don't. Rumplan leant against the bonnet of his big flash car, just as he did when he was kissing that secretary or whoever she was. He stretched, but then he stopped and pulled his arms down as if he must have caught sight of me as I stepped out the car. He turned to face me. He stopped stretching and just faced me, square on.

I had my gun in my hand. 'Rumplan,' I shouted. 'Rumplan, got your kids with you today, then?'

He just stared, but it spooked Mrs Rumplan and the kids. She saw me waving my gun about. I didn't really plan on using it, I just wanted to spook them, but she didn't know that, so she let out a scream. Half-way through she held it back, though, as if she didn't want to spook the kids more than I already had. I kind of admired her for that. You know, for having the strength to put her kids before herself. She reminded me of my mum. My mum was always doing that, putting me and my sister before herself. When Mrs Rumplan did that, I kind of felt bad about what I was doing; she seemed as if she might be a decent lady. A decent lady married to low down scum. I felt sorry for the kids too. It was Rumplan I wanted to hurt, not them, but it was too late. I was here, and I was waving my gun around.

She yelled over to them and they ran back, shouting 'mummy'. They hugged around her legs as they did when they were on the stage at one of Rumplan's rallies. They kept screaming 'mummy'.

'Todd, let him have the car, give him some money. Todd, please, please.' She thought I was some lowlife after their stupid money. As if I cared about money.

'Please, Todd, just give him the keys.'

Rumplan just stood there as cool as anything. He didn't flinch, he just stood there staring at me.

'He don't want the keys,' he said.

'Please, Todd, please.' His wife was trying to stay calm for the children, but she was starting to plead. She sounded as if she was used to pleading with him. He ignored her. He looked as if he was used to ignoring her.

'Shut up, Alice.' He turned and looked at her. 'Shut up, will you. I told you he ain't after the keys. He ain't after money either.'

She flinched as if she'd been hit by a stone and laid her hands on the hair of her children who just kept hugging her legs. They had started to cry, and she crouched over to try to soothe them.

Rumplan walked towards me. He walked as if he was a gunslinger who knew he was fast on the draw.

'You ain't come for money, have you, Bardell?'

Him saying that took me back. How did he know my name? How did he know it was me? How did he know I wasn't just some lowlife chancer taking an opportunity, out here in the middle of nowhere?

He kept walking towards me slowly, and the kids started screaming and yelling. 'Shut up,' he yelled at them, 'shut up or I'll come over there.'

It sounded like a threat. They looked scared to death, maybe of me waving this gun about or maybe of Rumplan, I couldn't tell. They looked as if they were trying to control themselves but didn't know how. Their mum crouched down further and whispered to them to try to be quiet.

To tell you the truth, I was shit scared myself. It had all gotten out of control. I just wanted Rumplan to face the music, but it had all gotten out of control. And how the hell did he know who I was? Thinking about that freaked me out, big style.

'Don't come any closer,' I yelled at him. I waved my gun around and yelled again. 'Don't take another step.'

I reached in my pocket and grabbed out the reel of film. I waved it around in my left hand whilst I kept the gun pointed at him with my other hand.

'You know what this is,' I taunted. I threw the reel of film across at Alice Rumplan. It fell on the floor a few inches away from where she was in a trembling huddle with the kids.

'Take a look at that,' I shouted at her, 'if you want to know what your husband is really like. If you want to know who he meets in hotels. Have a good look at it yourself, Rumplan.' I sneered as if I could outdraw him, but he took another step towards me.

'What is he on about, Todd? Dear, please, please tell me, what is it all about?'

'Don't take another step,' I shouted, 'not a step more or I'll shoot.' I waved the gun, as if I was some madman.

'Shoot away,' Rumplan said as cool as anything. 'I ain't frightened of blanks. I run this town, see, and some no-good scrawny kid like you ain't gonna get in my way.'

I was getting scared. I think I was more scared than the kids and just wanted to hug around Mrs Rumplan's legs too.

'They ain't blanks,' I yelled. 'Now listen, not another step.'

He moved closer. He had a look on his face, as if he thought he was Clint Eastwood.

'You should ask Sissy about that. See, she's been in your room and changed your ammo. That's what you call it, I believe.' He said it with a sneer. 'See, your ammo ain't even live. She switched it for blanks. Sissy saw to that. I told you I run this town.'

Alice Rumplan looked up from the kids. 'Todd, please tell me, what is this all about, who's Sissy? Who's this kid? Todd, please Todd, please.'

Rumplan moved a step nearer and pulled out a gun from his jacket inside pocket. It looked like mine.

'See, your live ammo is loaded in here. And this gun? This is the one you bought near Tuba City.'

He laughed. One of those horrid laughs that ain't got nothing to do with humour.

'Todd, please, tell me what's going on?' Alice kept shouting across at him, and Rumplan kept ignoring her.

Rumplan was about three steps away from me now and I didn't know what to believe. My head was spinning, and I felt as if I was gonna throw up. I hadn't meant for it to go this far. I just wanted his wife to see that film and know he was scum. To see him how I saw him as a no-good scumbag. I just wanted to get her to take that film home and for the whole thing to kick up in Rumplan's face. To tell the truth, I couldn't have fired that gun even if it was loaded. See, I told you I'm a coward and I just don't have the nerve. But now I didn't even know if the gun I was holding was loaded or not.

Rumplan looked as if he did, though. Now he had a gun pulled on me and he was just three yards away. Maybe he was just trying to spook me, or maybe he was gonna shoot me. Right here, in front of his wife and kids, then make out I was some lowlife who was gonna rob him. He'd probably make out he was some kind of hero and had saved his family but had to shoot me dead. Shoot me dead, to save himself and his wife and kids.

I'm telling you I was scared. I wanted a leak more than when I was in that airport in New York. I wanted to hug Mrs Rumplan around her legs. I started to tremble. But that's when he told me to turn around.

'Turn around and walk back to your shitty little car,' he said.

I hesitated. I wondered whether he was gonna shoot me in the back. Maybe, he was just bluffing, and my gun was loaded, and he was playing some crazy twisted game to get me to back off. I hated the guy, but guys like him are clever. Maybe it was a double bluff. Maybe my gun could kill him.

'Turn around,' he yelled. He yelled it and his wife flinched, the kids screamed.

If I fired my gun and they weren't live rounds, I'd be dead in a second. I had no choice. I turned around slowly and took a step back to the car. I didn't know if it was gonna be my last step, my last breath, but if I didn't do as he said, maybe he'd shoot me right in the belly. From three yards, right in the belly.

I took another step and then another until I reckon, I was only about four or five steps from the car. Then I heard him speak. He spoke in a quiet, soft tone, as if he was searching for words that were unfamiliar.

'I'm sorry,' he said. 'I'm sorry.'

I can't really explain what happened next. A shot rang out, I shook, everything seemed to shake, there was a scream. Another scream and then a second shot and then a third. They rang out in quick succession as if someone had thrown a handful of stones at a corrugated tin roof and they all landed at almost the same time. But not quite the same time, so it lasted longer than one hit, but only fractionally longer. But long enough to make you feel as if it lasted forever. And then there was silence.

I thought maybe I'd been hit, but I couldn't feel anything. But my mind kind of told me I must have been shot, so I stumbled and fell anyway. I was shaking and I felt parts of me with my hands. I felt my legs and back and side and arms. It was crazy really, cos I knew I hadn't been hit, but in my head, it was as if I was in some scene from *Paradise Lost* and I was falling. I stumbled to my feet and looked back and couldn't believe what I was looking at. Alice Rumplan and his kids were crumpled in a pile on the floor. Blood was draining from Mrs Rumplan's chest and the kids were lying still. Dead still. Lying dead in blood, still, clinging. 'You madman,' I yelled. 'You crazy madman.' I got up and ran at Rumplan. I still had my gun, so I fired it, but he was telling the truth. It was full of blanks. I reckon that was the only time he ever told the truth. I needed his lies. I needed him to be lying, I wished it had been a lie. I fired shots at him and then more shots, but they were blanks. I ran at him and punched him, but he was a giant next to me and he pushed me to the ground. He laughed.

I lay on the ground. His gun pointed at me. I wondered if it was my turn.

'Go ahead,' I said. I was scared as hell, but nothing seemed to matter now. I'd got to Texas and I'd screwed up big style. I was scared, but just then it didn't seem to matter.

'Go ahead,' I said and kicked the dust with my foot. It went over his cowboy boots and up the leg of his creased jeans. Only someone like Rumplan would wear creased jeans.

'You don't get it, do you?' He spoke in that soft quiet tone again. It spooked me more than his yelling.

'Now give me your gun.' It was full of blanks, so I threw it at him. It hit him on the shoulder and fell by his feet. He picked it up and put it in his jacket pocket. He pulled out a clean rag and wiped the gun he had been using and pushed it into my hands.

'It's empty, keep it,' he said.

'See, you've done me a big favour,' he grinned. 'See, I've been wanting to get rid of my wife and kids. She was fine 20 years ago, but she is rather plain now, don't you think? She don't smile much either and doesn't come across well. I need someone that comes across well.' He spoke of her as if he was replacing a car, as if she wasn't lying dead just ten yards away. 'You've seen Lucy. You know when you took those photos and all at the hotel. Lucy's more my type, but it wouldn't have looked good for me to get a divorce or anything. Over here, to win big, I had to play the family card and I was stuck with them. You've done me a favour. Now I have my perfect alibi. This paranoid crazed kid from England comes seeking revenge and tracks me down. Then he kills my wife and kids just to get back at me. A poor crazy kid from England who lost his parents and then lost the plot. Then bought a gun and shot my wife and kids with it. But didn't shoot me, cos it was revenge and he wanted to see me in pain. See, that's why I got Sissy to get your gun and ammo. When they trace it all back, it's gonna be on you. I reckon I would have walked to power in this State anyway, but now I've got the sympathy vote too. Me, a dedicated family man and all, losing his wife and kids to a deranged English misfit. Give it a year or so, and I reckon Lucy and me can get together in public. She knows how to smile. I can get a new family thing going then. You can think about that on death row.'

'You stinking bastard,' I yelled. To tell the truth, I didn't much care about myself just then, but I couldn't get how he could do that to his own kids, his own wife.

'But she was your wife, your wife, your kids.' I sounded hopeless.

'I can get more wives and more kids if I want them,' he said. He said it all matter of fact, as if he was Henry VIII or someone, and it made me think, we weren't even from the same time, of the same species.

'Don't think anyone's gonna buy your version either. See, we know when you left England, where you've been travelling around, we've been tracking you. You know, waiting for you to get here. You'll get your case heard. You'll get some two-bit lawyer, but I reckon we'll get Brad to tell the court about all the crazy questions you asked him and how you told Annie that you would 'hunt me down'. Oh, and by the way, Dave will let everyone know you are always off your head on acid and Bob will let them know how you asked him to teach you how to shoot. See, you thought diplomatic immunity was your problem, but diplomatic immunity ain't the half of it. You don't get to do what I do, win like I win, without friends and connections. People who look after things for me.' He looked as if he said all that sort of stuff before. As if he'd said it to a thousand other poor bastards who had tried to take him on and got nowhere.

'See, the world's full of two kinds of people. Those who are trying to make it better and those who are trying to make it.' He smiled. 'You would think politics would be about making things better, but it ain't. It's about making it. Making it to the top and getting what you want. About getting people to buy the bullshit you need them to believe until you need them to believe some other bullshit.' He said it as if he didn't give a shit.

'Enjoy the view. The cops will be here soon, and I'll tell

them how you ambushed us and gunned down my family. In cold blood before my eyes, just for revenge. I'll put on a bit of the distraught husband and father stuff, but that ain't no biggy. In my job, I'm acting most of the time. Anyway, I don't reckon they'll ask many questions. I told you, I run this town. I run the police. I run everything. Maybe the country one day.'

I was feeling sick. Sick, that he'd shot his wife and kids, sick, that I'd fallen for all that crap from Bob and Annie and everyone else who had been bought off by Rumplan. Sick, that bastards like Rumplan hold all the cards.

Sick, that he was right and that we all stand and watch while Brian Holloway gets his head kicked in. Sick.

'Aren't you gonna look at your wife and kids, you bastard monster?' I spat at him.

'Nah, I've seen enough of them.' He didn't even flinch.

'I'm gonna go over. Maybe they're still alive?' I said.

'Help yourself.'

I stumbled over and looked at the crumpled bodies. You could smell blood. You know, the metallic smell of iron. They looked calm. Calmer than they did when they were on those rallies with Rumplan. Alice Rumplan didn't look so plain so close-up, and her flowered dress looked like a garden in full bloom against the soil. The kids were lying clinging to her legs. Clinging like if they had to die, this would be the place they would choose.

Rumplan stood over by his car. He was looking at some papers as if he had more important things to do. As if he'd finished this job and needed to get some other stuff sorted. I saw the roll of film lying by the foot of one of Rumplan's kids. I reckon Rumplan had forgotten all about it with all that had gone on. He was too busy congratulating himself for being the master of the universe to worry about detail. I checked he wasn't looking and picked up the film.

'I think I'm gonna be sick,' I yelled.

He looked over. 'Help yourself.'

There was a tree nearby. A big glorious oak tree. It was waving in the wind and it made me think of Mr Bagshot and how he used to make us stand on the desk if we got our spellings wrong. I crept around the back of the tree trunk just out of Rumplan's view. I made the noise of being sick. It wasn't hard cos I was feeling as if I would throw up at any second. But I didn't. I held it back, while I dug. I dug a small hole next to the tree with the gun I still had in my hand. I wrapped the small roll of film in my handkerchief. It still had Lucy's plate number written on it. I buried the roll of film and the handkerchief in that small hole at the base of the oak tree. I made honking noises as if I was being sick. I finished and then made honking noises as I was sick. Sicker than when Mrs Cauldwell made me eat that shit for school dinners.

Rumplan didn't look up once.

Now, after my lawyer read that, he didn't say anything. He didn't say anything for about five minutes. He just kept shaking his head, and rereading bits of it as if he couldn't take it all in. 'The mad, crazy bastard,' he said. When he spoke, that's all he said.

'But I've been out to where it happened. I've crawled over everything there, looking for anything that would have helped us, and there ain't no roll of film under the tree. I've crawled all over that place and there ain't nothing by that tree, just a hole. A big hole.' He said all that as if he was trying to figure it out, and then shook his head, and then reread all the stuff about how I dug that hole by the tree and buried that film.

'I've crawled all over the place and there's just a hole. I'll get out there again and take another look.' He sounded anxious. 'Is this really how it was?'

'I think so,' I said, 'I think so.'

'But is it the truth? Are you telling me the truth?' He said it as if he was pleading.

'It's my truth,' I said. 'Then Rumplan will tell everyone his truth. Then everyone will make up their minds. I ain't holding my breath.'

'I believe you,' he said.

I smiled. I was glad he said it and wanted to say something warm. But I didn't. I just said 'huh'.

Chapter Twenty-Seven

Well, that all happened a long time ago now. I don't really remember when exactly, but that's how I wrote it all down at the time. You know, when my lawyer asked me to write it down to understand how it all happened. But I don't remember anything too well now, just bits, just hazy fragments. That's what happens to you in a place like this. In the end you don't really remember anything. You just know you get treated like shit and that's all you know, that's all you remember. In the end, you just have this smell in your nose all the time, a taste in your mouth too. To tell you the truth, I'll be glad when it's all over.

See, I've been beaten up so many times. Kicked in the head and punched in the guts and all. I reckon I've been kicked in the head more times than they got that Brian Holloway kid at my school. You know, the kid who wore shorts to high school and never lived it down. I reckon he didn't know what pain was in the end; I know I don't. You think someone would look out for you, protect you maybe, but no one does. They just treat you like shit.

I don't know what anything is anymore.

Sometimes I try and work it out by writing words down on paper as I used to. When I used to do that, sometimes, it kind of helped to make sense of stuff, but it don't work now. Best I can do is words. I don't join anything together, just words. You know, single words, single, lonely words on their own. I started writing these single words on little strips of paper. Loads of words, all sorts of stuff just as they came into my head and all. After I had about a hundred words or something, you know, on these little strips of paper, I stuck them in a jar. It's hard to get stuff like that in here, but I managed to get one and hid it under a panel in the bed. Sometimes, when I get chance, I just shake that jar, with all the strips of paper in it. I just shake it, you know, as if it's one of those crappy snow globes or something they have around Christmas. You know the ones I mean, where you shake them, and all the pretend snowflakes flutter down over some crazy Father Christmas or Christmas scene they've trapped in the crumby little globe. Well, I shake this jar just as if it's one of them snow globes and let the words just fall out on my bed. I just wanna see how all the words fall out. I wanna see if they fall out and make any sense, see if they make a sentence or anything. I've done it plenty of times, though, and it never makes sense. It's always just a lonely word next to another lonely word that don't make no sense. I just wanted one lousy sentence. That's all I wanted, one lousy sentence, but it ain't happened. Not once it ain't.

Anyway, I don't have much time now. They're coming at 5, then it happens at 6. I got four and a half lousy hours left and no words that make any sense. Just that smell up my nose and that taste.

I can just about see their stinking clock on the wall in the hallway. If I put my head right up against the wall, next to the bars and tilt it a bit, I can just about make out the numbers. It's got those green fluorescent hands and numbers so you can see it all night. It's like the one that crazy 'porcelain' Pete had, except this one has a second hand too. A real loud second hand that clicks each second by.

It's quiet in here. Sometimes you get people yelling and screaming and stuff, a bit like how I remember in the Y in New

York all those years ago. It don't last long, though. You get roughed up pretty bad if you carry on yelling, so usually it don't last long. I don't know what's worse. I hate all that screaming and stuff, but when it's quiet, you just hear this lousy second hand. Click, click, click. It does my head in listening to it, but once it's in your head you can't stop. I wanna stop. God knows I wanna stop, but I don't. It's as if it's got in my head and I can't do nothing about it. I reckon the sadistic bastards have put it here just to do my head in. You know, just to make me feel shit.

My lawyer says I shouldn't lose hope, but he ain't in here listening to that lousy clock. He still only looks about twenty or something. I know he ain't, he's loads older than that, but that's what he looks like. I feel so old now, you know, since I've been stuck in here. I tell you everyone looks as if they're only twenty now. I reckon if some old biddy who used to pee herself on the bus came in here now, even she'd look twenty. Next to me anyway, that's what she'd look like. As if she was only twenty.

This lawyer is well meaning and all, but he still feels young. He still believes in justice and truth and all that bullshit. He ain't worked out yet that the dice are loaded. You know, how some rich bastards get diplomatic immunity whilst the rest of us scratch about to squeeze by. Maybe he knows, but just doesn't want to admit it, cos he'd go crazy. He keeps telling me he's looking for a technicality which will lead to an acquittal. I reckon he's crazy, but he keeps looking anyway. I don't really listen to him much, to be honest. I just do that thing Rusty taught me years ago. You know, that crazy ginger-haired guy who was good with girls, cos he made out he listened and all. So, I just do what he taught me and just look at this lawyer guy and nod and say 'huh' and stuff. He smiles a lot and touches my arm when he leaves. He does it in a real affectionate way too, as if he really cares and wants to be my buddy. I think he really means it too. I bet he's sitting up right now making phone calls and reading all his clever law books for some crazy technicality. It's all a waste of time, though. I reckon he'll be sad when I go, though, you know, maybe for a day or so. Then he'll find someone else to save, then someone else and then one day he'll feel as old as me and work it all out. I bet he'll be really pissed off then, you know when he works out, he's been trying to make a difference and it was all just one big waste of time. Maybe not. Maybe he'll live in some big house with sprinklers on the grass and won't care too much. He looks as if he will care, though. Like one day, he'll admit it was all a waste of time and be so insanely furious he'll get a gun and blow someone's head off.

Click, click, click, click, click. That clock is really doing my head in now, with its stupid second hand and its green, fluorescent numbers. I wish it was lighter in here so they didn't glow so much. Or maybe darker so I couldn't see anything. It's kind of half dark. That's the worst when something is half anything.

There's a bit of a light in the hall and it just shines enough to cast shadows. Not deep intense shadows like when the sun is shining on you full blast and you can see your shadow as if you got a brother next to you. But just enough for me to twist my hands into shapes and try to create shadow animals on the walls. I ain't no good at it, though, and the light ain't that bright and my hands don't work properly. I keep trying, though. Keep trying to see if I can make some shapes on the walls just as my mum and dad did on that tent all those years ago. You know, birds swooping and flying away free. Butterflies heading south to Mexico. If my mum and dad were here, I bet they'd do it easy. My dad made it look as if was a piece of cake. I reckon he'd even get me out of here right now if he was around. He made everything look like a piece of cake.

I look at the clock. It's 4.47. I think about my lawyer loosening his tie and looking through his crazy law book. I bet even he's sweating now. I think about Pete and how his alarm will go off at 5.55. Five minutes to six. I wonder where he'll be and if he remembers me or cares. I think about my mum and dad and the glorious shadows on the wall of a tent. I think they'd still be proud. Proud I tried. Proud I called it out and tried to make a difference, that I too may have had the courage to eat at a lunch counter or sit on the front seats of a bus.

I think about all the people I've met and all the others too. Some still clinging to the vacant words of a vacant man and hiding with the sugar stealers.

It's time. I hear footsteps and a voice, 'Move it, boy, or are you just gonna sit there?'